KT-467-897

# Firebug

# Firebug

Stephanie Hale

ROBERT HALE · LONDON

© Stephanie Hale 2005
First published in Great Britain 2005

ISBN 0 7090 7878 1

Robert Hale Limited
Clerkenwell House
Clerkenwell Green
London EC1R 0HT

The right of Stephanie Hale to be identified as
author of this work has been asserted by her
in accordance with the Copyright, Designs and
Patents Act 1988.

2 4 6 8 10 9 7 5 3 1

| CORK CITY LIBRARY | |
|---|---|
| 04885330 | |
| LBC | 08/02/2006 |
| | £18.99 |
| | |

Typeset in 11½/14pt Dante Regular
by Derek Doyle & Associates, Shaw Heath.
Printed in Great Britain by St Edmundsbury Press
Bury St Edmunds, Suffolk.
Bound by Woolnough Bookbinding Limited.

*For Cormac*

# Acknowledgements

Thanks to:
My son, Cormac, who is a little whirlwind of love, joy and inspiration.

My husband, Shane, for his helpful comments on my manuscript; his countless cups of Earl Grey tea; and his love.

My sister, Chloe, who, in spite of living hundreds of miles away, continues to be a source of loyalty and support.

Keiren Phelan, Literature Officer of the South-East Arts Board, who has had faith in me over many years and has given me encouragement when my self-belief was waning.

Ed Button, Local Studies Librarian at Ipswich Record Office who has helped with research on Suffolk.

Dr Nick Hindle and Dr Simon Robinson who have helped with medical and psychological research – although, on occasion, I have taken liberties with the facts.

# PART I

# Chapter 1

I made my first fire when I was twelve years old. It was two months after my mother and brother Billy, died. It was a disaster, or a phenomenal success, depending on your point of view. The fire blew a hole in our roof and caused the chimney to fly off – a feat which shocked both my father and me.

I was stunned and awed by the power of the explosion. Until that day, I had only ever seen the sedate coal fires in our living-room and dining-room. I had imagined fire to be a domesticated creature like a lap dog or a cat. It never occurred to me that this docile pet might have claws or teeth. Even less, that it might bite. In the light of what had happened to my mother and Billy shortly before, I can only put this pitiful ignorance down to my youth.

I was born in the coldest December in a decade. An Arctic front had caused the temperature to plunge to minus 9. The Midlands was one of the worst hit areas. Freezing fog and black ice brought motorists to a halt. There were power failures on the trains. Rivers and fountains froze solid for the first time in years. Patrolling police officers had icicles hanging from their helmets.

The inside of our house was like a refrigerator in the weeks following my birth. My mother used to relish telling me about it. 'I was like a smoke-dragon!' she laughed. 'Every time I opened my mouth, great clouds of steam came out. We ate and slept in the living-room. We didn't dare go upstairs for fear of hypothermia.'

Every day revealed fresh wonders. Paisley frost patterns appeared inside our windows. A dripping tap in the bathroom froze into a glassy stalactite. Milk turned solid on the doorstep and split the glass bottles. Ice crystals flowered on the nail heads inside our letterbox. My father had to heat his keys over a match before he could set off for work.

As a baby, I knew nothing of these icy marvels. My world was one of warmth: an extension of the womb. My mother, anxious for my well-being, placed my crib in front of the roaring fire in the living-room. Fire then was my companion from the moment I entered the world. When I was born, my eyes focused no more than six inches away. But when the mists parted, the first thing to have caught my attention would have been our coal fire. As I grew up from babyhood to toddlerhood, my gaze must often have been drawn away from my mother's face to the golden glow in the grate. The blaze started at five o'clock in the morning and was not damped down until midnight – even in summer. I don't think I ever saw the fire in the process of being lit or extinguished while my mother was alive. The fire in the living-room was blazing when I went to bed, and I was forbidden to rise until it was well alight. In my innocence, it seemed like an everlasting flame.

My mother was expert at all things fiery. She knew when to let more air into the grate and when to cover up the air holes; when to put smaller lumps of coal on the fire; when to let it lie. She was one of the few people I knew who could hold a sheet of newspaper over the chimney breast, without it catching light. Every week, I would help her to polish the brasses – the poker, the dustpan, the handle of the horsehair brush. Then we would rub the coal-scuttle until it gleamed. Few things gave us more satisfaction than to see our faces reflected back as if from a gold mirror.

My mother never simply stoked a fire. She honoured it. She placed coals on top of a blaze as if she was laying precious relics in a glass case. The smaller coals first. Then, as the flames took hold, the larger ones. Coal was her utmost joy. The layered streaks of it. The shiny blackness of it. Each lump of coal as unique as a fingerprint. Some dusty as Turkish Delight; others smooth and shiny as pebbles on the edge of the sea. Some square. Some oval. Some multi-faceted. My mother was one of those infamous women who ate coal while pregnant. She tried to conceal it of course: she did it as secretively as she could, but I distinctly recall black marks on her gumline while she was pregnant with Billy.

My mother was a teacher at Bromsgrove High School before she gave birth to me. Rather than waste her skills, she used them to further my education, regaling me with delightful facts about coal from an early age. She would break open large lumps of coal with a hammer. Then, we scoured the surface looking for fossils. Her lessons, though scientific, were wonderfully lyrical. They had the beauty and simplicity of haiku. This is why I remember them so well; why the memories have not faded.

One day, for example, my mother put her diamond engagement ring in one of my hands and a lump of coal in the other.

'Which is the most valuable? Which, the most beautiful?' she asked.

I looked at the brilliant white diamond, then at the coal. I giggled. But when I held up the ring, my mother shook her head.

'This diamond can't keep anyone warm. It can't drive a steam train. It can't heat food.'

She held the coal up to the window so that its dull surface was transformed. Sunlight caught its facets and made them glitter. I saw beauty – *felt* beauty – where before I had only seen an ordinary lump of coal.

My father was an educated man who adopted the simple life of a farrier after being made redundant from a pharmaceutical company. To him, coal was convenient, functional, ordinary. He stoked his furnace with it. He made it roar to temperatures of 500 degrees. He curved horseshoes over it. He straightened crooked nails over it. My father loved fire. He loved melting and bending metal. He loved working with horses. But he could never understand my mother's passion for coal.

'Anyone would think there was a baby in that coal bucket, the way you coo over it! If you want to look at coal, then come to work with me! I've got a mountain of it stacked in the yard!' he laughed.

'You can mock! But where would you be without it, eh?'

'I wish I'd known this when we got wed. I'd have saved myself a bob or two on your ring.'

My father's ridicule did nothing to dampen my mother's enthusiasm. The arrival of the coal-lorry was always an event. A rattle on the front door signalled delivery. This was the cue for my mother to loosen the rusty bolt on the garden gate. Shortly afterwards, the coalman lumbered up the path with a coal sack slumped over his shoulder like a sleeping child. His feet crunched down the passage leading to our coal-house. Then came the delicious sound as the sack was tipped out; as lumps of coal grated against each other. For days afterwards, we would find bits gleaming in the passageway.

The smell of coal always makes me think of my mother. It conjures up her spirit in a single breath. A picture of her hauling in the coal-bucket: her hands dusted with black powder, a smudge on the bridge of her nose where she had pushed back her spectacles. No matter how carefully she carried the scuttle, the dust got everywhere. On the carpet. On the sideboard. Beneath the sapphire glass vase on the window sill. Whenever my mother lifted up an ornament, there was a black print around it. 'Uh-oh!' she clucked, before wiping it away. 'Another shadow.' There was no escaping the dust. It settled everywhere. It was not until I was orphaned and went to live in Suffolk that I realized spittle should be clear rather than black.

My mother was a great believer in first footing. Every New Year's Eve, she stayed up past midnight to carry a piece of coal through the house – from front door to back – and left it on the doorstep. She smeared our cheeks with this same lump of coal to ensure good luck for the coming year.

Towards the end of her pregnancy, my mother had to stay in Bromsgrove Hospital with pre-eclampsia. One of our neighbours, Maddie Jackson, collected me from school and cooked my tea. My father picked me up when he got home from work, but when he was travelling far afield I stayed overnight. It was an unsettling period. Until then, neither my father nor I had realized how much we relied on my mother. We had assumed our daily rituals happened of their own accord – as dependable as the rising and setting of the sun.

As a result of my mother being in hospital, we forgot to welcome in the New Year. When midnight chimed signalling the end of 1976 and the start of 1977, my father was in Southwold preparing to shoe a team of dray-horses for a local brewery. Meanwhile, I was tucked up in bed at the Jacksons', the only celebration there being the muffled chimes of Big Ben on the television downstairs.

When my mother came home a week later, with Billy wrapped in a shawl in her arms, she looked for the coal on the doorstep and was appalled by our negligence.

'No good will come of it,' she tutted.

And she was right. One month later, she and Billy were dead.

I will not dwell on such sad events yet though. First, let me enjoy the precious memories that remain. Often as we sat in front of the fire, my mother read to me. I snuggled into her coal-scented skin, and pillowed my head on her breast. Her voice boomed in her chest, reverberated pleasantly in my ear.

'Tell me the story of *The Little Match Girl*,' I begged.

The fairy-tale has always driven a chill into my heart. It is the tale of a motherless beggar who wanders the streets selling matches on a bitter Christmas Eve. As snow starts to fall, the little match girl – barefoot and dressed in rags – is left shivering in the street. The blizzard is so bad that no one is sure whether snow is falling out of the sky or blowing upwards from the cobbles. Eventually, the little match girl takes shelter in a shop doorway. Here, she discovers one last box of matches in her apron pocket.

Rather than sell the matches, the little match girl decides to strike them in the hope of keeping warm. As the first match blazes into light, the most wondrous of sights: a banquet table laid out with a Christmas feast. In the centre is a roast goose, honey-glazed and decorated with cherries. The little match girl is starving, so she reaches out for a little crackling. As she does so, the match burns out and the banquet disappears.

She lights a second match. Again, an extraordinary vision: a

Christmas tree sparkling with candles and silver baubles; gifts stacked underneath. As the girl stretches to touch a branch, the match dies and the fir tree vanishes. Again, she is left shivering in the shop doorway.

With trembling fingers, she strikes another match. This time, her beloved mother appears, dressed in pearly robes. The little match girl lights the rest of the matches, one after the other, until the box is empty.

'Don't leave me again. Take me with you while the light lasts,' she pleads.

The last match is dwindling, but her mother scoops up the little match girl in her arms. They soar to Heaven in a blaze of light. There, the angels wrap her in fleecy clouds to keep her warm and feed her heavenly delights.

Pedestrians wandering the snow-covered streets on Christmas morning find her body in a shop doorway. Her cheeks are frozen roses. But her lips are smiling.

# Chapter 2

I sensed something was wrong as soon as I ran to the school gates. I was expecting to see the sparkling wheels of Billy's pram, my mother jiggling the handle to soothe him. Instead, Mrs Jackson was waiting for me: her daughter, Jessie, at her side. Mrs Jackson grabbed my hand and squeezed it firmly.

'You're coming home with us today Angela.'

'Where's Mum?'

'Your dad's asked me to fetch you from school. He'll explain everything when he picks you up.'

Elm Road was a meandering street which snaked in a long S-shape. The Jacksons lived at one end. We lived at the other. As we arrived, there was a police car parked horizontally across the end of the road with its lights flashing. A policewoman was redirecting traffic. In spite of her efforts, a driver had parked on the grass verge and was already ambling down the road. A camera was dangling from his neck.

Mrs Jackson gripped our hands and ushered us up the alley leading to her back door.

'What is it? What's happening?' I asked.

Mrs Jackson pretended not to hear my question. 'Would you like some fairy cakes before tea, Angela? I made some specially.'

'I know what it is. I know what's happening!' Jessie chimed.

Mrs Jackson gave her daughter a fierce glance. 'That's enough! Remember what I said! One word out of you!'

She tugged us up the passageway between the houses and I did not resist. I felt uneasy, but not unduly so. I was sure to find out what had happened when my father collected me.

Usually, when I visited the Jacksons, Jessie and I were sent upstairs to play. On that particular afternoon, Mrs Jackson suggested that we help in the kitchen. She was preparing my favourite meal: sausages and chips. Mrs Jackson let me wash the potatoes, then prod the sausage skins with a fork. She prepared the potatoes with practised skill, poking out the eyes and paring the skin so thinly that it looked like shavings rather than peel. After this, Jessie and I took turns whisking a packet of strawberry Angel Delight. We poured the mixture into cut-glass bowls and decorated the tops with a rainbow of hundreds and thousands.

After supper, Mrs Jackson usually made us all tea in the best china cups and we settled in front of the hearth. She slipped off her shoes for half an hour before washing up. We would swallow our tea quickly. Then we would spin the leftovers anti-clockwise in our cups and tip them out in our saucers. Mrs Jackson would examine the leaves and tell our fortunes.

It had been an evening ritual for as long as I could remember. But when Jessie span her tea and passed over her saucer, Mrs Jackson answered sharply, 'Not today. I don't think it's a good idea. Not under the circumstances.'

'Why, Mum?'

'You know why! I'm not going to argue about it. So don't keep on!'

'Can we watch telly then?'

'If you like. So long as it's not The News!'

When I heard keys jangling and saw Mr Jackson in the doorway, I knew something was wrong. Jessie's father never came home early on week days. Even when I stayed overnight, I did not see him until breakfast.

Mr Jackson ruffled my hair and told me I was 'very brave'. He bounced me on his knee, chanting 'Ride a Cock Horse' and 'To Market, To Market' – although we both knew I was too old for such games. After this, I was given a pair of Jessie's pyjamas to wear and (in spite of her protests) was allowed to borrow her flannel and toothbrush. We climbed into bed and Mrs Jackson read aloud a chapter of *The Lion, The Witch and The Wardrobe* lingering over descriptions of the White Witch and the ice creeping across Narnia. I did not enjoy the story as much as I had done before. I wanted to know why everyone was behaving so strangely.

'When's Dad going to pick me up?'

'I'm not sure,' Mrs Jackson replied. 'When he's ready. He hasn't called yet. I expect he will do later.'

'Have Mum and Billy gone to hospital again?'

Mrs Jackson bit the inside of her cheek. She started picking at cotton threads on the eiderdown.

'It's not really for me to say. Your dad should be the one to tell you. Try to get some sleep. Hopefully, you'll see him in the morning.'

But my father did not fetch me the following morning. Nor the morning after that. Nor the next. I stayed at the Jacksons' house for over a week and during that time, I was kept off school. Mrs Jackson occupied me each day with activities ranging from candle-making to cross-stitch. Every time I asked about my family, or my father, my questions met with evasiveness. Jessie, who was usually a blabbermouth, was itching to share the secret. But she must have been bribed or bullied into silence. I promised to give her my collection of pony stickers, my tennis racket, even my bike. Yet nothing I offered would persuade her to breathe a word.

# Chapter 3

Our house reeked of smoke. It was not the agreeable scent of coal or wood smoke. It was the stench of burned plastic, polyurethane and rubber. We kept our coats on and stood shivering in the hallway, uncertain what to do next. It was damp – the house appeared to have been left unheated for several weeks. The air was heavy: like wet sand. The hallway felt grainy and uncomfortable.

Instinctively, I headed for the warm comfort of the living-room. The door was shut. I put my hand on the brass knob and was about to turn it when my father placed his large hand over mine.

'Don't go in there yet. There's something I want to tell you.'

He guided me to the dining-room, a room my mother rarely used except for entertaining visitors. It was my least favourite room in the house. It had a north-facing window with red velvet curtains from ceiling to floor. The lack of natural light accentuated the sombreness of the furniture which was carved from black mahogany. The chairs were straight-backed, stiff, with uncomfortable tapestry seats. The table was hidden beneath an embroidered cloth which hung over the edges. A glass cabinet stood in one corner, filled with tantalizing ornaments I was forbidden to touch: porcelain flowers, a china dray-horse, a bowl filled with sweets made from Venetian glass.

The first thing I noticed was that the furniture had been moved. The dining-table had been pushed to one side and a semi-circle of chairs had been placed around the hearth. My mother's address book was open on the table. Beside it was a notepad, envelopes and a pen. A pile of newspapers had been placed on one of the chairs. *The Bromsgrove Herald* was at the top of the pile. Clippings had been torn from its front page. There were gaping holes in place of headlines.

My father sat down with a heavy sigh. He motioned for me to sit on his lap. Instead, I sat on the chair opposite. I was angry to have been left at the Jacksons for so long, only to return to an unwelcoming home.

'Well, Angel,' my father said, as if he was alone and talking to himself, 'I don't know what I'm going to say . . .'

As I sat sullenly waiting for him to begin, my gaze was drawn to the fireplace. The silver fireguard had been pushed to one side and a box of matches had been left on the tiles. A sheaf of scorched black paper was in the grate. It had maintained its shape in spite of burning. My father picked up the poker and prodded idly until it disintegrated. Fragments of ash fluttered on to the carpet.

'Something's happened to Mum and Billy, hasn't it?' I said, helping him.

'Eh? That's right. Yes. Yes.'

'Are they in hospital?'

'They were. But they aren't now. They . . .'

'Are they dead?'

I did not know where the words came from: was not even aware I had been thinking them. All the time I was at the Jacksons', I had clung to the notion that my mother might be ill or injured. I had avoided thoughts of anything more serious. At home though, everything fell into place. The terrible silence. The darkness. The dread. The grate filled with ashes like crushed butterflies.

My father looked relieved. Words tumbled from his lips.

'There was an accident,' he gasped. 'A fire. The neighbours had to break down the door. When they got inside, it was too late. They were both . . . neither of them survived.'

'You mean they're dead?'

'I'm sorry.'

'Both of them?'

'A spark jumped out of the grate . . . set fire to the rug. They were asleep. It was the smoke. It happened so quickly.'

'I don't believe you!'

I did not fully understand what had happened. But I understood the ash-filled grate and the closed living-room door. I understood the coldness.

I started to cry. Not from grief, but from confusion. My father was lying. He was holding something back from me. I did not know what or why. I just knew, as children know these things, intuitively.

My father tried to wrap his arms around me, but I pushed him away. So he crooned: the lullaby-voice he used to calm horses at the forge.

'Come on now, Angel. It's all right. Come on. Let me hold you.'

He hauled me on his lap so that I was balancing on his knees, overlarge and clumsy, weeping against his shoulder. He stroked my hair in the sensitive spot behind the ear. Rhythmically. His middle finger tracing the same journey again and again, his fingernail occasionally catching the skin. Over and over. Stroking all the resistance out of me. All the anger. The disbelief.

Then, I was no longer crying, but was like a violin, wailing while someone else scraped the strings. The sobs wrenched me, stirring every part of my body. Up and down the scales without a music sheet to read from. Blind. The torture of inexperience and untuned strings.

Finally, the terrible symphony subsided. My ears stopped ringing. I discovered that I could breathe. My father's pullover was sodden beneath my cheek. He was still stroking my hair; still lull-lulling with his tongue.

I twisted my head to look at him. He had changed since I had seen him last. The rounded edges had disappeared from his face. His cheeks were angular and haggard. There was something about his eyes. Not just around them, but in them too. As if they were not eyes, but stones. They were empty, utterly empty.

'Do you believe in Heaven?' I asked.

'I don't know,' my father answered cautiously. 'Do you?'

'Not really. I think it's just a made-up place.'

'I think so too.'

'What will happen to them? Now they're dead?'

'I don't know. I don't think anyone does.'

'Do you think we'll ever see them again?'

'Yes, I do. Definitely. That's for sure.'

'Dad?'

'Mmm.'

'I'm cold. Can we build a fire?'

Some of the ashes were as powdery as icing sugar. Others were as crunchy as honeycomb. My father rattled the poker in the grate to break up the larger husks. Then, when the ash had fallen through, we scooped it into the bucket.

He fetched a pile of newspapers, wood, and coal from the outhouse. Then, he showed me how to twist the paper. We packed the kindling densely in the grate before placing the wood on top. After this, my father lit the base. The paper flared, the flames seeping along the newsprint like slow inkblots. But the wood would not catch light. Eventually, the fire sputtered out.

'The wood must be damp. Your Mum's always saying we should keep it indoors,' my father said flatly.

Several hours had passed since we first entered the house. It was growing dark outside. We were still wearing our coats. I was blowing on my fingers to keep warm.

'Maybe we should just go to bed, eh? Light the fire tomorrow? Do you know where the hot-water bottles are kept?'

I nodded and showed him the larder where the rubber bottles were hanging upside down on a hook.

While my father was boiling the kettle, I noticed what looked like a black garden bucket by the kitchen door. On closer inspection, I realized it was the coal scuttle. I rubbed it with my finger, hoping to spot a glimmer, a trace of its former splendour. But the polished brass which my mother and I used to shine to a mirror was no more.

We went to bed early that night. I slept in my parents' bed, on my mother's side. We did not undress. My father folded about me until

I stopped shivering in his arms.

'Try to get some sleep,' he whispered. 'It's one of the few things we can do.'

My mother's nightdress was under the pillow. The cool satin slipped through my fingers like liquid. From where I was lying, I could see a white baby shawl hugging the bedside chair like a ghoul.

# Chapter 4

I was not sure what I expected to find in the living-room. A charred crib? Scorched rags flapping around the windows? A television with melted knobs? A ceiling black as a midnight sky?

Instead, the room was empty. The brown and orange sofa, the armchairs, the crib, the television, the curtains, the oval mirror that hung over the fireplace were gone. As were the framed black and white family photographs which had lined the mantelpiece. A stepladder stood in a corner with a tin of emulsion on top. The carpet had been taken up to reveal the stained floorboards. A crescent of glossy paint had formed in the centre of the floor.

I had thought the living-room was white before. The repainted walls revealed that what I had previously thought of as 'white' was in fact the colour of old dentures or chewing gum. This colour – this new white – was startling. It was the white of doctors' waiting-rooms, of dental surgeries, of hospital wards. The white of winding sheets.

My father had done his best to whitewash over the soot, the burns, the smoke, which had blackened the walls. What he had neglected though was the smell. I was not destined to stay at Elm Road for long after this, but the smell of fire must have remained in the bricks for years.

For the first few weeks, my father made meals from whatever he could find in the pantry. One day, we ate Rice Crispies for breakfast, lunch and tea. Another day, we had salt 'n' vinegar crisp sandwiches, without any butter or marge. On another, we feasted on lemon curd and cream crackers. When we discovered a tub of custard powder tucked away on the bottom shelf, it was an excuse to eat nothing but variations of custard. Custard with cocoa powder, custard with bananas, custard with tinned pears, custard with raisins, custard with wafer biscuits.

What followed was a period of leniency in which I was allowed to indulge in all kinds of wanton behaviour. I wore the same pair of socks for five days in a row. I wiped my nose with my sleeve. I drank milk straight from the bottle. I licked butter off my knife. I 'forgot' to brush my teeth.

'What would your Mum say about this?' my father sometimes asked.

'She wouldn't mind.'

He did not have the strength to contradict me.

I missed my mother and Billy in so many ways it was impossible to count them all. I remembered the day Billy arrived: violet-eyed, with vernix in the creases of his skin. How he had a reflex which made his arms flap like a sparrow's wings when he was put down. How his fontanelle dipped if he was thirsty. I missed Billy's baby-grows steaming on the clothes horse. I missed his ancient face; his wise but innocent eyes.

My mother was harder to miss. Missing her was painful. Instead, I missed my mother's lumpy porridge at breakfast. I missed the tenderness with which she zipped my anorak right up, so that the teeth pinched my chin. I missed the way she slipped bananas into my satchel without undoing the buckle, so that the fruit was bruised by lunchtime. I missed wearing clean clothes which smelled of fresh-mown grass and the breeze. I missed hoovered carpets, plumped cushions, crumbless sheets. I missed the soft flesh pillowing my cheek as I listened to bedtime stories.

'Want to talk about it, Angel?' my father asked.

'Talk about what?'

'Whatever's on your mind.'

'Nothing's on my mind.'

'Well, whenever you want to talk about the nothing that's on your mind, you know where I am.'

'I know.'

'When you're ready then.'

Even after my father had finished redecorating the living-room, we did not use it. He filled a bowl with homemade pot pourri: dried rose petals and eucalyptus leaves sprayed with Old Spice. He replaced the sofa and bought a new black and white television. He hung a pair of Constable landscapes on either side of the chimney breast. Yet we still could not bring ourselves to sit in there.

'Maybe we should move house?' he suggested. 'What do you think?'

'I'd rather stay here.'

'Even with the smell?'

'I don't notice it much now. I've got used to it.'

'I suppose you're right.'

'Why don't we just swap rooms? Move all this stuff into the dining-room – and put the cabinet and dining-chairs in here.'

Finally, that was what we agreed to do. We carried the glass and china ornaments one by one into the living-room. We tucked the display cabinet into a corner. We stacked the dining-chairs in pairs: one upside down on top of the other.

Then, we turned the new sofa on its end and shuffled it along the corridor. My father rewired the aerial and put the television on the dining-table. We rehung the pictures of Flatford Watermill.

The dining-room was cramped, but it was more homely than before. We ate meals off our laps in front of the fire. We did not take our plates into the kitchen after meals, but instead left them on the floor. We slipped off our shoes and warmed our toes. Our heels occasionally brushed the plates, chinking the cutlery. The television murmured and cast shadows against the walls.

We were sitting in what my father referred to as 'our new quarters' one evening, when there was a bang and the window suddenly exploded. Glass sprayed around us. A missile skimmed past my father's ear. Then the floor was glistening, twinkling with danger. In the middle of the hearth was a housebrick, surrounded by a crazy paving of glass. I squealed: a shriek such as a hedgehog or a vole might make when pounced upon unexpectedly. I could smell ice. The tingly, almost chemical scent, of hawfrost coming through the broken window. The chill penetrated the room immediately, driving out the heat. I started to whimper. I had already come to associate cold with fear.

In the same instant, it seemed, my father was lifting me in his arms. Earlier, he had kicked his boots to the other side of the room and taken off his socks. His feet were bare. The skin was mottled, mapped with mauve veins. His toes were covered in toffee-coloured hair. The soles were calfskin soft. Yet he carried me across the broken glass with the same unflinching faith I have since witnessed in people who stride over coals. He did not put me down until he reached the bottom of the stairs.

'Go upstairs and get into bed. I'll be up in a minute,' he ordered.

I was still whimpering; afraid to be alone.

'What is it Dad? What's happening?'

'Nothing to worry about. Just someone acting as judge and jury.'

'I don't want to go. What if something happens to you?'

'Nothing's going to happen. It wasn't meant to hurt me: it was just a warning.'

'Your feet are bleeding.'

'They're scratches.'

'There's blood everywhere.'

'Go up to bed. Quickly. No arguing. Just do as you're told.'

I did not plan to get into bed: I intended to sit at the top of the stairs and wait. But it was so cold that I eventually pulled back the flannelette sheet and curled beneath it. I did not dare to switch on the light.

Other strange things had happened since my mother and Billy had died. The telephone clamoured late at night until my father pinched the plug out of the wall. The door knocker rattled but the doorstep was empty. Cigarette butts and matches were posted through our letterbox, together with other, less savoury, items.

Then there was the car parked on the grass verge at the end of our front garden. It was a distinctive car – a white MG with a dented wing. At night, its paintwork shimmered under the street lamps so that it became almost ghostly. The driver was faceless – a cigarette glowed in the space where his face would have been. Sometimes, two amber spots blinked like demon's eyes. It was unnerving and sinister: I had never known anyone to smoke two cigarettes at the same time.

When I first mentioned this car, my father became agitated.

'You haven't been peeping out of the curtains? You've got to ignore him, the same as I do. He'll only keep coming back if there's something to see!'

After this, I never raised the subject again. On the rare occasions I went outside, I trained myself to look away.

The housebrick changed all this. It was rust-coloured, with concrete still clinging to the dip in the middle. It was engraved with the words *LONDON BRIC–*. Concrete obscured the remaining letters. The brick was identical to all the other bricks used to build all the other houses on our estate. When it arched through the dining-room window, spraying glass like water droplets, it had landed on the hearth. It chipped the tiles around the fireplace. A message was attached, scrawled on a scrap of paper. It had been torn from a ring-binder notepad: all the holes were ripped in one direction. There was one word upon it: MURDERER.

That night, all sounds were magnified. It was as if my ears were compensating for the loss of sight after the lights went out. The faintest noises, unnoticeable in daylight, carried. A cat's nails clicking as it leapt on a garden fence. Our neighbour, Norman, emptying his dust-choked lungs on the other side of the wall. The yowl of a distant fire engine. A baby halfheartedly mewling on the other side of the street.

Downstairs, a cupboard door shushed as it was opened, dragging against the carpet. Plastic bags whispered. A brush chattered in a dustpan. My father shuffled back in the dining-room, glass grinding under his feet. Then, came the soft sweep of horse hair; the clash of jagged glass resisting jagged glass.

When the brushstrokes paused, there was a frosty thud. My father must have thrown the brick out of the window. Something – someone – yelped. The bark of a badger, a fox, a dog. After this, there was a steady thump of feet.

My father must have heard the sounds too, for he flung open the front door and shouted, 'That's right, you bastard, run away! As if we haven't suffered enough!'

I scrambled out of bed and parted the curtains. The windows were misted with a million polka-dots of condensation, all frozen against the glass. I made a peephole by holding my fist against the window, then scratching off the ice. Through this hole, our front lawn was elongated by the light flooding from the front door. The hydrangea bushes had disappeared into the bordering darkness.

I wanted to see what my father was doing; where he had thrown the brick; what he had done with the message. But I was too close to the glass and the peephole kept freezing over. Everything was ice-streaked, blurred.

Eventually, I returned to bed. I lay there for some time, listening to my father attempting the impossible task of repairing a broken window with newspapers and sticky tape.

# Chapter 5

My father was too educated to be a farrier. He knew the melting point of every metal on the Periodic Table. He could tell which metals gave off which flame colours; what happened when they were oxidized; which chemical reactions occurred if they were mixed with sulphuric acid. He could look at a metal amalgam and guess the elements it was composed of, and in which percentages.

He picked up interesting bits of rock and knew which metal ores they contained. He could match a shoe to a horse's hoof by sight alone – and it was rarely out. Unfortunately, this intelligence was coupled with a tendency to be introverted and abrupt. Had he been gruff but unintelligent, perhaps no one would have minded. As it was, anyone who met him for the first time thought him either arrogant or rude.

We were living in Bromsgrove, an unremarkable town in the Midlands, which was still small enough for most people to know one another's christian names. Bromsgrove was once considered a rural town: it was surrounded by broad swathes of agricultural and farming land, and had a weekly livestock market. But it was rapidly becoming more industrial. Birmingham was less than fifteen miles away. Factories were already springing up in new industrial parks around the peripheries of the town. Once, people had climbed to the top of the nearby Lickey Hills to admire the miles of rolling pastureland. Increasingly, they saw chimneys spearing the skyline.

My father was caught in the flux of this change. When he first started in business, he worked full-time at a traditional forge. As his list of local clients diminished, he realized it was more lucrative to take to the road. He purchased a van and a portable forge. He drove all over the country: setting up in the middle of market squares, at the side of busy highways, or in isolated churchyards. He was not short of work. Most horses needed their shoes replaced eight times a year due to the damage caused by modern roads.

One morning, my father reversed his van to the back of the house and put his leather apron on the front seat. I knew this could only mean one thing. I waited until he went to the shed to fetch his tool bag, then I climbed into the back. When my father returned, he looked at me quizzically, as if to say: 'What are you doing in there?' But he did not ask me to get out. Instead, he pushed his anvil in behind me and closed the doors. Shortly after this, we set off.

I tried talking at first, but the engine was too loud. I had to

shout, so eventually I gave up. My father was not in the mood for chatting anyway. He had talked less and less since the brick came through the window. When I asked questions, he would often respond with nothing more than grunts. Sometimes, he just stared for long periods of time at the carpet and I wondered if he knew I was there at all.

There were no seats in the back of the van, just a fragment of tatty carpet. As we drove down winding lanes into the heart of the Worcestershire countryside, I let myself roll from side to side, enjoying the exaggeration of my movements. When I tired of this, I sat on the wheel arch and felt the potholes vibrating through the metal.

I had been off school for over a month. At first, I had missed my friends and the routines of school. But then, to tell the truth, I got used to staying at home. In fact, I preferred it. So many strange things had happened, I wanted to be close to my father. As if somehow I might protect him, just by being there. I wanted to help him get his eyes back. His old eyes which had warmth and feeling in them. Not the dull pebbles that had replaced them.

I was worried how much time I had left before I was sent back to school. We had already received two letters from my headmistress. She made the mistake of sending her correspondence in envelopes embossed with the school crest. Given my father's state of mind, I doubt whether he would have responded, but I ripped up the letters anyway. My father needed me more than my teachers did.

The van turned off the road and up a muddy track which appeared to lead nowhere: through a copse bordered by silver birches, over a stream, through fields ravaged by winter. Magpies were tossing their tails and pecking at the dirt beside the track. They flew up as the van approached, then dipped down again a hundred yards ahead, as if waiting for us. We turned a corner through a thicket of brambles. Suddenly, we were in a muddy courtyard. We stopped in front of a large farmhouse which sprawled into a series of outhouses, stables and sheds. There was such a confusing number of doors, it was impossible to see the main entrance.

A middle-aged woman with broad hands, short nails and a wide trustworthy face, came out to greet us while we were unloading the van. She was small in stature, but had disproportionately large feet: the tops of her wellingtons came over her knees. Her name was Alicia Crawford, and it was a name I would remember for the rest of my life.

'Jim! I'm so sorry!' Mrs Crawford said, extending her hand.

'Well, they're gone and that's all there is to it.' My father's voice was flat and indifferent. His heavy Bromsgrove accent crushing all trace of emotion from his words.

'You didn't have to come today. I wasn't expecting you.'

'Life has to go on. I still have to earn a crust.'

'Well, at least you've still got a daughter. It must be a comfort to you . . .'

'Angela? Oh yes, I've still got her. Now where's this horse?'

A chestnut stallion was tethered to a fence not far from the farm-house. My father tied on his leather apron and removed the worn horseshoes with the pliers. He trimmed the hoofs using giant nail clippers and a file like a cheese grater. The clippings were the size of saucers.

My father had always been most at ease with horses. He said they were easier to talk to than people – that they talked more sense and knew when to hold their tongues. Perhaps because of this, my father was more communicative than usual. He even started to whistle – not a tune that I knew, but one of those meandering melodies which only mean something to the whistler.

I picked up one of the hoof clippings and held it like a dragon's claw.

'Can I have one, Dad? Can I keep it?'

'You can have all of them if you like.'

'Does the horse mind having its hoofs cut?'

'Don't be daft. It's like having your nails trimmed.'

Once the furnace was roaring, the labour began. My father poked a shoe in the flames until it was red-hot. He held it up against a front hoof to approximate measurements. Then, he hammered the metal on the anvil, before plunging it back in the furnace. After the shoe had reheated, he thrust it against the hoof. There was a puff of flame which was quickly extinguished. The air was branded black.

I soon tired of watching my father. I tight-rope walked on a stone wall, then tiptoed over a cattle grid. I pretended the hoof clippings were giant talons, and that I was a tyrannosaurus or a pterodactyl. My father was extraordinarily slow. Even after I had finished my games, he was only hammering the third shoe. He was still whistling though. A good sign. I might have been mistaken, but his eyes seemed to shine a little too.

'I'm cold,' I whined.

'Put on my coat then. It's in the front of the van.'

'I'm bored.'

'Go and find something to play with. I won't be long.'

'You always say that. I know you'll be ages.'

I wandered into the courtyard and saw some chickens pecking the dirt. I started chasing them – pretending not to be chasing them, pretending to be simply ambling in their direction, but chasing them nonetheless. The chickens fled into a barn, up into the rafters where they escaped me altogether. I was looking for something else to do when I spotted a silver Mercedes parked to one side of the farmhouse. I was peering through the windows admiring the polished dials and buttons, when Mrs Crawford came outside carrying a tray of steaming cocoa.

'I thought you'd like something to warm you up,' she said cheerily.

'Can I sit inside your car?'

'If you like. But you can't take your drink in there. And no muddy feet on the seats!'

Mrs Crawford hooked a bunch of keys out of her pocket and unlocked the driver's door.

'Can I try the horn?'

'OK. But not too loud. I don't want you frightening the livestock.'

Mrs Crawford put the drinks on the wall and climbed into the passenger seat. She leaned across to show me where the indicator was; how to switch the windscreen wipers on and off; how to tune the radio. I tooted the horn a couple of times; changed channels on the radio; experimented with the water squirter, the windscreen wipers, the electric windows.

I had discovered the foot pedals and was pumping the accelerator when my father shouted, 'Ho there! Can I have a hand?'

A brisk wind was gusting and the horse was becoming skittish. We could see it capering on the spot through the back window.

'I'd better go – your dad needs some help. Will you be all right here on your own? Or would you rather come with me?' asked Mrs Crawford.

'Can I stay here?'

'OK. But no touching the handbrake!'

Mrs Crawford took the keys out of the ignition. Then, she lumbered across the courtyard, her wellingtons making a heavy *clud, clud, clud* on the dirt.

I scrambled into the back of the car and pulled out the arm rest, my legs straddling either side, to watch. Mrs Crawford was a short woman, but she was strong. The horse was several hands taller than her, but she pinned it against the fence so that my father could resume his work.

The ashtrays in the back were jammed with cellophane wrappers which smelled faintly of Murray Mints. So I clambered into the front again and fumbled with the catch on the glove compartment. It contained a folded newspaper, a pair of leather gloves, a chamois leather, an AA handbook, a lipstick – but no sweets.

I was putting these items back, wondering whether Mrs Crawford would notice if I 'borrowed' her lipstick, when something caught my eye. I looked. Then, looked again. My father's face was staring at me from the front page. Above the picture, printed in large typescript was the headline: FARRIER QUIZZED OVER BLAZE DEATHS. I read no further. My father's mouth was half-smile, half-snarl. His eyes were crazed.

I staggered across the courtyard clutching the newspaper. My father had his back to me. He was hunched over, hitting nails into the final shoe. *Ching! Ching! Ching!* The leather apron had pulled tight: a thin noose around the back of his neck.

'What's this?' I gasped.

I was choking. There was water in my throat and on my lip. Salt water. The taste of an ominous grey sea: a presage of what was to come. My cheeks were stinging. I felt betrayed. As if something momentous had happened and I had been excluded from it. My father stopped whistling. His face faded to the colour of suet.

'So you've found out then! I wondered how long it would be.'

He threw down his hammer and peeled off his leather gloves. I would not say that he hugged me, rather that he crushed me to him.

Mrs Crawford hesitated. 'Jim, I'm so sorry. I meant to throw that out ages ago. I'd forgotten about it. She must have got it out of the car.'

My father did not answer. He was squeezing me against him, his brute hands full of love and force.

'Come on now. It's not worth crying about. There's no point getting upset. That won't change anything. What's done is done. We've just got to be strong . . .'

I did not listen to much my father said that day. But I remember his desperation. The way he whimpered rather than crooned. It was pitiful. If he could not convince me, a 12 year old, how was he ever to convince anyone else?

By the time I stopped crying, Mrs Crawford and her horse had disappeared. My father tipped his coals into the ditch and splashed water over the portable furnace. Then, he motioned for me to climb into the front of the van while he collected his money.

It was late afternoon when we finally left. The sun was already setting, but there was no brilliant flare on the horizon. The sky was wan and overcast, as if all the colour had drained from it. My father's eyes were the same dull grey as the shingle beach near my aunt and uncle's home in Suffolk.

'What are we having for tea, Dad? What are we doing when we get home?'

He did not answer. As we bumped along, I saw what the magpies had been pecking on the edge of the track: the carcass of a young deer. We drove home in a silence heavier than any known metal.

# Chapter 6

We used to have an old-fashioned coal-fired boiler to heat the water. It was a temperamental appliance. Sometimes it heated the water so hot that it scalded our hands. On other occasions, it extinguished itself without heating the water at all. There was an art to lighting this boiler and keeping it ablaze. My mother claimed the flue had been misconnected to the chimney. Gusts of rain and wind, however slight, always managed to find their way inside and tamper with the flames. It was the reason why my mother got up at six o'clock – it took this length of time to coax the boiler into life and ensure hot water by breakfast.

After my mother and Billy died, my father did not bother lighting the boiler. We boiled water in the kettle and had flannel washes. When we ran out of clean clothes, we retrieved items from the laundry basket and aired them on the backs of chairs. On the rare occasions we left the house, my father sprayed our clothes with deodorant. Eventually though, our clothes had been recycled so many times that they did not just look dirty but smelled dirty too.

Our neighbour, Maddie Jackson, had dutifully visited us ever since the fire. Sometimes she came with a baked bean casserole or a shepherd's pie. Occasionally, she ran the vacuum cleaner and a duster around the house. Other times, she washed and tidied away crockery which had been left for days.

Mrs Jackson was discreet, non-judgemental. If she had an opinion about our hygiene, she never mentioned it. Even when her nostrils flared at the stale body odour, she remained tactful.

'I'll take Angela's clothes home with me if you like. If you could put them in a bag, I'll do them tomorrow. It won't be any problem. I'll put them in the tub with Jessie's clothes,' she offered.

The suggestion was sufficient to stir my father out of his lethargy.

'Don't worry about it, Maddie. I've been meaning to do some washing myself. Sunday. That's when I'll do it. Ah yes, that's decided then.'

Thus, without knowing it, an unalterable chain of events was set in motion. We had two months' laundry. All our clothes, the bed linen, the towels, the tea towels, were in varying states of grubbiness. We needed large quantities of water – *hot* water – to clean them. There was no escaping the fact that we would have to light the boiler.

It was a joyless Sunday morning when my father prepared for the task ahead. As the boiler's metal door screeched open to reveal the soft delight of the ashes, the sound instantly conjured up the ghost of my mother. There was exquisite pain and pleasure in that moment. I held the shovel, dipped it in the ash, tipped it in the bucket, in the full knowledge that my fingers were tracing the same surfaces where my mother's had been, gliding over the same dents and depressions as hers.

There was once a time when my father would have patiently coaxed a flame, cajoled it, teased it into life. He would have viewed the boiler as a contest, a battle of wills. He would have been undaunted by the challenge. In fact, he would have rather enjoyed it. But that time was gone. It was a sign of my father's anguish that fire had become tedious to him. It was a chore he would rather have done without. As a result of this malaise, he did something he had never done before – he purchased a bottle of paraffin.

Let me tell you about paraffin. There is a certain luxury to it: a velvety smoothness, a gentle blueness, an iridescent shimmer. My mother never used paraffin while she was alive, but I know she would have loved it. It would have been an indulgence. She would have reserved it for special occasions.

My father though was too depressed to appreciate the finer qualities of paraffin. He had become increasingly withdrawn since the visit to Alicia Crawford. Now, he haphazardly stacked the kindling and fuel in the boiler, then dribbled paraffin over the top. He tossed in a match, then slammed the door. There was no poetry or finesse to these preparations. My father performed the operation resentfully: in the same way that he squirted washing up liquid over a bowl of dirty dishes.

'Just going to put my feet up for five minutes!' he muttered, and disappeared into the dining-room. 'Reading the paper,' he would once have added. Except that 'newspaper' had become a dirty word. Something unmentionable. Even the sight of the newspaper boy was enough to make my father look ashamed.

The living-room door clicked shut. I knew he would not look at the boiler again unless the water pipes were cold or if it needed extra fuel.

The boiler went out in less than five minutes. It was not difficult finding the paraffin bottle. It had been left on the sink with the lid off. It was a large bottle and surprisingly heavy. I lifted it unsteadily and somehow managed to spill paraffin on the lino. I mopped the floor with a tea towel with the toe of my slipper as I had seen my father do. I opened the boiler door and stuffed in more newspaper. Then, I squeezed the paraffin until the bottle folded in the middle and the plastic made a sucking sound. I doused the paper and kindling thoroughly. I was determined that this – my first fire – should not go out. I emptied the entire bottle.

The box of matches was on the draining board. I had never lit a match without supervision before. I broke two matchsticks before I managed to strike a light. For a moment, I stood transfixed admiring the quivering flame: the mauve tinge around the base; the space just above the head of the match where there seemed to be no flame at all. I twisted the wood as the flame crept along, leaving charred cinder behind it. I held the match until I could hold it no more. As the flame approached my fingertips, I tossed it into the boiler.

Nothing.

The match had extinguished itself as it somersaulted through the air.

I struck another match. This time, I crouched down to drop the flame inside the boiler.

What happened next, happened all at the same time. There was a brilliant white light and intense heat. My eyes, my nose, my mouth were filled with it. Searing, scorching white light. Instinctively, I raised my hands. But I had no face. Or rather I had no hands. Or perhaps my hands melted into my face. Or my face melted into my hands. My throat was sizzling. My lungs were roaring. My ears were shrieking. Every breath was white light. Every pulse was white light. It was light so hot, it screamed. Or perhaps I was screaming. I was the white light: the white light was me.

Just as suddenly it was gone.

Then, I was no longer on the face of the sun. I was on the far side of the moon. Where no light can penetrate and human blood freezes. I was plunging through space. Down, down, down. I landed on the cool relief of kitchen lino.

The first thing I became conscious of was someone clawing at my clothes. There was weightiness. Weightlessness. Then, my arms and legs were bouncing. Jolting. A slow rhythmic pace which was oddly familiar and unfamiliar at the same time.

I opened my eyes and saw the primrose-yellow diamonds of my father's favourite pullover. We must have been in the hallway. The door latch, the security chain, rattled. I was tilted to one side. My head pressed against my father's chest. The front door clicked open. His grip tightened again. We were outside.

I was surprised to see the chimney pot in the middle of the lawn, together with a mosaic of scattered roof tiles. My father was muttering wordlessly. He had placed me on the grass and I could see him clearly against the darkening sky. His lips moving, but no words came out.

'My hands!' I gasped. 'My hands!'

My tongue was too large for my mouth. My lips were swollen. I made two further attempts at speech, before realizing I was deaf.

One of my slippers had fallen off. Soot from the chimney pot mingled with frost on the grass. The chill was already pricking my skin. Someone had put gloves on my hands. Thick uncomfortable mittens, several sizes too big. I tried to tear them off. Then, I realized, I was tugging skin.

A row of shadows appeared at the end of our garden. They were neighbours: parents and children who I considered to be my friends. They must have run out of their homes at the sound of the explosion. They formed a straight, almost military, line along the bottom edge of our front lawn. My father cried to them. He lifted his hands, imploring like a beggar. Wordlessly.

They stared back with accusing eyes. Not one of them stepped forward.

PART II

# Chapter 1

While my mother was alive, we visited Uncle Harry and Aunt Rose every summer. In spite of this, I did not know either of my relatives very well. Although we regularly visited their home in Suffolk, we usually saw more of their housekeeper, Hilary. Uncle Harry was a marine archaeologist and an author. When he was not giving academic lectures or writing books, he was diving for artefacts in the underwater ruins off Dunwich. Aunt Rose was a history professor at Essex University and often stayed overnight in Colchester to give lectures. My aunt and uncle were generous with their home, but less so with their time. They were passionate about East Anglian history, but seemed less interested in the living.

I was therefore surprised to see my uncle strolling down the ward at the Queen Alexandra Hospital to visit me. His knees were doing a knit one, purl one – the bones in the early stages of arthritis. I had, by this time, been in hospital for many months. My only contact with my aunt and uncle had been a 'Get Well' card and a bouquet of yellow carnations. My father told me about the carnations: they had wilted by the time I was conscious again. The card had long since been thrown away.

Uncle Harry patted the bed covers and sat down.

'Do you know who I am?' he asked.

'Of course I do. You don't need to shout though. I can hear you.'

'Oh, your Dad told me—'

'That was ages ago. You just sound a bit odd: like I have cotton wool in my ears.'

'That's good. Very good. I thought—'

I interrupted again: 'When did you speak to Dad? Have you seen him?'

It seemed a long time since I had seen anyone from the outside world, the non-hospital world. Even after all this time as a patient, the ward seemed alien and surreal. I remembered my horror when I had first opened my eyes. My hands were sealed inside plastic bags filled with fluid. The bags were like the ones used to carry goldfish home from fairgrounds. The sight of my hands, quivering like marine creatures at the bottom of the bags only heightened this impression.

I had been sedated to prevent the after-effects of shock. I had lost my hair, my eyebrows, my eyelashes. My palms had been seared off. I had three skin grafts in as many months. The consultant told me it might be years before my skin healed: I would need an intensive programme of physiotherapy to regain the use of my hands. The doctor had a kind face, but I did not trust her. She had an unnerving habit of staring over my left shoulder as she talked.

Uncle Harry reached over to hold my hand – a gesture of intimacy unusual for him – then finding dressings rather than skin, he touched my arm.

'The nurse told me you've been asking about him. I expect you've been wondering where he's been . . .'

My father had been visiting me on and off since I had regained consciousness. He had tried to entertain me by sketching caricatures and comic strips on a notepad. He played Snakes and Ladders against himself for my benefit. He brought me bags of sherbert lemons and cola cubes. The atmosphere was strained though. There had been a distance between us ever since I found the newspaper. I did not trust him and he knew it. Eventually, his visits had become more erratic. He excused his absences, saying he had started to take commissions away from home again. I suspected he was avoiding me. Secretly, I was relieved. It is not a nice feeling wondering if your father is a murderer.

'The staff here tried to contact your father . . . They were worried. They thought he might be ill.'

I knew this already. Although I would hardly have described

anyone as 'worried'. The consultants, the nurses, the auxiliaries, knew what had happened to my mother and Billy. They knew who my father was. Who *I* was. I could see it in their faces. The suspicion. The pity. I heard the hushed and not-so-hushed whispers.

'When they couldn't get hold of him, they called the police. They called me . . . There's no easy way of saying this . . . but I think it's only right that you should know . . .'

I knew already. My father was beating out his feelings on metal. Making the air sing. Curling iron into metal shoes. Burning black crescents on to horses' hoofs. Because it was easier being around horses than it was being around me.

'He took his own life.'

Uncle Harry had never been what my mother called a 'people-person'. While his books and lectures were full of academic sensitivity, he lacked tact in matters of a personal nature. He shifted in his chair and stared at the polished hospital floor. He had broken the news to me as gently as he was able. Now, he was waiting for me to respond in some way.

'He took his own life,' he repeated.

It sounded like a newspaper headline.

The lady from the newsagent wheeled a trolley loaded with newspapers on to the ward each morning. Patients would read them in their beds, arms outstretched, faces hidden behind the headlines. When the visitors came, they would have the same stiff paper truncheons in their hands. When they had finished with them, they left them lying on chairs, on beds, in the bathrooms, in waste-paper baskets.

Late at night, long after everyone else was asleep, I crept along the ward and found them. I felt a deep shame reading these newspapers. As if I were doing something deeply wrong – like steaming open someone else's letters, or unlocking a personal diary.

I read that my father's eyes were blue and that they were also green. That my mother was thirty-two and that she was thirty-six. That we lived at Oak Road and Elm Road and Elk Road. I believed everything and I believed nothing at all.

Now I had another headline. Another story which might have been a truth or a lie. In a strange way this comforted me. It was not my father who was dead, but the dot matrix father. The black and white father whose picture stared from the front pages. The headline concerned a different 12 year old. Another girl – with unscarred skin, with pigtails, eyelashes, eyebrows – had become an orphan.

'Are you all right?'

'I should have guessed,' I whispered.

At the far end of the ward, an orderly wheeled in a silver trolley rattling on its hinges. The smell of steamed cod, mashed potato and tinned peas wafted towards us. A spoon jangled in a stainless steel tureen: the chime of metal on metal. With my eyes closed it might have been my father rattling a poker in the grate.

'I'm afraid he didn't leave a letter. I suppose he was too distraught. So we'll never know the exact whys and wherefores. He just left this . . .'

Uncle Harry drew an envelope from the inside pocket of his coat. It had been folded in four – a crude fan shape – to make it fit. My uncle smoothed out the concertina creases and turned it over. He pulled back the flap and emptied the contents on the bedcover.

'I haven't looked at anything yet. I thought you'd better be the first . . .'

Newspaper cuttings fluttered across the bed like the papery leaves which signal the onset of winter. Some stories were not much larger than oak leaves. Words threaded across them like spidery veins. Others had banner headlines which branched across two pages.

Our home was filled with newspapers after my mother and Billy died. Locals, nationals, broadsheets, tabloids, advertisers, free sheets. The delivery boy arrived at six o'clock each morning, unaware of my father waiting invisibly on the other side of the door. He caught the papers as they slipped through the letterbox: they seldom hit the floor. He sneaked them into the dining-room and scanned the headlines before breakfast.

Sometimes, when I crept to the door, I would hear the squeak of scissors, the tearing of paper on the other side. I turned the handle as swiftly as I could, but it was too stiff. By the time the door swung open, my father would be pretending to read a book or scanning through his accounts. What betrayed him was the agitation in the air. This, and the holes in the newspapers hidden at the bottom of the bin bags.

I made a gesture which, had my hands not been in plastic bags, would have shunted the cuttings to the floor. I felt angry. A hard, cold fury, sharp as flint.

'I don't want to see them. Can you put them away?'

'Perhaps when you've had time to let it sink in. When you feel more able . . .'

Uncle Harry gathered up the cuttings swiftly, as if he had just realized his insensitivity. He stacked the papers unevenly and stuffed them back inside the envelope.

'I'll be taking you to Dunwich with me this weekend. The doctor says it'll be OK. They'd prefer to keep you in longer, but under the circumstances they're prepared to be flexible. They'll send your case notes to the Norfolk and Norwich. You can have any further treatment you need there.'

The lunch trolley trundled at the end of my bed. The orderly heaped a sloppy white mound on a plate and brightened it with mustard-coloured peas. She tucked a serviette into my nightgown, then hunted for a spoon to feed me.

Uncle Harry fastened the buttons on his coat, but made no effort to leave. He lingered by my bedside as if there was something he wanted to say, but was uncertain how to go about saying it.

'I don't suppose you noticed anything strange about my brother – your father – before you came into hospital?' he asked quietly. 'I know things have been pretty difficult since your mother passed away. But was there anything . . . anything which might have pushed him over the edge?'

With dull shock, I remembered that Uncle Harry and Aunt Rose only read *The East Anglian Daily Times*. They were proud to say they did not watch television or listen to the radio. 'Most news is bad news' was the principle. They would only have known what my father told them.

In short, they knew nothing at all.

# Chapter 2

Dunwich was alien to me. If I was a child of earth and fire, Dunwich was a place of air and water. A gale was blowing on the day I arrived at my new home on top of Dunwich cliffs. As we pulled into the narrow lane which led to the house, waves were casting in to shore in relentless white crests. It had always been sunny when I had visited the village before. Now, with the sky so black and the sea pounding the shore, I was reminded of the area's history and the way in which an entire city had been lost beneath the waves.

Four Winds was a tall Victorian building with a high porch, gabled roof, and wooden balconies. The house was in a poor state of repair. The outside walls were covered in grime and badly needed repointing. The window frames were cracked and split. The house was bordered by a copse of trees, but had open views to the sea. On a sunny day, you hardly noticed the shabbiness. You only noticed the sky and sea. Yet on this particular day, Four Winds looked forbidding. The lightning conductor on the red-tiled roof was poised like a harpoon. The surrounding trees had distorted into all manner of shapes, pointing towards the house like the gnarled fingers of witches.

Uncle Harry got out of the car first. As the door swung open, an icy wind swept through the car driving out all warmth in a single breath.

'Ah, smell that sea air! That'll drive a few cobwebs away,' he said cheerily.

He unloaded my suitcases and placed them in the porch, before returning to fetch me. His clothes were spotted with rain and his hair was flapping wildly.

'Come and have a look at the garden before we go inside! You'll be surprised how much has disappeared.'

I tried to protest. But my uncle had taken off his jacket and wrapped it around my shoulders. I let him guide me to the back of the house.

The garden had always been one of Uncle Harry's favourite subjects. My aunt and uncle had purchased Four Winds shortly after they married some thirty years before. At the time, the house was fifty yards from the cliff edge. A surveyor had warned them about the dangers of erosion, but they had no savings and the property was cheap. Besides, they had fallen in love with the village and were fascinated by its history. They calculated the rate of subsidence in the area and took a gamble.

I had seen evidence of the garden slowly disappearing each time I visited. Yet I was shocked when I looked towards the North Sea. There had always been a small boathouse at the end of the garden, together with a wooden bench. Both of these had vanished: the edge of the cliff was less than twenty yards away.

'Did they go over the edge?' I shouted. The wind was driving in hard and my words were blown away in the crash of the sea. But my uncle had anticipated my reaction.

'Last September!' he beamed proudly. 'After a storm.'

He started to stride down the pathway to the end of the garden. Although I would have preferred to go inside, I had no choice but to follow.

We did not stand on the edge of the cliff. Even my uncle with his eccentric enthusiasm must have known this would have been madness. We stood several yards back and peered down towards the beach, while the wind wailed around us like a banshee. I had expected to see the broken shell of the boathouse on the sand. Instead, mounds of white foam had piled on the shore. The sea had breached the shingle bank protecting the beach, and was gnawing at the sandy base of the cliffs. Before the end of the week, another chunk of land would disappear.

The North Sea was usually grey rather than blue, so the colour of the water did not surprise me, but I had never seen the sky assume the same gloomy hue. There was no horizon – it was impossible to tell where the sea left off and the sky began.

'Is there a storm coming?' I shouted.

'No. It's just a squall!' There was merriment in my uncle's face. Yet he must have sensed my fear, for almost immediately he started to lead me back towards the shelter of the house.

Aunt Rose was waiting for us in the porch, her brown hair scrambled by the wind.

'You'll catch your deaths!' she cried. 'What were you thinking of, Harry? Haven't you any common sense?' She ushered me through the front door and lifted my uncle's jacket from my shoulders.

I had always remembered the Four Winds' kitchen as unnaturally cold, but after the blustery conditions outside it felt warm, even homely. The lamps were on and the kitchen was bathed in an amber glow. The smell of roast chicken and rosemary wafted from the oven. On the work surface, an apple pie had been left with a note written by the housekeeper: *Thirty minutes at Gas Mark 6*. A bowl of whipped cream beside it was already starting to melt. Roast parsnips fizzed in fat behind the oven's glass door.

'It's lovely to see you, Angela. It's a shame it couldn't be under better circumstances.' Aunt Rose's cold lips fluttered on my cheek. Then, she opened her arms and embraced me. She was a bony woman without a bust. She was not naturally demonstrative, and her ribs were as uncomfortable as a washboard. Yet in spite of this, I felt soothed. I wondered what sort of a mother she would be. Perhaps I would not mind living here after all.

'Would you like a biscuit? Or a cup of tea? Supper won't be ready for another hour.'

'I'm not hungry, just tired.'

'You must be shattered. Go and lie down. I'll bring your food up as soon as it's ready.'

There was no need for my aunt to show the way. I was to have the room I had always shared with my parents when we visited. They had slept in the double bed, while I used a camp bed.

Although officially the guest room, it was used mainly for storing historical artefacts. My aunt and uncle dived regularly on the ruins off Dunwich, recovering relics from the sea bed. Some of the artefacts were donated to Dunwich Museum. Other mementos – bits of masonry, coins, a human skull, pilgrim's badges – lined the shelves in this room.

A collection of photographs and sketches of Dunwich had been hung haphazardly on the walls. There was a faded postcard of All Saints Church, dated 1903, before it fell down the cliffs. Another photograph showed the dilapidated ruins of Greyfriars Monastery. An inkprint sketched the lines of the Leper Chapel near St James's Church.

On the bedside table was a colour photograph of my mother, father and I the summer before Billy was born. We were on Dunwich beach. I knew when the picture was taken because my mother's dress was pulled tight against her stomach to reveal the early contours of pregnancy. She looked relaxed and happy, as did my father. I was squeezed between them. My father's hand rested protectively on my right shoulder, my mother's caressed the left. I tried to remember the day when the picture was taken; to establish its significance. What had we been doing? Collecting shells? Walking? Picnicking? I could not recall.

That summer holiday had been idyllic. My parents had left the bedroom windows open in the evenings. They sat on the balcony with a bottle of Frascati, scanning the horizon for yachts and fishing boats. I kneeled between my mother's knees while she brushed my hair. The rhythm soothed me, the bristles prickling my skin, tickling my scalp. I rested my ear against her swelling belly, straining for a second heartbeat. If only I had known then what was to come. That I would lose my family. That I would be left alone with so many unanswered questions.

Now, the wind rattled the window frames and smeared the glass with salt water. The withered tendrils of a Virginia creeper flapped wildly. The sea leered, vast and empty. I could not unpack my suitcases and bags. My dressings made it impossible to open the clips. I keeled heavily on to the double bed. The picture of my parents was inches away on the bedside table. I could not bear to have it so close. I tried to turn over the frame with my wrists. Instead, it clattered to the floor.

As the frame came apart, wood separating from glass, it revealed the hidden section of the photograph. I remembered the day then vividly. We had spent the afternoon collecting driftwood on the beach. Then, my mother had skewered marshmallows and placed them in the swaying flames. My excitement had risen as the smell of hot sugar filled the air and the mallows browned.

'They're too hot to eat straight away. You'll have to blow on them until they cool down,' my mother warned. But I didn't listen and, in my eagerness, popped them straight in my mouth. The blisters were instant. I had swilled my mouth out with cold water. But the small red sores stayed for days.

'Try not to think about them,' my mother said. 'Things only hurt if you let them. If you stop thinking about it, the pain will go away.'

So I deliberately made myself stop thinking about the pain and, as if by magic, it did.

# Chapter 3

During my first weeks at Four Winds I stayed in bed. I felt helpless. The things I took for granted – wiping my nose, scratching my ears, picking food from my teeth – were impossible. I could not dress, undress, eat, drink, wash. The troupe of nurses and auxiliaries who had cleverly hidden my inadequacies from me, were no longer there. The tiniest exertion tired me: I realized how weak I was.

In truth, bed was probably the best place to have been. Although there was a fireplace in every room, these were for decoration only. In some rooms, the chimney breasts had been blocked up. My aunt and uncle warmed the rooms individually using Calor Gas heaters which were moved about on castors to whichever room was being occupied. 'This house is a huge money pit,' Uncle Harry grumbled.

'The heat goes up the stairs and out of the roof. I might as well burn the money!' While some rooms were warm (notably my bedroom and my uncle's study) most of the house was cold. The effect of this was to discourage me from going anywhere else. Even trips to the bathroom were best delayed. Everything felt damp. Carpet. Toilet paper. Towels. I knew better than to complain. Uncle Harry would only have told me to wear a pullover over my nightdress and to put on a second pair of socks.

As soon as I felt well enough, I set about inventing ways of doing the things I had done before. Uncle Harry and Aunt Rose had hired a television to entertain me while I was convalescing. I flipped the channels with my big toe. I taught myself to flick on the bedroom light with the tip of my nose. I tugged the light cord in the bathroom with my teeth.

Mealtimes were my greatest triumph. I tipped cornflakes from the box and poured on milk with my elbows. I fed myself by means of a spoon (supplied by my physiotherapist) attached to my arm. Any food which could not be balanced on the spoon – peas, grapes, cherries, peaches, tinned pears – was puréed. There were accidents, spillages and breakages. But these were a small price to pay for sparing Aunt Rose the exasperation of helping me.

My aunt had taken unpaid leave from the university in order to nurse me. But there were moments when I was aware of the firm set of her jaw, the granite in her face. Perhaps I was super-sensitive: my awareness heightened by tragedy. When I was around her, the air sometimes crackled. My bedroom would be filled with the faintest of scents, metallic, toxic as ozone, as if a thunderstorm was approaching.

Her anger – for I think that was what it was – was exacerbated by the fact that Uncle Harry had handed over all responsibility for me. While my aunt had taken leave in order to look after me, my uncle's routine was unchanged. His excuse was that nursing and childcare required a womanly touch; that he should not be involved in dressing, undressing, and bathing a 13-year-old girl. His excuses for avoiding washing clothes, cooking meals and making beds, I could only guess at. Whatever the reasons, my uncle did little for me, his blood relative, while my aunt was responsible for me twenty-four hours a day. It was no wonder that she became angry and resentful. While her husband snored beside her, she helped me to the bathroom in the middle of the night. While he studied in his office, she carried my umpteenth puréed dinner upstairs. While he planned his diving schedule, she telephoned the hospital to arrange my next appointment. He laid out his wetsuit, while she was pegging my washing on the line.

Aunt Rose was an academic who had chosen to be childless in order to pursue her career. Through no fault of her own, she had become unwitting mother to a girl not even her own. Of what I was never sure was whether her anger was directed towards my uncle or me.

One of my aunt's main grievances was that Uncle Harry started solo diving soon after I arrived. They had always dived as a pair, scouring the sea bed around All Saints Church (about twenty yards offshore) and St Peter's Church (about a quarter of a mile out). However, Uncle Harry had abandoned this familiar territory, and was instead investigating an area more than a mile out to sea. He was hoping to establish evidence of a Roman fort beyond the medieval boundaries of the city.

Before my arrival, Aunt Rose had been an equal partner in any such diving expeditions. All the discoveries made (and there were plenty of them on display in Dunwich Museum) had been accredited to both of them. She felt betrayed by my uncle. She was also worried about his safety: solo diving was dangerous.

I heard my aunt and uncle bickering frequently, their voices buzzing through the floorboards: hers angry as a trapped wasp; his, stubborn as the hand holding the glass. They fought where they thought they would not be heard: behind closed doors, down long passageways at the other end of the house, outside in the garage. But these early quarrels were mere trickles: water seeping out and spilling over. It was inevitable that the hostility would eventually erupt like an overheated geyser.

I had been at Four Winds for about six weeks, when I woke to the sound of a door being slammed. My uncle (I knew it was him from the knitting needle click of his knees) marched into the bathroom. My aunt followed with a shiver of silk. The bathroom was only a couple of yards away. The water pipes travelled through the walls and passed through my room. The sink served as a microphone and speaker, transmitting their voices along the metal.

'You know what the guidelines are – you dive in pairs in case anything goes wrong. Why can't you wait another month? If you'd only hold off, I could go with you. It wouldn't make any difference.'

'That's crap and you know it. The weather could change. The silt could move. Anything could happen.'

'My point exactly – *anything* could happen.'

'Don't be so melodramatic! I've been diving over twenty years. Nothing's gone wrong before.'

'No? You've got a short memory! You've almost knocked yourself out on the ruins. You've been dragged out by drift currents. You've been tangled up in fishing nets. You've been hit by falling masonry. Shall I go on?'

'I might have known you'd bring all that up!'

'You need someone to help – even if it's just with an inflatable and a radio. You're taking too many risks!'

'I've made up my mind, Rose. That's all there is to it. I want to put a surface buoy out there.'

'Ask someone else to go with you then! That way you could take some air bags and a sling; bring it up at the same time.'

'You know that isn't an option. If anyone else gets to hear about this, the font'll be whisked away as soon as it's out of the water. They'll put it straight in the museum.'

'Get yourself killed then. Don't let me stand in your way!'

Aunt Rose usually spent her afternoons downstairs, either marking students' essays or reading in the living-room. She came upstairs after lunch to collect my dishes, then disappeared almost immediately. That afternoon, she came into my bedroom with a jigsaw and a tray which she placed on the bedspread. Her usually proud head was a daisy on a wilting stalk.

'I thought maybe we could do this together,' she suggested.

'Together?' I looked at my hands. 'I can't!'

'I'll do it and you can watch. We'll keep each other company. It's not terribly exciting, but it's the only jigsaw we've got.'

It was a picture of Southwold lighthouse overlooking the North Sea. It had 5,000 pieces. Four thousand different shades of brown. One thousand white. My aunt managed to put the lighthouse together very quickly. But the sea was unfathomable. She found the four corners, but struggled with the edges. The aroma of fresh pinewood stirred from the tray. My aunt picked up pieces, put them down again, started sighing. After an hour, she had constructed two edges and a lighthouse. The rest of the puzzle stayed scattered in the tray.

Aunt Rose had positioned her chair so that she was facing the balcony. She kept glancing at the window. Raindrops tap-danced on the panes. As if through a blurred lens, the sea loomed beyond the rivulets of water. Only the day before, ten-foot waves had been rearing black and menacing. Today, tamed white horses galloped to shore.

'It's very calm,' I ventured. 'At least, it is today.'

'Days like today are sometimes the worst. It can be smooth as a mill pond on the surface. But you never know what the current's like at thirty feet.'

My room was filled with artefacts – I woke up with them, spent the day staring at them, slept with them. But what I knew of my aunt and uncle's underwater expeditions had been gleaned from snatches of overheard conversations and half-remembered discussions. I wanted to ask about the font. But if I did, Aunt Rose would know I had been eavesdropping.

'What's it like under the sea?' I asked.

My aunt did not answer immediately. She held a segment of puzzle in her palm, opening and closing her fingers around it like an oyster.

'I can't give a single answer to that. Most of the time it's so dark you can't even read a compass. It's like being blind. You have to use your fingers, or a grappling hook, to find your way around. Other times, if you're lucky, it's clear as crystal. You can see up to twenty feet.'

'Don't you get bored?'

'Doing the same thing, you mean? No, the ruins are different every time. Sometimes the walls are taller than houses. Other times, everything vanishes under the mud and it's like the face of the moon.'

'Are there sharks?'

'Oh no, they keep out of the way. It's the crabs you have to watch out for. They give a nasty nip if you're not careful!'

'Is it your favourite thing in the whole world?'

'Oh no, I don't like *diving*!' my aunt exclaimed, as if offended by the suggestion. 'It's the *ruins* I like. Nothing can match it . . . recovering things that haven't been touched for hundreds of years. It's just that . . .' Here, she faltered. 'There's a high price to pay if anything goes wrong.'

She turned her attention back to the puzzle and started pushing pieces together with forced concentration. She gave a sigh of satisfaction as she fitted four segments of chocolate-coloured water. I did not have the heart to tell her the edges did not match.

# Chapter 4

The following day, Aunt Rose announced that she would no longer be looking after me. The housekeeper, Hilary, would be taking over until I was well enough to return to school.

'Harry's found something, you see. Something important. If we don't bring it up now, we won't get the chance again. It might be washed away. Do you understand?'

'Yes, Aunt Rose.' In truth, I felt like crying. As if I had been placed on one side of the scales and the font on the other. That for whatever reason, I had been found lacking.

'Good girl. Hilary will do a good job looking after you. She's got daughters of her own. She's had to bring them up because her husband... well, her husband isn't around any longer. I'm sure you two will get along just fine.'

For the first time since arriving in Dunwich, I wanted to be touched, held. Aunt Rose's bony kiss and cold embrace had sufficed when I first arrived. I had barely registered her distance and reserve. Now, unexpectedly – so sharp it almost took my breath away – I longed for the warmth and comfort of flesh. My mother. My mouth was suddenly filled with the fire of plump marshmallows. Don't think about it, I told myself. Don't think about it and it won't hurt.

'What is it? What have you found?' I asked.

'I can't tell you. It's a secret. You'll just have to wait and see.'

I flicked on the television to hide my disappointment. There was to be no consolation. She would not even share their secret.

My aunt had been carrying what looked like a pile of cotton sheets. She unfolded these across the floor. They were so large that they covered the rug and I had to get out of bed to see them properly. I tried to seem interested. I wanted her approval; for her to like me, trust me.

'What are they?'

'Old maps of Dunwich. I thought they might interest you.' My aunt was kneeling. She flattened the creases and traced a line with her finger.

'Here's the King's Palace . . . and the Mint . . . The Town Hall . . . The Maison Dieu hospital . . . All Saints Church . . . St Martin's, St Peter's, St John's . . . Knights Templars' . . .'

Amid the sprinkling of dots and squares, a huge city was beginning to materialize. In the centre was a market square with thoroughfares spiking off it like spokes around a wheel. Within the intricate cross-hatching of roads was a bishop's mansion, a monastery and a convent. There were shops, homes, hillocks topped with windmills. In the outlying areas were orchards, meadows, broad swathes of woodland.

'Is all this under the sea?'

'What's left of it. Most of the homes have rotted – they were just built from wood and plaster. It's the public buildings that have lasted. Even with them, the stones keep being washed away.'

'What about the people? Did they drown?'

'Oh yes, hundreds of lives in a single night. If there was a bad storm, they were swept away with their homes . . .'

Aunt Rose was more animated than I had ever seen her. History was her great passion. It was for history that she was prepared to dive and risk her life. I tried to let myself be carried along by her enthusiasm. But I felt nothing. I was still hurt she had not trusted me with the secret of the font.

'Could it happen again?'

'Of course. You've seen the shingle bank on the beach? That's all that stands between the village and the sea. All those houses and just a stretch of marshland in between.'

'Why does everyone stay then? Why don't they move away?'

'For the same reason that people live near volcanoes or in tornado alleys . . . because they think it'll never happen to them.'

'What about Four Winds?' I ventured.

'Oh, it'll happen one day. You've seen what the cliff's like. Hopefully, it won't be for a few years yet!'

On the map, numerous pencil marks undulated through Dunwich like rings in the centre of an oak. Each line showed the encroachment of the sea for a particular year. I calculated the losses – a hundred yards of land every hundred years. One yard per year. However, not all the lines were evenly spaced. There were sizeable losses which could not possibly have been predicted.

'How do you know we're safe?' I persisted. 'How come you're so sure?'

'There's a simple answer to that: I'm not. We're taking the same gamble as everyone else.'

Aunt Rose got up and walked to the window. She drew the curtains, shutting out the daunting vision of the sea. She gave me a wet kiss, which glanced off my cheek like the touch of seaweed in water. Then she left me alone again to look at the maps by myself. To contemplate the past – and whatever the future might, or might not, hold.

# Chapter 5

I woke up in darkness the following morning. A golden bar of light was sliding across my ceiling. The car was being reversed on the driveway. Footsteps crunched. The gravel cracked. Bags were zipped and unzipped in the hallway.

My aunt usually left a breakfast tray in my room so that I could help myself if I woke up early. That morning, there was no sign of cereal, orange juice or milk. I waited patiently for more than an hour. Eventually, at seven, I crept downstairs to find some breakfast.

The hallway was frosty. The front door was ajar letting in the spiky air. Outside, voices murmured in the dull morning light. I padded to the doorway in my bare feet and waited. The cold flag-stones stuck to the soles of my feet. I called out, but no one answered. Finally, I went back upstairs.

I had only been in bed for a few minutes when I needed to go to the toilet. I decided to go to the bathroom by myself and lift my nightclothes with my elbows. My confidence was short-lived: I ended up wetting the hem of my nightdress and the bathroom carpet.

Hilary arrived at nine o'clock. She was wearing a loud orange blouse, with stonewashed jeans and cowboy boots. Her copper-coloured hair had been teased into a pony tail. She bustled into my bedroom carrying a large holdall.

'I've brought you some dresses. They're cast-offs from my daughters. I know you're not out of bed yet, but you'll need other clothes eventually. The less buttons and zips you have the better. I've brought you some loafers too. I wasn't sure about the size, but they'll be all right for wearing around the house. You can just slip them on and off.'

She held a small velvet box towards me and opened the lid. There was a gold locket inside engraved with a strange-looking bird.

'A welcome present. It belonged to my daughter Fiona. Her nickname's Phoenix – Fi for short.'

One of my mother's stories came to me. How a fabulous bird, the Phoenix, had thrown itself on a funeral pyre when it was 500 years old. How everyone on earth had wailed and tugged out their hair. How another bird, more magnificent than before, had risen out of the ashes. Its eyes were like black sapphires and its feathers were golden flames.

'Fi's my oldest. I've got two others – Isobel and Daisy. You'll have to come and meet them when you're feeling better. I'm sure they'd love to meet you.'

'Great,' I said. But I was wary.

Hilary had eyes like freshly budded bluebells and a trusting smile. I was grateful for the clothes and the locket. But she was only being friendly because she was being paid. It was just a job to her, the same as any other.

By this time, I had been sitting in my nightdress for nearly two hours. The urine had dried, but the fabric had a sweet revealing scent. I was embarrassed by the thought of Hilary helping me undress. Yet in contrast to Aunt Rose's awkwardness, Hilary had a reassuring confidence. After pulling a fresh nightdress over my head and tying the belt on my dressing gown, she fluffed up my pillows and shook the quilt.

'You might as well come downstairs and keep me company.'

'I usually stay in my room.'

'Nonsense. You can't sit up here all day. It's not healthy. You should have a change of scenery. It'll do you good.'

'What if I need to sleep?'

'You can sleep on the sofa.'

'But—'

'If you don't like it, you can come back up.'

It was so cold in the kitchen that I started shivering in spite of my dressing-gown and slippers.

'Have they switched off the central heating again?' Hilary tutted. 'I've told them before – I won't work when it's like this. It's colder in here than it is outside! And you so poorly too! Wait here while I go and find a heater.'

To my dismay, Hilary disappeared into my uncle's study. Uncle Harry's office had always been something of a Bluebeard's Chamber. It was an unspoken rule that no one was allowed in there except my uncle. My mother and father used to joke about it when we visited Four Winds. A cannonball was used as a doorstop. From the doorway we would see my uncle bent over his desk, a white crocheted blanket wrapped around his shoulders, even in summer. The carpet – except for a small triangle near the door – was covered with stacks of paper-work. The slightest breath disturbed them. It was impossible to set foot inside without my uncle knowing.

Imagine my feelings then, when Hilary returned with the same musty blanket that my uncle used to keep himself warm. She held it towards me, but I shook my head.

'Uncle Harry doesn't let anyone go into his study. I don't know if he'd like—'

'Oh, don't worry about that old skinflint. I'm not afraid of him!' She lifted up the blanket, opening her arms wide like a clothes horse.

'I'm not surprised you don't want this dirty old rag on you! It stinks!'

I was startled by her tone: I smirked. Encouraged, Hilary flapped the blanket so hard that flakes of skin flew off it.

'Ugh! Dandruff and who knows what else! It could do with a good wash,' she sniffed. She shoved the blanket in the washing-machine, holding it at arm's length, as if it was bedding from a mangy dog's basket. She set the dial and filled the drawer with so much washing powder that it spilled on to the floor.

Hilary rolled the Calor Gas heater into the kitchen, then fetched my quilt from upstairs.

'If there's one thing I hate it's the cold,' she grumbled. 'Gets right into my bones. Makes my joints ache. Budge over will you? I think I'll join you until it warms up.'

She lifted the quilt and snuggled beside me on the settee. At first, her jeans were cold against my leg. But then, her body heat started to seep through the denim. We huddled under the cover together until the blue flames turned orange and filled the grid.

'It's madness diving on a day like this if you ask me. But I suppose if they waited for a good day, they'd only dive once a year. What've they found this time?'

'I'm not supposed to say.' I was too embarrassed to admit they had told me nothing. That I was as much an outsider in this house as Hilary was.

Hilary smiled wryly. 'They've bound you to silence, have they? Worried I might pass on their secrets?'

'Oh no. They didn't say—'

'It's all right. I understand. There are plenty busybodies who'd love to know what they're up to. I might add I'm not one of them.'

She gestured towards part of an ancient stone coffin, leaning against the kitchen wall. Her lip curled disdainfully.

'If you ask me, it's a lot of fuss about nothing. Just a few bits of rubble and old bone!'

After lunch, Hilary pulled a large box out of her bag. My heart sank. Another dull afternoon watching someone else fiddling with a jigsaw.

'You'll trip over that lip if you're not careful! Don't judge until you've tried it. My girls love this game!'

The box was filled with brightly coloured fish: pike, trout, carp, perch, minnow and stickleback with metal rings in their mouths.

'It's for little kids! Anyway, I can't use my hands.'

Hilary pulled out two fishing rods with magnetic hooks. She poked one towards me.

'Nonsense – it's for all ages! Put this in your mouth and stop whinging.'

Pike and trout were worth five points. Carp and perch, four. Minnow and stickleback, three. If a boot was caught by mistake, all the fish had to be thrown back.

I gripped the rod between my teeth and halfheartedly levered it with my tongue, hoping Hilary would feel sorry for me and put the game away. But she was having none of it. She either did not notice me struggling or deliberately ignored it. She thrashed me for six games before I became so incensed that I was determined to beat her. After that I started to concentrate. When I won the eighth game, I yelped with excitement. Hilary's beam was even wider than mine: I was not sure if the triumph was mine or hers.

Aunt Rose and Uncle Harry arrived home at four o'clock. The moment I saw them, I knew they had not recovered the font. Uncle Harry lugged two rucksacks into the kitchen and dropped them without saying anything. He switched on the immersion heater. Then he tugged the diving log book from his rucksack, and disappeared into his study. Aunt Rose was more gracious in her disappointment. She chatted politely to Hilary, catching up on the events of the afternoon, before indicating that it was time for her to leave.

Hilary winked at me before she headed for the door.

'I'll leave the game here. You'll need the practice if you're going to beat me next time!'

After Hilary had gone, I lingered in the kitchen. But now there was no one to perform to, my aunt gave up her pretence. She heaved open the back door and slapped the wet suits over the washing line. She flicked the wet towels with such force that they snapped the air.

I was an unwanted presence in the room. I knew this without a word being said. My aunt preferred me to stay out of the way.

'I'm going back upstairs!' I said.

'OK. I won't be cooking tonight. It's been a long day and your uncle and I need to talk over a few things. I'll bring you up some soup later.'

I hoped that my aunt would offer to carry my quilt up the stairs. It was stuffed with eider feathers, twice my size, impossible to carry. I made a half-hearted attempt to drag it with my elbows, hoping she would intervene. But my aunt was crouching in front of the washing-machine, puzzling over what looked like a crumpled white rag.

I was still wondering how to approach my aunt when my uncle

thundered out of his study.

'That bloody woman's been in my office! What the hell's she been up to? Is that my blanket you've got there?'

I abandoned my quilt and crept up the stairs.

That night, I dreamed I was diving alone under a frozen sea. The waves were solid and I was trapped under a layer of glass.

A cry started up, lonely and haunting as whale song. I recognized this desperate lament as my mother's. She was searching for me, frantically calling my name. Her cries vibrated sharply through the ice. The sound bounced on the seabed and echoed back.

As I looked up, I spotted the silhouette of a boat on the skin of the sea. My mother was directly above me, trapped on the other side of the ice. I hammered at the iceceiling with my fists. I tried shouting. But the ceiling would not give and all that came out of my mouth were bubbles, round and beautiful as pearls.

# Chapter 6

It was during my visits to Norfolk and Norwich Hospital that I realized how lucky I had been. In one corner of the waiting-room, was a woman whose face looked as if it had been held over a naked flame until her nose, cheeks and lips had dripped off. Her companion's chin and upper lip had been burned away to expose the roots of his teeth. On the opposite side of the room was a child of indeterminate sex and age, whose skin was as white-grey as a gargoyle.

Aunt Rose had accompanied me on that first visit. She selected a magazine from the coffee table and passed it to me.

'Read this! Stop staring!' she whispered.

We had been sitting opposite a woman whose head was split like a grotesque theatrical mask. From the left, her face was unblemished, beautiful. Yet when she moved slightly, the other side of her face had melted. Her right eye seemed to have slipped from her face.

The longer I gazed at this woman, the more her features softened. Then her face seemed like a waning moon: one side shadowed by the earth, the other illuminated by the sun.

'Is this your first time here?' she asked.

'Yes,' I said nervously.

'I thought so. Who are you seeing?'

'Mrs Sanno.'

'Don't worry. She's really nice. I've got Mr Smyth.'

We did not have a chance to talk further. The door of one of the adjacent treatment rooms opened. A grim-faced nurse leaned out and beckoned in that authoritative way nurses have. I glimpsed briefly the inside of a torture chamber. A bed covered in paper towelling. A wall lined with surgical instruments. A trolley sparkling with silver. Coiled white bandages next to a sink.

My hands started to prickle. My skin felt clammy. I reassured myself that I was seeing the nicer of the two consultants.

Half an hour later, the same brusque nurse leaned out of the same treatment-room and beckoned me inside.

'Mrs Sanno's off sick, so your file's been passed to Mr Smyth,' she said.

I managed a timid smile as I entered the room, but Mr Smyth was not looking at me. He was reading my medical notes.

'Been playing with paraffin eh? Don't suppose you'll be doing that again in a hurry!'

He peered over the top of my file in a way that suggested my appointment was an inconvenience arranged to irritate him. Then he scribbled something indecipherable on his notepad and started unwrapping my dressings.

'Let's take a peek and see what we're dealing with,' he said.

I concentrated on providing answers to his questions. I was trying hard to ignore the trolley and the nurse hovering over it. I did not want to know what they were planning to do. It was better to avoid knowing until the last possible moment.

Then a plastic wrapper crackled. I spotted a cluster of small glass vials. A syringe. I had learned to hate local anaesthetic. I often wondered why something that was supposed to numb the pain should hurt so much. I started to cry.

'Don't be silly now – a big girl like you. Just a few little pinches and then we can examine you.'

The fluid was like a bee sting each time it entered my flesh. I had five injections on each wrist. My chest was heaving. I remembered that while I had been in hospital, one of the nurses had always stroked my arm or let me sit on her lap. I looked at Aunt Rose for comfort. But she was staring, fascinated, at the meaty flesh that had been hidden under my bandages.

I went to the hospital three times with Aunt Rose, then Hilary accompanied me. Though these visits were always traumatic, Hilary was a better companion than my aunt had been. My consultant changed too. Mrs Sanno returned from sick leave and I was able to avoid Mr Smyth.

An additional, but unexpected benefit, was that Hilary and I were able to carry out a small but pleasurable deception.

'If anyone asks, we'll say I'm your mother,' Hilary said. 'I don't want anyone making decisions over our heads. You're a person, not part of some production line. Believe me, it's for the best. I've had enough experience of hospitals to know what I'm talking about. A little white lie won't hurt anyone.'

After that, every time we went to the hospital we pretended that Hilary was my mother. The word was honeycomb-sweet to my tongue. Indeed, I sometimes laced my conversation so liberally with 'Mom', 'Mum' and 'Mother' that she had to nudge me to prevent me giving away the truth.

If I had to have a local anaesthetic, Hilary pulled up a chair close to mine so that we sat side by side. She put her arm around me and massaged the top of my spine, pressing my face against her chest. As I felt the familiar sting of the needle, I buried my face in her clothes. Cat hairs tickled the end of my nose. But it felt dark and safe. Reassuring.

'Keep your eyes closed,' Hilary soothed. 'Don't open them again until I tell you. Imagine you're in your favourite place . . . somewhere nice. Concentrate very hard and stay there. No matter what you hear or what you feel, don't open your eyes until I say.'

At first, my 'safe place' was my home at Elm Road. I imagined my mother tending the fire, Billy burbling in his crib or my father hauling in the coal scuttle. Unfortunately, there were as many sad memories as good ones. I was fantasizing about raking leaves on the front lawn when I spotted the MG parked at the end of the garden. In another daydream, I was playing hopscotch when I stumbled over the housebrick with the note attached to it.

I never considered Four Winds as an alternative refuge. Instead, I pretended I was in Hilary's house. I had never been there before, but I conjured up a rustic cottage with a rusty swing and a seesaw in the garden. Coal fires crackled in all the downstairs rooms. Upstairs, there was a bedroom specially for me. This room was not filled with historic artefacts and books. Instead, the shelves held all my heart's desires: a Spanish flamenco doll; a bubblegum dispenser; rollerskates; a record player; spangly silver shoes just like Mrs Jackson's.

In my daydreams, Hilary had signed adoption papers and her three daughters were my sisters. We made flapjacks together, picked the icing off fairy cakes, ate cubes of raw jelly, dipped bananas in caster sugar. We rifled through Hilary's wardrobe mixing cowboy boots, lurid blouses and flamboyant dresses in outrageous combinations.

Occasionally, I was tempted to open my eyes. I would hear tuts and mutters. Surgical instruments jangled like cutlery in a canteen. Whenever I felt like this, the pressure on my spine increased as if to reassure me. So I would concentrate again, until Hilary said, 'It's all right. You can look now.'

Then, I was back in the hospital again with my hands in fresh bandages. Hilary smiled and told me how brave I had been. We agreed a time for my next appointment. After this, we would go to the cinema and I would be treated to ice-cream and popcorn. I would fall asleep before the opening credits started to roll.

★

There was no single day when I woke up and realized I was better. The pain – the physical pain that is – lessened with each passing week. I started to reduce my painkillers. My appetite improved. Though I still needed my afternoon sleep, I was able to watch feature films, without dozing off during the adverts.

Even so, I was surprised when Mrs Sanno discharged me.

'I don't think I'll be seeing you again,' she beamed. 'It's time to pass you on to my colleagues in physiotherapy.'

'Does this mean she can go back to school?' Hilary asked.

'Not yet. She won't be able to pick up a pen for a while.'

'What about her hair?'

'What about it?'

'You said it'd grow back.'

'Yes I did. But I didn't say when. It might take months or even years.'

'She can't go back to school without any hair. Can't you give her something? Some sort of ointment? A cream?'

'There's no reason why it shouldn't grow back in due course. I'd be reluctant to intervene unless it's absolutely necessary.'

'But you must know a girl's hair is her—'

'I think the best thing would be to carry on wearing hats and scarves. I'm afraid it's a case of letting nature take its course.'

Mrs Sanno closed my medical file and squeezed it between her bulging rack. Then she ushered us towards the door.

Before I left the Burns Unit, I took one last look around the waiting-room. Over the months, I had seen a horrific variety of burns: gas burns; electric burns; acid burns; water burns.

I remembered a legend my mother had told: that of Prometheus who was caught stealing the secret of fire from the gods at Mount Olympus. His punishment was to be chained to a rock while vultures ripped out his liver. Every night, it grew back so his torture could be repeated.

It seemed to me that the waiting-room was filled with people like Prometheus. The vultures had not pecked out their livers, but their eyes, noses, mouths, feet, hands. These people would be preyed upon, scarred, for the rest of their lives.

In comparison, I was fortunate: I had escaped such a punishment. I imagined the gods had overlooked me.

# Chapter 7

It was difficult to cope with the loneliness when Hilary went home to her family at the end of each week. Weekends were like long treks through fog. I knew my starting point and destination, but all landmarks that might have made the journey bearable were wreathed in cloud.

My aunt and uncle never had much respect for weekends. To them, they were just extra days for working. Sometimes, Aunt Rose stayed in Colchester so that she could mark dissertations or prepare coursework for the coming week. When she was home, she and my uncle went diving. When she was away, he stayed in his office and ate breakfast, lunch, and supper at his desk. But for the rare jangle of the telephone, I would never have known he was there.

I looked out of the window, read books, listened to music, slept and practised magnetic fishing. But no matter how hard I tried, time never passed any faster. Sometimes, I played a guessing game. I guessed what time it must be. I waited and waited and waited. When I could not wait any longer, I looked at my watch to see how accurate I was. Surely it had to be eleven o'clock. Surely quarter past. Surely half-past. Quarter to twelve. Midday.

It was a relief on Monday mornings when Hilary gusted in full of goodwill and told me where she had taken her kids at the weekend. How they had seen seals on the beach near Minsmere; visited the brewery at Southwold; built sandcastles at Felixstowe; been crab fishing in Cromer. Hilary would bring small objects which she thought might interest me. A dried starfish. Snap seaweed. A black mermaid's purse. A rabbit's tail. Photographs of her family.

Although I had never met Hilary's daughters, I felt as if I knew them. The oldest daughter, Fiona, was an adventurer who loved rock climbing and crab fishing. Isobel, who was the same age as me, hated school but loved sport. She had swum five miles length-to-length in the school swimming pool and could already dive from the top board. Daisy, the youngest, was the most reserved of the family: she hated insects, heights and getting wet. She even had to have her hand held going up the short spiral stairwell in Orford Castle.

I was drowsing in my bedroom one afternoon when I heard children's voices. At first, I thought it was part of my dream. But when the volume became insistent, I pushed away the bedcovers. I looked out of the upstairs window – Hilary's daughters were playing in the garden. They were so much a part of my internal life, my wish world, that they appeared to have been conjured from my imagination. I recognized Isobel and Daisy from their pictures. Fiona was missing.

Isobel had her hands over her eyes and was shouting, 'Three thou-sand! Four thou-sand! Five thou-sand!'

Daisy ran towards the house and squeezed behind the dustbins.

'Six thou-sand. Seven thou-sand.'

Hide and seek was one of my favourite games. My mother had been seeker while Jessie Jackson and I ran off to hide. We were expert in squeezing into tight spaces. We could fit under the bed, behind the wardrobe, in the blanket box, in the coal shed. My mother stalked us, stealthily as a panther. Making us squeal with delight.

'Eight thou-sand! Nine thou-sand!'

I would have loved to join in. But I felt exposed and awkward. I wondered what they were doing in the garden. Whether I would be expected to meet them. I felt shy.

'Ten thou-sand. Coming whether you're ready or not!'

Daisy was so excited that she kept poking out her head from behind the bins. It would have been impossible to miss her, even if she had not been hiding in the most obvious place in the garden. Isobel made a pretence of searching elsewhere before creeping up and grabbing her.

Shortly after this, the floorboards groaned outside my room. Someone was coming up the stairs. I bolted to the bed and pulled the sheets over my head. The door opened and the curtains clattered. It was Hilary.

'Wake up Miss Lazybones, it's time for tea. My kids are here. My sister's had to go to the dentist, so she dropped them off on her way. We're having a picnic in the garden. Why don't you come downstairs? They'd love to meet you.'

I made a great show of stretching and yawning.

'I don't feel very well. My head's hurting. Can I have my tea on a tray?'

I had expected a fight: for Hilary in her usual way to persuade me that she knew best. Surprisingly, she did not.

'When you're feeling up to it then. I'll bring you a Distalgesic with your sandwiches.'

After the picnic was finished, Hilary's daughters stayed in the back garden. Isobel wanted to play games like double Dutch, cat's cradle and elastics. Daisy kept spoiling them because she was too small. She complained that the elastic rubbed the back of her legs. She tangled the string in cat's cradle. She could not keep up the height or pace of the skipping rope for double Dutch.

Gradually, the girls wandered towards the end of the garden. Watching from the upstairs window, I felt a wistfulness, a yearning. It was a long time since I had played tennis against the wall of Jessie Jackson's garage, British bulldog in the playground, swapped bike stickers in the park. I wanted so much to be friends with Hilary's daughters. But it was not just that I wanted to join in their games: I wanted to be part of their family.

When I looked out of the window again, Daisy was lying on the lawn with a scarf wrapped around her head. She had white socks on both hands; a stick in her mouth like a thermometer. Isobel was taking her pulse. Perhaps it was wishful thinking, but I was sure that Daisy was pretending to be me.

I felt giddy, like the times when I spun around with my arms outstretched, then flopped to the ground to look at the sky. A pleasurable but sickening feeling. Excitement, nerves and nausea all at once. Fear of wanting something too much. I wanted Hilary's daughters to like me. Or rather, I wanted them to view me as a sister as well as a friend. I took their game of patient and nurse to be a good omen. Perhaps they would accept me after all.

My thoughts were broken by the slam of the back door; a crack and a judder as the glass trembled in the rotten wood frame. Uncle Harry had warned me about the back door. The paint was peeling off in strips and the putty was coming away around the window. 'I don't want to replace that door unless I have to,' he said. 'It's lasted us this long. If you treat it gently, it should last us a few years more.' He always treated it with exaggerated care.

There was a silence. Then, the door groaned and keeled like a drunkard clinging to a wall to stop himself falling. It hung there, tremulous, suspended by a rusty hinge. Glass chimed as it hit the paving, a single peal of splintered sound. All this happened in a moment. But this was not all. As the door was falling, Hilary was striding down the garden. Waving her arms.

'AWAY! AWAY from the edge! AWAY!'

She was still wearing rubber gloves. Ridiculous brighter-than-bright pink gloves. In her right hand, a dinner plate. A white disc dripping soap suds down her elbows.

'Come here! HERE! Now! NOW!'

She waved her arms, as if the plate, the gloves were not there. There was something odd, unnerving about it. But it was her voice which frightened me most. Not so much a voice as a sword slicing the air.

'Leave your toys. LEAVE THEM! Come here! NOW!'

The blade touched Daisy and Isobel. Their faces were as startled, as frightened, as mine must have been. For suddenly, they were on their feet. Running towards their mother like chicks to a hen. Seeking the sanctuary of her embrace.

'Oh girls. Girls . . .'

The dinner plate bounced on the grass, spun, landed upside down. Hilary scooped her daughters towards her. She clung to them, or rather enfolded them. Smothered them in her arms.

'You frightened me. Don't ever do that again!'

Hilary's chest was heaving. The girls were shaking with emotion too. The three of them stood in the middle of the lawn. Sobbing. Each one comforting the other. Hilary stroking rubbery gloves over her daughters' backs; they rubbing their small hands over hers. I felt excluded. Like a stranger watching something strange and forbidden. I stepped away from the window. I could not help thinking I had missed some vital detail.

# Chapter 8

A fortnight later, I found five sunflowers in the kitchen sink. The faces were dark brown, pocked with tiny pits and craters. The delicate petals frayed around them. Perhaps it was my frame of mind, but there was something ominous about them. It might have been the way the centres dominated, the petals tiny and irrelevant on the outside. Or perhaps it was the fact that they had no scent. The leaves and stems were covered in a soft fur; a down fine as sable. Yet when I touched it, it pricked my skin.

'Are you admiring Fi's flowers?' Hilary asked.

I sucked my hand. The skin was already itching in the curve between my thumb and index finger. I gnawed it irritably, as if to draw out the poison. I did not have the heart to say I hated them.

'Mmmnnn.' It might have been a yes or a no, skin taut between the teeth. Only the acutest listener would have noticed. Only an acute listener, or a cynic, would have taken it for a no.

'I'm popping in on the way home. I always make a point of visiting on her birthday.'

I stopped biting the edge of my hand. I rubbed it on my thighs instead. Up and down my trouser leg. Anything to distract from the soreness of the skin.

'I thought she lived with you?'

Hilary twisted the cold tap to allow more water on the sunflowers. She turned it too fast. Spray spattered over the wrapping paper on the draining board. It began to stick to the corrugated surface.

'I thought you knew.'

'Knew what?'

A smile spread across her face. Not a real smile. More of a twitch or a stretching of muscles. All other parts of her face – her eyes, nose, chin – did not flinch. The deeper the smile became, the more it betrayed itself. Hilary unpeeled the wrapping paper and hung it over the back of a chair.

'It's not a proper birthday – not like you're thinking. I'm going to see her at St James's.'

'The church?'

The smile was so wide that it was starting to lift the flesh beneath her eyes. It must have taken years to perfect that smile.

'She died five years ago.'

The news shocked me. In every tale I had been told, Fiona had been vibrant, alive. The photographs too had been full of movement. Wind in her hair. Legs skipping. Arms swinging. It never occurred to me that Hilary might have been resurrecting a ghost.

'No one told me.'

'Don't take it to heart. There's no reason why they should. You've got enough on your plate.'

'What happened to her?'

'A cliff fall,' Hilary said simply. 'She was out walking and the land gave way. Her Dad was killed too.'

The best thing to do with wet wrapping paper is to leave it until it dries. Any idiot can tell you that. Even the largest tear will mend if you leave it alone. That is how it is with paper. The edges will seam together like the two sides of a scar. Instead of doing this, the sensible thing, Hilary kept fussing. Stroking rhythmically, her hands like an iron. Inevitably the paper puckered. Ripped not just one or two ways, but in several directions. A daisywheel of rips. And still Hilary's fingers kept gliding over it.

'I used to block it out. I thought that if I stopped myself thinking about it, then it wouldn't have happened. They wouldn't be dead.' She paused to poke her finger through the hole. The paper moulded around her knuckle. A perfect 'O'.

'It was only when I stopped pretending, that I started to feel better. I thought I was helping myself by blocking it out, you see. Really, I was stopping myself from healing and moving on.'

I knew exactly what Hilary was referring to. Every time I started to think of my parents and Billy as 'dead', I stopped myself. I tried to avoid thinking about the past, my life in Bromsgrove. I knew there was a coalbed inside me, but I did not rake it over for fear of stoking the flames. Better, far better, not to think at all than face it.

Hilary looked at me expectantly, affectionately. Her smile deepened. This time, her cheeks puckered and her nose quivered. Genuine lines curved around her mouth and chin. There was no doubt about it. She was willing me to cry so that she could wrap her arms around me as she had her daughters that day in the garden. So that we might share our grief. So that she might console me. So that I might find comfort. Solace.

I did not deliberately stop myself: I could not cry. I did not have the energy for it. Or perhaps I had forgotten how to. I could have pretended I suppose. I could have made the effort. But I felt nothing. Only a numbness as when you have been sitting by a roaring fire for hours, then walk outside to find snow.

# Chapter 9

I was indebted to Hilary in many different ways. She demanded that the central heating be switched on during the day; that the water should be heated in the evenings; that I should be allowed to flush the toilet in spite of my uncle's anxiety about the septic tank. She exchanged the shabby brown curtains in my bedroom for a pair decorated with daisies. She ran up a patchwork bedspread on her sewing machine to hide the old-fashioned quilt. She made cushions appliqued with daffodils and primroses.

My aunt and uncle had the best intentions of helping me with my schoolwork. But somehow they never got around to it. In the evenings, they were always too exhausted. At weekends, they were usually immersed in paperwork or diving. Hilary, on the other hand, was determined that I should not fall behind. Her daughter Isobel was going to the same school as I would be. So Hilary asked her teachers to supply books, exercises and homework.

We worked through the subjects together. Hilary read to me, then wrote down notes as I dictated them. We were given assignments, practical exercises and essays. We split sunlight into its myriad of colours using a glass of water. We made a model of the solar system using a shoebox, plastic straws and balls of plasticine. We built a rocket using a balloon and an empty lemonade bottle. We learned the positioning of the planets by remembering the phrase 'Most Violet Evening Moths Jitter Slowly Until Night Passes'. Hilary looked forward to receiving the teachers' comments as much as I did. We read the red ink in the margins together. When I received a good grade, she was as excited as I was.

I enjoyed these lessons. I was confined to the house, unable to use my hands, yet I felt as if a pair of wings had unfurled on my shoulders. I was able to fly, escape the boredom. Of course, these things are better appreciated with hindsight. For a long time, I kept Hilary at arm's length. All those things children are supposed to need – love, affection, praise – I temporarily dispensed with. Hilary offered them like tempting purple grapes. But time and again, I waved that bowl of sun-ripened fruit away.

After I moved to Dunwich, I found it hard to fall into a deep sleep. The house was the noisiest place in which I had ever lived. The windows rattled and shook with every gust of wind. The chimneys bellowed like great blow pipes. The beams groaned above and below me. There was always a draught around the curtains or the fireplaces, so that if you left a book there its pages ruffled. As a result, I was always on edge. The house seemed like some giant decaying creature we were living inside. I never slept properly. When I woke, I often felt more tired than when I fell asleep. I sometimes felt as if I was still dreaming.

One afternoon, while I was taking a nap, I heard something in the bedroom. A slight creak. The whisper of fabric. Sounds so soft, they might have been wind mutterings or products of my imagination. As if through a gauzy veil, I opened my eyes.

Near the dressing-table, with her back to me, was Daisy. It took a moment to realize who she was and what she was doing. She was holding a dress Hilary had given me. A brushed cotton dress, delphinium blue, with a pocket on the front. She turned the dress over in her hands as if searching for something. Then suddenly, she lifted it to her face. It was not as if she was sniffing it, rather as if she was nuzzling it. She put it down, then noticed the loafers under the chair. She examined these too, then slipped her feet inside them. She shuffled over to the bedroom door, and back again. Then she took them off.

I pulled the covers slightly so that I was still hidden beneath, peeking out. The movement must have caught her eye, for she seemed to notice the bed for the first time.

'Fi?' she whispered. 'Is that you?'

There was a soft padding on the carpet. A hushed breathing. I closed my eyes, nervous how she would react, what she would say. I was not Fiona, but I was alive. I could be just as good a sister.

My neck tickled as the bed covers were drawn back. I smelled pickled onions and bubblegum. Warm breath on my face. The time was right to open my eyes.

'Hello Daisy!' I said. I smiled lazily and sat up.

This was when the threads holding the dream began to tear apart. Instead of smiling, Daisy's mouth formed a wide circle. The marble of pink gum dropped from her mouth. She screamed.

'It's OK,' I said. 'I'm not Fiona.'

The more I tried to reassure her, soothe her, the more upset she became. I tried stroking her, patting her back. But, she writhed in my arms, twisting and turning this way and that. The tighter I held her, the more she struggled. Finally. she bit me on the forearm and I was forced to let go. By this time, she was squealing like an injured rabbit.

As she bolted towards the door, she ran straight into her

mother's legs. Hilary picked her up, clutching her as I had intended to do. Daisy did not struggle.

'Calm down,' she said. 'Calm down, you silly girl.' She hoisted Daisy on to her hip and let her bury her face in her shoulder. She stroked her hair, making clucking noises.

'You frightened Angela more than she frightened you. I told you to stay downstairs.'

'I thought . . . she was . . . Fi. You gave her . . . Fi's clothes . . .'

Words flew from her mouth like dried peas from a blow pipe. I could not see Daisy's face. But I could hear her despair.

'It's what Fi would have wanted, darling. She wouldn't have wanted them left in the wardrobe.'

'I hate . . . you . . . I . . . hate you . . .'

'Don't be silly now. Hush . . . Hush.'

A thin watery blood was already gathering on my skin. It might have been pale-red lipstick. A kiss print from my mother. Except that I could see individual teeth marks. It was already throbbing.

'Oh my goodness, look at Angela's arm! What've you done?' Hilary said. Her tone changed. 'That was naughty! What were you thinking of? Say sorry!'

Daisy turned to look at me. Her eyes were red-rimmed. Saliva bubbled on her lip like cuckoo spit.

'Sorry!' she said, clearly unrepentant.

She tightened her legs around her mother's waist and pushed her face into her shoulder.

'I'm going to get some Germolene from the bathroom,' Hilary said. 'After that, I'm going to call my sister and get her to take the girls home.'

She loosened Daisy's arms in spite of her protests and put her down. She led her along the landing. As she was doing so, feet clattered on the stairs. It was Isobel.

'What is it, Mum? What's happened?'

'A misunderstanding, that's all. Back down the stairs, both of you.'

By the time, they reached the bottom of the stairs, Daisy had stopped whimpering. I even heard her giggling while Hilary was on the telephone. Shortly after this, a car pulled up, snapping the gravel on the drive. I heard the girls chattering as they got inside. The exchange of women's voices. Then, the door banged shut. The car swept away as swiftly as it had arrived.

While this was happening, I took off my headscarf and crept into my aunt and uncle's bedroom. There was a full-length mirror by the window.

Looking into this mirror, I had the strangest sensation as if I was seeing myself for the first time. Someone, or rather something was staring back at me. Half-human, half-fish. A Red Snapper with a shiny body. Wide unrimmed eyes. No hair. Pink scales instead of skin. I stuck out my tongue and waggled it. The fish-girl poked a tongue at me. I blinked an eye: she winked back.

I recalled Mrs Sanno saying, 'It isn't a pretty sight at the moment, but it's not as bad as it looks. When your hair grows back, it'll make all the difference.'

I had not realized – or had chosen not to realize – what she was saying. I had merely compared myself with the other patients and been grateful. I had become so used to looking in the mirror each day, that my reflection had lost its horror.

Now, I took a fresh look at my hands. First my left hand, then my right. There were no lines on my palms. The whorls, loops and arches on my fingertips had disappeared. As had the peacocks' eyes on my index fingers.

Once, when I visited Jessie Jackson's house after school, I asked her mother to tell my fortune. She beckoned me to kneel beside her, and grasped my hands so firmly that her long nails pinched my skin. She looked at my life-line, heart-line, head-line, fate-line – checking for gaps; for the criss-cross of new branches or bars; for islands.

'I've never seen hands like this before,' she said. 'They're unusual. But palms change every day of the week. People think I can look once and tell their fortune. If only it was that simple! Lines appear overnight, then vanish again. Hands should be read at least once a week to get an accurate reading.'

Mrs Jackson frowned, squinted, poked and prodded my skin. She muttered: 'Now where's that gone?', and, 'Where have you come from?' Her nails tickled. She did not share the secrets with me.

She was delighted by my index fingers which both had peacocks' eyes.

'Lucky girl! You've heard of cats having nine lives? Well, peacocks' eyes are much the same. They're very special. Mark my words – one day you'll remember this conversation and realize I was right.'

I was still in front of the mirror when adult hands suddenly folded around mine. The fingers were short and stubby, the skin around them ragged with hangnails. The cuticles had been pushed back to make the nails look longer than they were. They were covered in chipped purple polish.

Hilary's arms encircled me like wings. She held me so tightly that I could hardly breathe. The fibres of her blouse tickled my nose. A button pressed against my cheek. I could smell vanilla custard, salt and gravy. She stroked my back. Stroking my skin, as if she might softly, softly rub the pain away.

And still I did not cry.

# Chapter 10

Norman Bradley, the wigmaker, smelled of smoke. It whispered about his clothes and hair. It was not the oily scent of coal, the smoked mackerel of wood or the bitterness of pre-rolled cigarettes, but the mellow fruitiness of pipe tobacco. I had not been looking forward to the wigmaker's arrival at Four Winds. Yet, as he breezed into the kitchen, I found myself looking at him with unexpected interest.

Mr Bradley flicked open the silver catches on his briefcase and pulled out a brochure.

'As you'll see, we've got a range of styles to suit every budget. We've got long curls, short curls, long straights, short straights, long waves, short waves, mid-lengths, close crops. They can all be individually styled for either formal or casual occasions . . .'

'Whoa there!' said Hilary. 'You can save your sales patter for your other customers. We just want something simple.' She handed him a picture that Aunt Rose must have given her. 'This is the sort of thing we're looking for.'

Mr Bradley tugged at the frayed ends of his moustache, twisting them into points.

'Natural or synthetic? There's quite a price difference.'

'Natural,' Hilary said emphatically.

'Made-to-measure or off-the-peg?'

'I don't care how much it costs. It's just got to look right. We don't want something that looks like a wig.'

'In that case, it'd better be bespoke.'

Mr Bradley pulled out his tape measure and expertly removed my headscarf. He took three measurements: a circlet around my head; ear to ear; and a line from my forehead to the nape of my neck. His index fingers were yellow. Specks of tobacco ash clung to the knees of his trousers like delicate snowflakes.

'It's going to be difficult getting the right colour. I'd normally cut a strand of hair and match it. In this instance, we'll just have to make an educated guess.'

'What would you suggest?' Hilary asked.

Mr Bradley held my photograph to the light and squinted at a chart of dyed hair samples.

'My guess is that it falls somewhere in this block here. As you can see, there's quite a lot to choose from.'

The samples were labelled. *Pale golden blonde. Light brownish blonde. Medium golden blonde. Light beige blonde. Light golden blonde. Light brownish blonde. Medium ash blonde.* I selected one swatch. Hilary chose another. There were five shades between them. We wavered and changed our minds again. We were still three shades apart.

'If I can be of some assistance,' Mr Bradley interrupted. 'I do usually recommend that customers buy at least two wigs! A wig needs to be washed after ten wears. It makes sense to have a spare.'

'We'll take two then,' Hilary said.

'How much will it cost? What will—' I interrupted.

'Let me deal with them. If they make a fuss, it can come out of my wages.'

Mr Bradley bent over the table and filled in an order form in neat arched handwriting. He opened another suitcase containing a selection of combs, styling brushes and shampoos.

'We offer a full range of accessories to care for our wigs. You appreciate it could take up to four months to process your order?'

'No it won't. If you can't do it in less than a month, we'll go elsewhere,' Hilary said firmly.

'But most of our natural hair is shipped from abroad.'

'I don't care where it comes from. This poor girl's had to wear scarves and hats for over a year. She's going back to school this September. I think she should have the best start possible don't you?'

While Mr Bradley was negotiating the delivery date, a box of matches dropped from his trouser pocket. It must have been empty or very full, because it fell without rattling. It landed under the breakfast-table, the *England's Glory* crest facing upwards. I watched, breathless, to see if either adult would notice. The floor tiles were terracotta brown; the matchbox, red, blue and white. But neither Mr Bradley nor Hilary scooped it up.

I gave the matchbox a small kick so that it slid like an ice skater towards the newspaper rack. It skidded over the tiles too easily: I was still uncertain whether it was empty. When I was certain neither adult was watching, I bent down and slipped the matchbox in my pocket. It had a promising weight.

## Chapter 11

My new school was a daunting nineteenth-century building with latticed windows and a sharply-angled roof. When the windows steamed up, they showed up messages invisible to the eye: *Mr Cox picks his nose* and *Sarah-Jane wets her knickers* and *Katie L. loves Peter J.*

My classroom smelled of wax polish and disinfectant. There was a display of hermit crabs at the front of the class, a diagram of the water cycle from sea to land, an aerial photograph of the spit at Orford Ness. The desks were wooden fliptops with deep grooves scratched with names, and inkwells filled with rubber shavings. There was a pencil sharpener attached to the teacher's desk. Bits of coloured chalk covered the floor beneath the blackboard.

The form teacher, Mrs Tyler, made me stand at the front of the class while I was introduced.

'Attention please! This is Angela Burnett. She's going to be starting school with us from today. I hope everyone will do their best to make her welcome.'

Children hunched over their desks. Some rocked on the back legs of their chairs. Others leaned forward, resting their chins on their arms. They were outwardly attentive. But a note was being passed across the back row: surreptitiously read, folded, then slipped to the next person.

I stared at the floor. Somewhere along the school corridors, my shoe had picked up a drawing pin. It made a tap every time my heel moved. I rolled a piece of yellow chalk underfoot and started to grind it.

Mrs Tyler beckoned to a pupil sitting at the back.

'I want you to give Angela a guided tour of the school. Show her the tuck shop and the dining-room. Look after her and introduce her to some of the other children. Just while she settles in.'

There was a groan of objection. A chair shuffled. A desk was pushed forward. But I did not look up to see who this reluctant pupil was. I was examining Mrs Tyler's legs. She was wearing flesh-coloured stockings and the brown hairs on her legs were poking through the nylon.

Mrs Tyler handed me a combination padlock with the number attached on a label. I took it, still looking at the floor.

'Go to the cloakrooms and find an empty locker for Angela's coat. After that, you can take the register to reception.'

Mrs Tyler patted my shoulder in a gesture which could only have been construed as favouritism: 'If there's anything you need, even if you just want to talk, you know where I am.'

The other kid was impatient. He, or she, was already in the corridor outside. I could hear them kicking at something – the skirting-board, a wooden bench – as I stepped outside the classroom. I looked up with what I hoped was an apologetic smile. I was astonished to see Hilary's daughter, Isobel.

Isobel Franklin marched several steps ahead carrying the class register. She had the haughty disdain of someone who had been in the school a long time, had many friends and knew all there was to know.

'Assembly hall . . . Science block . . . Art block . . . Staff Room . . .'

The register bumped against Isobel's thigh while she sauntered along the scuffed parquet corridors. She pushed open doors with it, bending back the wallpaper cover. She did not hold the doors open, but let them close behind her so that they swung in my face.

'Bike sheds . . . Netball courts . . . Playing fields . . . Bogs . . .'

As I followed Isobel around the concrete playground, I wondered if she knew I was the same Angela Burnett her mother looked after; if she knew I lived at Four Winds; if she remembered the incident with her sister, Daisy.

I wondered if I should mention Hilary. Whether I should thank her for letting me borrow her school books. Or whether I should pretend an interest in swimming and sport. I was a poor swimmer, but I could always practise. I was determined she should like me.

'Gym . . . Changing Rooms . . . Reception . . .'

Isobel slipped the register into a wire tray behind some sliding glass doors, then made her way back across the courtyard. I trotted behind, struggling to keep up.

'The lockers are over there! You can find your way back, can't you? We're in room 1-03.'

At break-time, I experienced vertigo, as if I was in the branches of a tall chestnut tree and the earth was smirking beneath me. It was a cold morning. Smoke poured out of the children's mouths as they tore around the playground. There was a cluster of kids around the climbing frame, waiting for their turn to twirl crazy loops over the bars. A group of boys had taken over the ropes: hurling themselves across the mud, then clinging, climbing, swinging like spider monkeys. A couple of kids had linked arms, hoping to start a game of British bulldog before they were spotted by the teachers.

I squeezed the *England's Glory* matchbox in my pocket so that the corners nipped my skin. I nudged the drawer out with my thumb, stroking the matches inside. The heads were rounded, inspiring, smooth. Hilary had masked my face with foundation cream and concealer, and pencilled in eyebrows. My scalp was hidden beneath my new wig. I should have felt confident. But I could not help remembering the day Daisy came into my bedroom. I wondered how the other pupils would react if they saw me without my make-up. So I paused on the edge of the playground, unable to move, feeling the terror of falling. I turned the matchbox over, snagging my fingers on the edges. The glossy cover. The sandy sides. Smooth: rough. Rough: smooth.

Isobel sauntered towards me, a rescuer scaling my tree.

'Just the person I was looking for. Come and meet Bernadette and Tina. They'd love to meet you.'

My limbs came loose and I followed her to the playing-field. The grass had been cut so short that it was possible to see worm casts on the surface, spikes from football boots, cigarette butts. Two girls were scuffing their feet at a spot where the field met the concrete verge. Tina was scrawny, wearing clothes several sizes too large. Her cardigan was a shapeless garment with lopsided sleeves which could only have been knitted by her grandmother. The hem of her skirt was unravelling, a thread of cotton dangling to her knees.

Bernadette had ginger hair and glasses thick as paperweights. She was wearing the formal school blazer rather than a cardigan, under-knee socks rather than tights, an A-line with panels rather than a straight skirt. When she smiled, her mouth was full of silverwork.

'Hi. I'm Angela.'

'We know,' Bernadette said. 'We're sorry to hear about your Mum and Dad – you know – being dead and all that.'

I was taken aback. My aunt and uncle used phrases like 'passed away' and 'no longer with us'. Most of the time, they dodged the subject. I was happy to do the same. I was unprepared for tres-passers: strangers trampling over the edges of my grief.

'How do you know about my parents?'

'Everyone knows. It isn't a secret, is it?'

'No, I s'pose not.'

'My gerbil died,' Tina said. 'My brother squeezed it too hard. We buried it at the bottom of the garden. We've got a rabbit now. A black one. When that dies, Mum says we can have a dog.'

'My gran died last year. She had a heart attack. She was buried in a shoebox,' Bernadette volunteered.

'A shoebox?'

'Well, not a shoebox. But a teeny box with her ashes inside. We buried it just like a proper funeral.'

'That's sad,' I said.

'No, I'm glad she's gone. She never washed and she smelled funny. She always gave me sweets that tasted of sick. I had this box of Quality Streets one year and all the chocolates were white. I wasn't allowed to say anything in case she got offended.'

We had moved away from the edge of the playing-field to the playground. There was an invisible circle around us which no one entered. A group of boys was playing football nearby. When the ball came rolling in our direction and Bernadette threw it back, no one wanted to touch it. The first boy who did – the goalkeeper – wiped his hands on his pullover afterwards.

'Are you wearing a wig? Can we see?' asked Tina.

'I can't take it off. It's kind of glued on with sticky strips.'

'It looks real,' said Bernadette helpfully. 'You'd never know.'

'I wish my mum would let me wear make-up,' said Tina. 'Not that I'd want to wear that much powder. Couldn't you wipe some of it off?'

'It's supposed to, you know, cover up my skin,' I mumbled.

'It'd look better if you just left it. Wouldn't it, Tina?'

'You could wear false eyelashes though.'

'Yeah. They might help. Make your face look a bit more—' Bernadette did not finish the sentence.

Shortly after this, the two girls lost interest and moved away. They did not invite me to join them. I wandered across the playground looking for Isobel and eventually spied her with a group of girls loitering near the bike sheds. Their eyes darted shiftily. Their hands kept dipping down like swan's necks in water, as if they were concealing something. Smoke drifted from behind their backs.

I felt a thudding against my collar bone just inside my blouse: the gold locket Hilary had given me. I hooked it out and let it rest against the knot of my school tie. I realized this might be the key to making friends with Isobel, to her accepting me. I imagined it winking there, lending me luck, strength. Isobel would recognize it: I need not say a word.

The school bell rang and everyone started to form crocodiles ready to go inside. I followed Isobel to where our class was standing. We stood in line. Someone at the back of the class blew up an empty crisp packet, then popped it. Heads swivelled to look at the culprit. As Isobel's gaze fixed on the locket, I imagined it glittering, blinking its message: I was a sister, a friend.

I waited until Isobel stopped staring. Her gaze caught mine. It was full of hate.

# Chapter 12

I did not realize it at the time, but I was fortunate to have stolen a box of *England's Glory*.

An *England's Glory* match is unrivalled. It is the longest and easiest match to strike. The head does not disintegrate when damp, and the wood does not split in two as with inferior matches. It is one of the few brands that have a distinctive aroma before a single match is set alight. If you don't believe me, try it. Sniff a matchbox before the seal is broken. The chances are you will smell nothing. Not the faintest whiff. What a disappointment this is! Like pressing a delicate spray of jasmine to your nose – only to discover a genetically engineered strain without any scent. A box of *England's Glory*, on the other hand, has a wonderful aroma. If you rub it, the scent tattoos your skin. The perfume lasts for several washes.

During my first weeks at school, I developed a habit of sniffing my fingers. I kept the matchbox in my cardigan pocket, wrapped in a cotton handkerchief, and squeezed it when I needed reassurance.

When I got home, I opened the matchbox and played with its contents. With their bright pink heads and slender bodies, the matches were like miniature dolls. I twirled them in my fingers like ballerinas; lined them up; tucked them in their box as if in an over-cramped bed. I had a roll call, counting all forty-two matches in and out of the box, to make sure none was missing. At night, I slipped the matchbox under my pillow before I went to bed. In this way, I protected them from harm even while I slept.

I might never have been tempted to strike one of these matches, but for a fact that I have mentioned before – there was an empty fireplace in every room at Four Winds. Many of these were original Victorian fireplaces with colourful tile surrounds swirling with tulips and arabesques. The fireplaces had been blocked up and the ornate grates were filled with what could only be described as abominations. There was a pyramid of silver pine cones in the living-room fireplace; a vase of teasels in the kitchen grate; twisted willow in Uncle Harry's office; and an arrangement of brown poppy heads in my aunt and uncle's bedroom. A vase of dried lavender filled in the hearth in my bedroom.

I could not express – nor would I expect anyone who does not love fire to understand – how much it incensed me to see these fireplaces. Many people consider gas heaters or central heating to be perfectly acceptable. Some prefer them. For me, there is no comparison with the sheer glory of a coal fire. Just looking at those faded flowers in my bedroom grate made me want to cry. I tried to ignore it. But it was impossible. It was a constant reminder of all that I had lost.

I waited for a weekend when my aunt and uncle were diving. I found out what time they intended to return and dutifully waved goodbye. Then, I raced upstairs to my bedroom and plucked a match out of the box. I held it with trembling fingers.

The last time I had struck a match, the consequences had been terrible. There had been paraffin on the floor, on my clothes, on my hands. A paraffin fire was mean and hungry as a wolf. It snapped your hands, snarled, slathered, the instant it was lit. But I was older now. I knew that paraffin, petrol, solvents, thinners, all types of liquid fuels, were unpredictable. I would never take the same risks again, however beautiful the iris flames.

I ran my fingers along the edge of the matchbox, the sandpaper snagging my skin. Suddenly prominent were the words: KEEP AWAY FROM CHILDREN. My palms were clammy. I sensed I was holding the key to a door that ought to remain locked. Yet my fear warred with a need – yes, a need – to strike it. As if one flickering flame could ease my pain; could hold back the overhanging darkness just for a moment.

The match felt very brittle, liable to break at any instant. I was aware how precious, how precarious, life was. I wiped my hands on the back of my trousers. I was not sure if I would remember how to light a match. If I still could.

A scratch.

Another scratch.

There is no sound quite like the joy of a match flaring into life. The whoosh as wood and sulphur give birth to a flush of flame.

The match shimmered like a jewel: a tiger's eye. It lasted three seconds. But for that fleeting time, I experienced a glow which was more, much more, than the heat of a single match.

My second attempt was more successful. The wood curled into a charred C. When the heat started pinching my fingers, I dropped it into the hearth. After this, I lit several matches in quick succession. Three burned to the end of the stick. Four burned halfway. Two gave off twirling candytufts of smoke.

A box of white tissues was on the dressing-table. The first tissue set alight instantly. Flames blossomed, bright as marigolds. I held the burning tissue as long as I could, then tossed it in the grate. After this, I scrunched up several other tissues and fed these to the fire.

The flames did not last long. The tissues changed from white to charred black almost as soon as they were lit. But then a marvellous thing happened. After the flames died, hundreds of yellow sparks began squirming like bees dancing over honeycomb. These sparks skittered, flittered and jittered for several minutes. Every time, I thought the display was over, they flickered into life, wings twinkling as if covered in magic dust.

Looking at this grate, I forgot everything. I could have been at Elm Road, sitting by the fire waiting for my father to come home. My mother might have been in the room behind me, flicking through a newspaper or picking cradle cap from Billy's hair. It was a rare moment of tranquillity. It was the first time I felt any sensation of warmth – *real* warmth – since arriving at Four Winds.

I was still kneeling by the grate when I heard the cow's bell chime of keys. The front door shuddered open. There was a slap as *The East Anglian* fell from the letterbox on to the tiles. Outside, Hilary's car was on the driveway. Isobel was sitting in the front; Daisy in the back.

Then, Hilary's voice: 'Hallo-oo. Anyone at ho-oome!'

I was suddenly a whirlwind; a blur of movement. I ran to the top of the stairs.

'I'm just getting changed. I'll be down in a second.'

The ashes were still warm, but I scooped them on a sheet of paper and took them to the bathroom. I tipped them down the toilet and tugged the chain. I sprayed the air – and myself – with rose water, and went downstairs.

Hilary was already on her way out. Half-in, half-out of the front door.

'I'm not stopping,' she explained. 'I just dropped by to pick up my coat. I'm taking the girls to Thorpeness for the day. How about you? Doing anything nice?'

'Don't know yet.'

'Your folks about?'

'They just popped out.'

'You could come with us if you like.'

I thought of Isobel. The way she had looked at her sister's locket: as if she had wished to strangle me. Daisy: the bubblegum dropping from her mouth as she screamed. Then, I thought of the ashes in the bedroom fireplace. The windows still open upstairs.

'No, it's OK. They'll be back soon.'

'See you on Monday then.'

I stood in the doorway as Hilary crunched across the drive. I tried not to look at the car – or rather *inside* it – but the harder I tried, the more I was drawn towards it. Isobel was glowering in the front seat. Daisy was hiding behind the upholstery in the back.

Hilary unlocked the boot and tossed her coat inside. I forced myself to concentrate on her alone as she wound down the window.

'Don't you let your aunt catch you with her perfume,' she said. 'She can be a bit funny about anyone borrowing her things.'

Hilary turned the key in the ignition and started the engine. The car eased down the drive. I waved, trying to pretend no one else was sitting with her.

After I had gone back upstairs, I scoured the carpet and hearth in my bedroom to make sure I had not dropped any matches. Then, I checked the bathroom. I was glad to have taken this precaution: ashes were floating on the surface of the toilet; clinging to the edges of the bowl. I flushed the toilet and still they bobbed to the surface. I pushed a shroud of white tissue over them, and pulled the chain again. Finally, they disappeared.

This, I think, was the day on which the firebug was conceived. The day I took the lavender out of the grate and replaced it with fire. The day I drove the darkness out of my bedroom and let in light. The day I felt warmth instead of draughts. The day I sensed my family with me again.

Where the firebug came from I do not know. Nor why it chose me. Nor who planted it. It must have been invisible to the eye when it first embedded in my flesh, its tiny embryo multiplying cell upon cell. Growing to the size of a blackberry. Growing bigger and bigger still. If only I had known then, as I know now, how swiftly the firebug would begin flexing its limbs. How we would both fight for the same air supply, the same blood. For control of the same body. Eventually, this parasite would grow so large that my heart would be pushed to one side. Its appetite would be formidable.

# Chapter 13

It was my aunt and uncle's custom on Sunday evenings to sit in the living-room in subdued companionship, reading *The East Anglian Daily Times* or weighty volumes about history and archaeology. These encounters were silent. The passage of time was marked not by the popping of sparks in the grate or the replacement of coals, but by the steady rhythm of a brass carriage clock ticking on the mantelpiece. Occasionally, I would join them in the living-room, spreading my homework across the table. There was no television. The new radio was seldom, if ever, switched on. It was an unspoken rule that if we chose to speak, we should do so in hushed tones as if in a library. The natural consequence was that we talked very little, if at all.

One evening, Uncle Harry broke the silence by asking, 'Did you ever look at those cuttings?'

I was reading a Chemistry textbook, and jotting notes on a piece of paper:

*Most fuels are hydrocarbons (compounds containing hydrogen and carbon only) such as petrol, paraffin and natural gas. Complete combustion of a hydrocarbon fuel always produces carbon dioxide, water vapour and energy.*

*Methane is a prime example of a fuel. Ethane, propane, butane, pentane, hexane, heptane all have similar molecular structures – as have petrol, kerosene, gas, oil and petrol.*

*Thus, the chemical reaction for methane from natural gas, could be denoted:*

$$CH_4 (g) + 2O_2(g) \rightarrow CO_2(g) + 2H_2O(g) + energy$$

*Pentane from petrol thus:*

$$C_5H_{12} (l) + 8O_2 (g) \rightarrow 5CO_2(g) + 6H_2O(g) + energy$$

'I said: "Did you ever look at those cuttings?" '

The chemical equations were like necklaces threaded with amber beads. I did not understand all of them, but I understood their beauty.

*Ethane. Propane. Butane. Pentane. Hexane. Heptane. Pentadecane. Hexadecane. Heptadecane.*

I had learned to recite these alkanes. One long exhalation. An incantation like supercallifragilisticexpialidocious. Depending on my mood, it could be enunciated quickly or slowly. *E-thane. Propane. Bu-tane. Pen-tane. Hep-tane. Pent-a-de-cane. Hex-a-de-cane. Hep-ta-de-cane.* How magical the words sounded. They could be strung on one long thread. Or each jewel could be appreciated separately, light reflecting from its own facets.

'Did you hear me?'

I put down my pen, looked up from my book.

'Which cuttings?'

'The ones your father left behind. I gave them to you at the hospital that time . . .'

'I don't know where they are. Why?'

'I wouldn't mind taking a look at them myself.'

'They're in my room somewhere. Anyway, you said I could read them first.'

'That was nearly two years ago. I just wanted to know that they're—'

'They're in my bedroom! OK! I'll read them when I'm ready!'

Aunt Rose interceded now. She forced a smile.

'I'm sure they're somewhere safe. She'll let you see them in her own good time.' She looked directly at me. 'Won't you, Angela?'

'*When* I've finished with them!'

I pretended to read again. My hands hidden under the table, I fumbled in my pocket for my lucky matchbox. I rubbed it for comfort, stroking the silky surface again and again. I stared at the page in front of me and picked up my pen. But the words blurred. I could not concentrate.

*Ethanepropanebutanepentanehexaneheptanepentadecanehexadecaneheptadecane.*

I muttered it under my breath, hoping it was a strong enough spell.

I went to bed earlier than usual that night and lay fretting for some time. Just the mention of the cuttings made me feel dirty. Unclean. The envelope containing them was locked in a suitcase on top of my wardrobe. But I suspected it would not be long before my uncle came looking for it. I had to make sure it would not be found.

I tried to think of other hiding places: under the flap of carpet near my bedroom window; behind the framed picture of All Saints Church; beneath my chest of drawers; in the blanket chest in the hallway; in the loft. But my aunt and uncle knew every musty and dusty corner of the house better than I did. They would be sure to find it.

I toyed with the idea of taking the envelope to school and hiding it in my desk or locker. What if another pupil discovered it? This was even worse.

I did not hide my lucky matchbox under my pillow as I usually did. Instead, I held it in my palm and kept my hand under the covers.

*Ethanepropanebutanepentanehexaneheptanepentadecanehexadecaneheptadecane.*

As I was falling asleep, inspiration came. I remembered the deserted ruins of Greyfriars Monastery.

## Chapter 14

The shopping bike in the garage had not been used for years. The chain was rusty and the back tyre was soft to the touch. A spider with striped markings had built its web in the wicker shopping basket. At first, the bike looked beyond repair. But Hilary helped to oil the chain and pump up the wheels. I put the spider in another corner of the garage – on a shelf lined with paint pots and turps bottles – where it was unlikely to be disturbed. Then, I wiped down the paintwork.

On my first bike ride, I pedalled across the clifftop to Dunwich Heath and freewheeled down the hill into the basin of the village. I explored the narrow lanes and alleys around Dunwich – the beach, the fishermen's huts, St James's Road, Dunwich forest.

The bike gave a profound sense of freedom. Aunt Rose and Uncle Harry were relieved that I was getting out of the house and entertaining myself. I was less dependent which gave them more time for diving. As a result, they were lenient about my comings and goings. As long as I turned up for meals and went to bed on time, they let me do more or less as I wished. The only 'rule' was that I was ordered to keep away from Greyfriars Monastery.

'We don't want you playing around the ruins. They're ready to fall at any moment. So stay away! Is that clear?' Uncle Harry said.

Later, Hilary followed up my uncle's warning by telling me ghost stories about Greyfriars. How campers who had pitched a tent on the clifftop had seen a mysterious monk crossing the meadow after dusk. How Sea Scouts sleeping on the beach below had seen a woman in a Victorian gown wading into the sea. How villagers had reported strange green lights at the spot (which was after all, only yards from All Saints graveyard) and heard children's voices singing late at night.

I did not go through the ornate arch that formed the main entrance to Greyfriars on the Westleton Road. I was sly: I turned off at the track stretching along the edge of Greyfriars' boundary wall. The track followed the line of the cliffs, but anyone who did not know it was there would easily have missed it. It was barely a foot wide and overgrown with brambles. Below, the shingle rattled as the sea tossed stones to shore. A narrow band of trees was all that separated me from the fifty-foot drop.

I had put a trowel in my coat pocket. A spade would have been better, but there would have been no way of concealing it. The metal blade swung against my thigh. A pendulum marking each jolting step. I felt angry that day. Angry at having to pull the cuttings from their hiding place in the suitcase. Because I had hoped to forget about them; because they made me feel vulnerable and ashamed. I was angry with everyone: my mother and Billy, for dying in the fire; my father for killing himself and leaving the cuttings behind; my aunt and uncle, for wanting to read them.

I was cross with myself too, that I did not have the strength to destroy the cuttings altogether. To burn them or tear them up. But the truth was that they had a powerful hold over me. I was afraid of them. I felt humiliated by them. Yet I knew they were my history. They held a hidden message; an uncracked code. I could not let them go until I had deciphered it.

The trees were still wet from an earlier shower. When I brushed against them, the branches trembled leaving wet patches on my anorak. I felt the rain trickling through my hair, tickling my scalp. Brambles kept snaring in the spokes of my wheels. If I slowed down, the wheels quickly became tangled. The track was slippery and the hems of my jeans were soon rimmed with mud. I carried on, my anger pushing me forward.

Eventually, the track became clearer. Ivy and moss replaced the long grass. Here, among the trees was a solitary gravestone which I recognised from a photograph hanging in my bedroom at Four Winds: *In Memory of JACOB FORSTER who departed this life March 12th 1796 Aged 38 Years*. One of the last remaining gravestones from All Saints Church before it tumbled into the sea. I leant my bike against a tree and stopped. I knew nothing about this man.

But for some reason, it seemed important that the grave should have flowers. I searched around, hoping at very least to pick a handful of lady's lace. I found none. Instead, I tore up some lengths of ivy and fashioned them into a bouquet. It was not much, but it was better than nothing.

I picked up my bike again and wheeled it further along the track. I had almost reached the end of the boundary wall. Ahead of me, the crumbling parapets of the old monastery loomed against the skyline. The ruins were taller, gaunter, more desolate than I remembered. Darker. There were two main walls running parallel to one another, with a narrow corridor between. The grey light filtered through the many windows and arches. But somehow it made no mark on the mottled flintstone.

I had visited the ruins three summers before when my parents were alive. Then, we had been more interested in the dappled mare in the adjacent meadow. My father had tugged up a handful of grass and stood at the gate clicking his tongue. Although the horse was knee-deep in grass, she had pricked up her ears and loped towards us; her nostrils flared, making that reassuring half-purr, half-croon that horses do. She blew hot air over our hands, drooled green slime over our clothes, tickled our fingers with her whiskers. I tore up grass until my fingers ached, just to keep her at the gate.

The horse was gone now – probably in a warm stable. Perhaps because of this, I noticed things I had not seen before. Over one of the windows, was a gargoyle with bulging eyes, which looked as if it was singing or screaming. Beneath this was a sign saying DANGER – KEEP OFF THE RUINS.

I climbed into a window arch and sat swinging my legs. With the trees bare, it was possible to see out across the cliffs. Out to Walberswick in the north and Minsmere in the south. I knew I would have to be careful. With a clear view of the cliff to the east, and open stretches of land to the west, it was possible for anyone to spot me long before I saw them. I knew exactly where I would bury my package. Under the shrieking gargoyle on the north wall.

I had expected it to take minutes to bury my envelope; instead, it took over an hour. The black soil was hard and my trowel kept chiming against pieces of flint. I had never buried anything before, so I had not considered the size of my envelope nor thought what a large hole would be needed to conceal it.

I wanted a deep hole to be sure the package would not be exposed by wind or rain. But I hit a bed of white flint and could not dig any deeper. I was tired from the journey uphill; the mud; the overgrown path. In the end, the hiding place was just under a foot deep.

I had already wrapped the envelope in a cellophane bag and sealed it with parcel tape to keep out the damp. Now, I placed it in the hole and scooped the soil back in. I placed a clump of uprooted grass on top and tramped it down. I marked the spot with a clover leaf of stones.

I thought I would feel relieved when I had finished. Instead, I felt a gnawing anxiety. I had been so intent on digging the hole, I had forgotten to keep a look-out. What if someone had seen me? The clifftop was popular for villagers to walk their dogs. What if they told my aunt and uncle? What if the package was unearthed?

No sooner had I buried my cuttings, than I wanted to pull them up again. To dig a deeper hole. To dig a safer hole somewhere else. But my hands were bubblewrapped with blisters, and my fingers were aching in every joint.

In the end, I was distracted from such thoughts. As I pushed my hands into my pockets, I felt something crumple. I tugged it out. BLAZE ORPHAN TO LIVE WITH RELATIVES. A page torn from *The Birmingham Post* during my time in hospital. I had looked at it the night before, but had hidden it in my pocket when I heard foot-steps on the stairs. I had intended to put it in the envelope with the other cuttings, but must have forgotten. I felt a searing hatred. I hated all newspapers. All reporters. All photographers. *The Birmingham Post. The Bromsgrove Star, The Droitwich Herald, The Stourbridge Times, The Worcester Gazette. The Sun, The Mirror, The Express, The Mail, The Star.* These were just the names I could think of. The list went on and on.

I wanted to do something dramatic. Counter-attack. Revenge if you like. As if this one cutting was responsible for all my pain. It had to be destroyed. Obliterated.

I took the cutting to a wire-meshed litter bin near the boundary wall. Although the top of the bin was speckled with rain, the rubbish in the middle was dry. I prodded around until I found a paper bag and screwed it into a taper. The wind was blasting in off the sea and my matches went out as soon as they were alight. I squatted behind the stone wall and used my coat as a windbreak. I cajoled the flame like an invalid, cupping my hands protectively, nursing it. Once the paper bag was alight, I carried it to the bin and tossed it in.

An empty Silk Cut packet was the first thing to flare. The wrapper curled back as if unwrapped by an invisible hand. The white and purple box began to twist, before setting fire to a Cornetto wrapper, a brown paper bag, an envelope. The fire might have been stopped by a limp banana skin and a child's woollen hat. But it leapt over these to a cardboard sheet and (I noted with grim satisfaction) a faded *News of the World* magazine.

It was then that I added the cutting from *The Birmingham Post*.

Within seconds, the bin was an amazing sunflower. Petal upon petal unfurled, each more brilliant than the last. The air was dusted with pollen. Sparks danced in the air; bees sipping nectar, dripping honey. And I was happy again. Yes, *happy*. Ecstatically, euphorically, rapturously happy.

My neck started to tingle. I sensed something – a shadowy presence – behind me. At either side, just beyond my line of vision. I could not see my parents. But I knew they were with me.

I wanted to turn around: to wrap my arms around them, to kiss them, to touch their faces. But I knew instinctively that if I did they would disappear. We stared into the heart of the flames for some time. Sharing love, warmth, companionship. The joy of fire. I sensed that they approved of what I had done: destroying the cutting to prevent anyone reading it. My longing had summoned them from the Other Side.

I stood absolutely still until the flames died away. Until the paper and cardboard had disintegrated to ashes. I did not dare to look up. Then, I felt the light touch of fingers on my shoulder. I turned around. They had already vanished.

# Chapter 15

When my mother was alive, we would peer into the flames to watch the fire sprites at work. We stood so close to the fireguard that the heat snapped at our skin. 'Look!' my mother would whisper, 'there's a pair of eyes peeping out from behind the coal. See that spark jump? That's one of the babies throwing its rattle out of the grate.' We invented stories for every colour in the flames. Red flames were robin feathers in the fire sprites' caps. Green flames were willow leaves stitched together for the menfolk's trousers. Blue flames were cornflower petals in the ladies' petticoats.

During my chemistry lessons at school, I discovered the unromantic truth. Fire was the combustion of hydrocarbons and oxygen in the air. Its by-products were carbon monoxide, carbon dioxide, carbon, water vapour and various carcinogens. Flame colours were the result of chemical reactions known for decades.

Rather than disenchanting me, these scientific facts only strengthened my interest. I combined the poetry of my mother's tales with the unflinching facts of chemistry. After experiments with a selection of chemicals and a Bunsen burner, I noted my findings in a school exercise book.

*Sulphur – pale yellow solid, melts to amber liquid. Burns with bright blue flame to form misty gas with choking smell (sulphur dioxide).*

*Red phosphorus – red powder rapidly reacts when heated, burning with a white flame to form a white smoke.*

*Carbon – black powder only reacts when red hot, then smoulders or burns with white flame.*

*Aluminium – does* NOT *burn even when heated strongly. (This was underlined several times.)*

*Magnesium – dazzling white flame.*

*Zinc powder – blue-white flame.*

*Calcium – dull red, like a Victorian housebrick.*

*Iron – powder sparkles as it oxidizes like a fountain.*

*Copper – blue-green like a peacock.*

*Lithium – poppy red.*

*Potassium – lilac.*

*Sodium – bumble-bee yellow.*

*Barium – yellow-green like a firefly.*

I was the delight and despair of my chemistry teacher, Mrs Selbey. Although I was one of her most promising pupils, I did not select Chemistry as one of my 'A' level subjects. Instead, I chose History, English and Geography – a disastrous combination as she saw it. But although I enjoyed the sciences, I had set my heart on a more creative course.

In English, my imagination had been gripped by fictional events such as Mr Krook's spontaneous combustion in *Bleak House*; Ayesha's immortalization in the eternal flame in *She* by H. Rider Haggard; Dante's journey through the Inferno in *The Divine Comedy*. In History, I had read accounts of events including the Great Fire of London, the devastation of Pompeii, the burning of Moscow and the bombing of Berlin. In Geography, I had learned about the molten core of the earth; the seething face of the sun; the glowing Will-o-the-Wisps caused by marsh gas.

I told Mrs Selbey, somewhat grandly, that I had chosen the subjects that most appealed to me. I was not certain which path my career would take, but was confident the answer would come with time.

My chemistry lessons were not entirely wasted though. They provided the fundamental principles for my own experiments. I had learned how to draw up scientific tables, analyse results, establish principles. So I put my learning to good use outside the classroom by devising my own tests and trials.

## MATCHES

*England's Glory (Moreland) – Longest matches. Easy to light on most surfaces, even shoes. Smoky. Score: 9.*

*Swan Vestas – Shorter. OK to light. Head disintegrates if damp. Can flick in the eyes if not careful. Score: 7.*

*Safety Matches – Sometimes spit when lit. Can occasionally be lit by striking on glass. Score: 5.*

*Courtesy matches (The Ship Inn) – Difficult to light. Matchsticks bend even when dry. Use only when desperate. Score: 1.*

After raiding the medicine cabinet and kitchen cupboards, I had a number of other results to add to my findings:

## SPRAYS & LIQUIDS

*Hairspray – Extremely flammable – orange flame – needs wick, but once alight burns well. Score: 8.*

*Hair mousse – As above. Explodes if tossed on an open fire. (Similar result if left in hot sun.) Score: 8.*

*Perfume (Chanel No.5) – Highly flammable – blue/orange flame. Only suitable for emergencies due to smell. Easy to trace??? Score: 5.*

*Nail polish remover – Flammable. Burns fiercely. Large flame. Cheap. Easy to obtain. Score: 9.*

*Gin – Useless. Extinguishes match unless used with wick. Ditto other alcohol??? Score: 3.*

*NB. Test brandy, vodka and whisky when the decanters are full so Uncle H. won't notice.*

## PAPERS & WRAPPING

*Walkers Crisps packet – Burns, but shrivels to miniature size – could be used as brooch?*

*Cellophane – Horrible smell – shrinks rather than burns.*

*Greaseproof paper – Sets alight – paper becomes brittle, but cracks rather than crumbles.*

*Aluminium foil – Scorches black but doesn't melt.*

*FABRICS*

*Viscose – Cigarette held against the fabric for several minutes, but wouldn't light. Match held underneath and fibres smouldered. Would not catch light, even when blowing to increase air flow.*

*Wool – Buds of wool caught light giving oily smell. Fabric glowed, but no flame with either cigarette or match.*

*Cotton – Burned best of all – evenly and brightly if blown on. Impossible to raise a flame using cigarette or match.*

*Acrylic – Fabric would not smoulder. Melted away from both cigarette and match.*

I was meticulous in my record-keeping: noting the time, date and whereabouts of my discoveries. I also collected stories from *The East Anglian* which caught my interest and stuck them in the back of my notebook: a hospital patient who set herself alight by smoking inside an oxygen tent; a pensioner who burned down his home after leaving nightlights on the side of the bath; a man who intended to kill himself with exhaust fumes, but instead blew up his garage.

I knew it was dangerous to keep this notebook. It was lunatic. But I could not bring myself to destroy it. Instead, I took measures to protect myself. I disguised my handwriting. If the book was ever discovered, I would pretend it belonged to someone else.

# Chapter 16

The firebug which had been conceived inside me was growing. It was forever hungry, forever making demands. The small fires on the cliff tops near Greyfriars Monastery never really satisfied it. No sooner had the flames gone out than it was gnawing my insides again, as if crying out: 'More! More! More!' It was hankering after something bigger.

I made my fires as the inclination took me. I was careful to ensure no one saw me. They would never understand. I knew this because a Fire Officer had visited my school after a series of grass fires one summer. He used phrases like 'playing with matches' and 'the dangers of discarded cigarettes'. There was no link between his words and the fires I made, but it made me realize that my innocent pleasure would be misinterpreted and misread. Others would see ugliness where I saw beauty.

My High School was ten miles away in Lowestoft – a shipping town with an endlessly changing population. Sometimes the community was made up of fishermen, sometimes sailors, sometimes workers from off-shore oil rigs. In the summer, tourists, holidaymakers, and day-trippers added to the confusion.

I caught a bus from Dunwich every morning, then walked from Lowestoft bus station to school. This arrangement suited me as I grew older because I travelled the distance alone and was subject to the vagaries of public transport – a convenient excuse if I needed one. I was given money each week for bus tickets and refreshments. In short, I had finances, transport and a degree of independence.

I looked older than my years. After concealing my school blouse and tie under a jumper, I was able to buy matches, firelighters and paraffin without shopkeepers so much as blinking. Sometimes, by chance, I would catch the reflection of myself in the shop windows. I was always amazed when this happened: I was starting to look like a woman rather than a girl.

My deceit was made easy by Aunt Rose and Uncle Harry's relaxed attitude toward my upbringing. As long as my grades remained high and my school reports excellent, they let me be. They never nagged me to spend time with them as other parents did. Nor did they interfere or give unwanted advice. I saw little of them during the school week. But when they were home at the weekend, they rarely asked where I had been or what I had been doing. As long as I was at breakfast by eight and my lamp was out by 10.30, they believed all was well. I got little praise from them. But I received little criticism either.

The threat of discovery came from an unexpected source. It was Hilary who asked questions when I arrived home late one evening claiming to have stayed for an after-school club. She peered at her watch and wondered aloud if I had started courting. Then, she sniffed me (I had already changed my clothes) and gave me a lecture about the dangers of underage smoking. But I never considered Hilary to be a real threat. She had two daughters of her own to watch over, without interfering with me.

So fire marked the passage of time as it had since my birth. My journey from childhood to adolescence. From adolescence to adulthood.

PART III

# Chapter 1

There was only one thing more frightening than a black sky: that was a red sky. One morning, in early January, I opened my curtains and the sky was like a giant eye with a burst blood vessel.

I was seventeen. Six yards of land had been shaved off the back garden since I first arrived at Four Winds. The sea had twice breached the shingle bank and flooded the marshland in front of the village. A herd of pigs grazing on low-lying land had drowned.

'Wonder how much garden we'll lose this time!' my uncle said cheerily, peering through the curtains at the back lawn.

'I knew we should have moved those shrubs. Now we're going to lose them!' my aunt answered.

'I don't think so! They're half-way up the lawn.'

She glared at him in answer as if he was personally responsible. 'Since when has *that* ever made a difference?'

I went to school nervous, expecting news of a catastrophe before the day was out.

When I arrived home, the storm still had not broken. The sky was no longer red but black – the colour of a raven's wings, but without the glossy sheen. The North Sea, on the other hand, was white. There were no waves: only a continuous turmoil of milkiness.

My uncle was not in his office. He was perched on the kitchen table warming his hands on a mug of steaming coffee. Hilary was sieving flour, which was odd. She was a sloppy cook and usually claimed sieving was a waste of time. Now, she was pushing lumps through the wire mesh with the back of a tablespoon as if her life depended upon it. Her recipe book was propped open at the page for steak and kidney pie.

'It's just a legend,' my uncle said. 'All the church towers have fallen down. There are only foundations and walls now. If there were any bells left, they'd be silted up! They wouldn't make a sound.'

'What's he talking about?' I mouthed at Hilary.

We were used to communicating like this. Silent conversations that no one else could hear. Mere lip movements. On this occasion though, my uncle intercepted them.

'What I'm talking about is the bells!' he snapped. 'Hilary thinks she heard them this morning when she was fetching in the milk.'

'Which bells?' I asked, although I knew perfectly well what he was referring to.

'The Dunwich bells, of course! Don't they teach you anything at school?'

'We studied them in the first year,' I said indignantly. 'I'm in sixth form now!'

Eighteen churches lay on the sea bed off Dunwich. Most of them had been lost overnight with bells still hanging in their towers. There were fishermen in the village – *sober* fishermen, as opposed to pickled yarn-spinners – who staked their lives that they had heard them. The bells were supposed to toll when storms were brewing, or if land was about to be flooded.

Hilary sliced a lump of butter and weighed four ounces on the scales. She nudged her glasses up her nose with one finger, leaving a buttery smear on the lens.

'You can poke fun all you like. I know what I heard and I know where it was coming from!'

'I'm sure you heard *something*,' my uncle replied, 'but it was coming from the land rather than the water. In all my years' diving, I haven't found a single bell on the sea bed. For that matter, I haven't heard one either.'

He started to laugh dismissively, and I'm ashamed to say I joined in because I believed Hilary and was afraid.

## Chapter 2

The Robinsons were asleep when the sea surged on to the marsh-land in front of their home, near Walberswick. The first sign anything was wrong was when the family cat, Marmite, jumped on the eiderdown in the middle of the night. Martha Robinson never allowed the cats to sleep on beds, let alone to go upstairs. After several unsuccessful attempts at shooing the animal out of the room, she finally got out of bed. When she flicked on the light in the hall, she was surprised to see a quivering circle at the bottom of the stairs. It took her a moment to realize that this circle was a reflection and that the hallway was filled with water. She tugged back the curtains to confirm what she already suspected: the garden shed, the car, the children's climbing frame, the slide, were already half-submerged.

The Robinsons had known for years that they were living on a flood plain. They kept a rowing boat and CB radio for such an emergency. They did not use the boat for fear of being sucked out to sea. Instead they summoned help across the airwaves. Twenty minutes later, they were back on the safety of dry land.

Hilary talked about the flooding loudly and often. Especially, it seemed to me, when the door of Uncle Harry's office was open. She just couldn't help crowing. Other people had heard the church bells, not just her. She had not forgiven my uncle for his mockery. Now, the Robinsons were lodging with one of her friends in Dingle, so she was able to give regular updates. Martha and Ian Robinson were planning to move back to Walberswick as soon as they could put down replacement carpets – in spite of the threat of future flooding.

'It's the kids I feel sorry for,' Hilary said. 'Those poor mites were watching from the window while their dog was washed away. Martha says they saw him being sucked under. I don't suppose they'll forget that in a hurry.'

I wondered why she seemed so surprised. The sea had always seemed to me like an unpredictable monster slumbering on the shore. Drownings and sinkings were regularly reported in *The East Anglian Daily Times*. If the sea could devour fishing boats and sailors, why would it spare a dog?

'You'd think the parents would see sense and move inland. But that's sea folk for you. Always lived by water. Won't live anywhere else.'

I tolerated these noisy conversations with Hilary, although I suspected they infuriated Uncle Harry who hated what he loosely termed 'the village grapevine'. I did not want to be thought a conspirator, so I lowered my voice in the hope Hilary would do the same. Unfortunately, she did not take the hint. I let her continue to confide in me though. I was lonely, curious, eager for conversation. Although I had lived in Dunwich for four years, I had no companions of my own age. Hilary was the only person I would have honoured with the title of 'friend'.

'I'm popping over to Walberswick tomorrow, if you fancy coming along,' Hilary said. I imagined my uncle in his office, stiff with resentment. There seemed no purpose to the journey other than nosiness. He would have expected me to have the sense to stay at home.

'Yes, please.' My voice was too eager, but I would not have missed the trip. I wanted to see what the sea was capable of.

A white salt mark ringed the outside of the Robinsons' cottage where the water had been. What appeared to be the body of a sheep was hanging in the lower branches of a tree. When I looked more closely, I realized it was a sodden rug.

We circled the cottage peering in the windows. Inside, the living-room looked as if it had been ransacked. Dining chairs were lying on their sides. Wet cushions were scattered across the floor. There was no carpet, only a covering of brown silt. In the hallway, a telephone dangled from its hook; an ornamental fig tree was upturned with its roots washed clean. The kitchen was the only downstairs room in which nothing had moved: the cooker and fridge too heavy to have overturned.

Hilary walked towards the tree and started to tug at the sheep-skin rug. Every time she pulled, the branches shook. Water pattered like rain.

'I'm glad you decided to come along,' Hilary began. 'You see, I'm going to launch an appeal for Martha and Ian, and I wanted to ask you a favour.'

'Oh yes. What?'

The rug suddenly came free and flopped on to the soil. It was too heavy to carry. Hilary dragged it towards the washing line, which only made it muddier. She motioned for me to help. It took several attempts before we managed to fling it over the nylon.

'I wondered if you'd help me write something for the local papers. Just a short piece asking for clothes and furniture; toys for the kids.'

'I don't know if I'm the right person to ask. I haven't got any experience . . .'

Hilary found a stick to prop up the line. Then, she started wringing out the rug, twisting her wrists as if she was milking teats. Streams of water stringed on to the earth, forming shiny puddles before soaking into the ground.

'You'll do it for me, won't you? You know I can't put two sentences together.'

'Why don't you just call the papers and give the information over the phone?'

'I don't trust them to do it properly. I don't want it to sound like Martha's begging for handouts.'

The sheepskin felt wiry in my hands. Like fibreglass. I felt as if my skin was being shredded every time I touched it. I stopped wringing and let it hang. It looked as wet as when we started.

'I don't know how to. I wouldn't know where to begin.'

'Just explain what the appeal's for and why it's being launched. You'll only have to write a page!'

'I'll try,' I said doubtfully.

'You're an angel! I told Martha I'd ring her tonight. We can come back tomorrow when the light's a bit better to take the pictures.'

Hilary gave the rug another squeeze. Sea water splattered over her feet, turning her shoes a shade darker. The following day, the brown leather would be spotted with salt rings like crusted barnacles.

# Chapter 3

Hilary passed me the copy of *The East Anglian Daily Times* jabbing it with her finger. I folded the paper over. It felt more manageable that way; less unwieldy. I sat down to read it.

*TRAGIC pensioner Nancy Peters has died after lying for two days within inches of her telephone. The 82-year-old widow, who lived in an isolated cottage on Dunwich Heath, fell down the stairs during this month's devastating storm. An inquest has heard that Mrs Peters dragged herself to the telephone, but was unable to call 999 because the lines had been blown down. Newsagent, Mr Sam Hodgson, of Westleton, alerted police after the pensioner failed to collect her daily newspaper.*

'Is this Mrs Peters with the orange hat?' I asked.

Hilary frowned. 'I can't say I remember her hat. She used to make jam. Damson jam. We bought some last summer.'

'Yes – Mrs Peters with the orange hat who lives up on the heath. That's who I mean.'

'Poor dear. What a way to go! With her phone lying right next to her, too. Who knows what must have been going through her mind. I wasn't meaning for you to look at that though. I meant the story underneath!'

*A SUFFOLK family is lucky to be alive after a terrifying ordeal when the sea flooded their home. Ian and Maria Robinson and their two children were trapped upstairs after the sea smashed through defences at Walberswick. They radioed for assistance but had a nail-biting wait of more than an hour before help arrived. The two children, Emma and John, watched in horror as the sea swept away their beloved Jack Russell. Friends and neighbours are launching an appeal to replace all the furnishings, clothes and toys lost during the flood. Anyone wishing to contribute can contact Mrs Hilary Franklin on Dunwich 282.*

'The phone hasn't stopped ringing all day,' Hilary said. 'I've had one woman offering a second-hand sofa. Another's giving a suitcase full of clothes. I've got someone else giving their kids' old toys.'

'But this isn't what I wrote. It's nothing like it.'

'If you're worried what Martha will say, I shouldn't worry. She's over the moon.'

'I know. But you'd have thought they'd stick to the facts . . .'

'They've had reporters knocking on the neighbours' doors apparently. Got the story from them. I agree it's a bit melodramatic. But we've got what we wanted, haven't we? I suppose they just wanted to tug the heartstrings.'

It was the same in *The Suffolk Advertiser* and *The Suffolk Herald*. The story about the Robinsons was there, but I hardly recognized it. I rifled through my duffel bag and read the opening paragraph of my press release.

*An appeal's being launched to collect clothes, toys and furniture for a family in Walberswick. The organizer, Hilary Franklin, is asking people to turn out their attics or to make a donation. She is organizing the appeal for her friend Martha Robinson and her family. Martha's children, Ella and John, lost their pet dog, Skippy, when their home was flooded a few weeks ago.*

When Martha Robinson telephoned later that night to thank me for my help, I did not know whether to feel proud or embarrassed.

Two weeks passed. Three. Then four. My brief dabbling in journalism was forgotten. One afternoon, Hilary hauled her handbag on to the table and unzipped it. It was a large denim bag with silver studs.

As the zip opened, a hairbrush clattered on the table top. This was followed by a bottle of cherry-coloured nail polish.

'I've got something for you,' Hilary said. 'I thought it might be of interest. Hold on a minute. It's in here somewhere.' Hilary rummaged through her bag, tossing items on to the table: crumpled tissues; a packet of fruit pastilles; sticky plasters; a book of first class stamps.

Eventually, she tugged out a crumpled ball of newspaper.

'Here we are! Just what I was looking for!'

The paper was covered in rusty blotches. I hesitated.

'It's got blood on it!'

'Blood?' Hilary squinted, furrowing her brow. She held the paper under her nose, close to her eyes. She had lost her glasses.

'It's biro I think, or ketchup. No, it's lipstick. Definitely lipstick. The top must have come off.'

Hilary straightened the paper on the flat surface of the table. She beamed and pointed with her finger.

'There!'

'What? Where?'

'There! The advert of course. Read it.'

The paper was Dalmation-marked with lipstick. Red blotches smeared into one another. I held the edges gingerly. Beneath the red circles was an *Appointments Section* ripped from a newspaper. In the centre of the page was an advert for a newspaper based in Birmingham.

CUB REPORTERS REQUIRED
- *Are you fascinated by current affairs?*
- *Can you write attention-grabbing stories?*
- *Are you hard working and self-motivated?*

*Each year, we offer two school leavers the chance to train as reporters at* The Birmingham Bulletin. *We have two award-winning newspapers –* The Daily Bulletin *and* The Evening Bulletin *– and the successful candidates will have the chance to report for both. If you think you have what it takes, then write and convince us. Salary: £8,000 per annum.*

'What do you think? You've been wondering what to do after you leave school.'

'But I'm not taking my A levels 'til next summer!'

'I don't mean for you to apply now. I was thinking of next year. Look! They take on two trainees every year.'

'I don't know.'

Hilary grinned. 'It's perfect. You're good at English and you like writing. It'd suit you down to the ground. And look at the pay! I wouldn't mind earning that.'

'I don't know. I'll have to think about it.'

Hilary folded the advert into a lopsided rectangle and handed it back.

'You've got nothing to lose and everything to gain as I see it. You won't know unless you give it a try.'

I had homework to do so I went upstairs. I wedged the newspaper in the letters rack at the back of my dressing-table. I pulled my school books out of my satchel and spread them out. I was working on an essay about *The Old Man and The Sea* when I noticed a smudge on the paper. I put my pen down. There were red marks under my nails. It must have come off the newspaper. I picked at the substance and examined it closely. It had no reflective sheen. It was not slippery. Nor did it smell of pear drops. Whatever it was, it was not lipstick.


# Chapter 4


One of my few memories of Nancy Peters was of a woman with a dried apricot complexion sitting on a deckchair at the end of her drive beside a hand-painted sign saying *Eggs for Sale*. Then, there were the annual carol concerts at St James's when she wore a tangerine beret with a hedgehog pompom and sang several octaves higher than the rest of the congregation.

After Nancy Peters died, her cottage on Dunwich Heath became a source of morbid interest. I cycled along the winding lanes to her home and peered through the nets at her windows. I was haunted by the stories I had read in the newspapers. How the old woman had tumbled down the stairs. How she was found when the newsagent in Westleton noticed she had not collected her *Sunday Times*. Her body was slumped by her telephone. She was too weak to dial even after the line was reconnected.

There were no immediate neighbours so I was able to visit Nancy Peters' cottage as often as I wanted. For a long time, the furniture stayed where it was behind the net curtains and the mail piled up in the porch. Then, one weekend, a large skip appeared on the driveway. A red hatchback and a transit van were parked along-side it. A couple – presumably the son and daughter-in-law mentioned in Mrs Peters' obituary – were carrying boxes to and fro.

When I returned to the house a couple of days later, the windows were gaping and the light bulbs were bare. Six wooden chairs with red cushions were lying on the lawn, together with a television in a mahogany cabinet, and a wicker sofa someone had made a poor attempt at crushing.

The skip was piled high. A set of china teacups decorated with rose buds had been tossed on top of the skip, together with some matching dinner plates, a teapot without a handle and a pair of tarnished candlesticks. These things saddened me. I did not know Mrs Peters, but each battered item must have marked a year in her life: a tablecloth stained with wine from a dinner party; chair legs scuffed by her grandchildren; a coffee table marked with white mug rings.

Even Mrs Peters' Christmas decorations had been thrown out. Tinsel strands spilled out of a McVitie's biscuit tin, together with faded baubles and a plastic angel. Foil lanterns and paper chains dangled beside them.

Inevitably, the sight of these things set me thinking about my own family and how I had lost them. About the Christmases I used to have at Elm Road, and the Christmas I had just had at Four Winds.

*

Aunt Rose and Uncle Harry had tried their best to make Christmas an 'occasion'. Aunt Rose bought a six foot tree from Westleton and decorated it with white ribbons and silver pine cones. We ate Christmas dinner in the dining-room rather than the kitchen. The table was laid with star-shaped serviette rings, red napkins and the best silver cutlery.

We snapped crackers and wore gaudy paper hats. We ate turkey until we were stupefied: then ate some more. But by the time the Christmas pudding reached the table, my aunt and uncle were exhausted with the effort of being merry. My aunt poured brandy over the pudding, but she did not set fire to it as my mother had done. She let it soak into the pudding, before breaking it up with a spoon.

After dinner, I opened my presents. My aunt and uncle gave me a dressing-gown, pyjamas and slippers. Hilary gave me a polar bear sculpted from white chocolate and a fluffy reindeer with a hot water bottle in its belly. Hilary's gifts made me smile. But Christmas was not the same. On Boxing Day, we watched the hunt go by, then walked over the heath at Minsmere before eating a cold turkey buffet. Once this was done, Christmas was tacitly understood to be over. The decorations which were put up three days before Christmas were taken down three days later.

The simple fact of the matter was that neither my aunt or uncle were really 'Christmas people'. They tried their best to pretend they enjoyed lazing around, eating rich foods, and playing Monopoly. But idleness did not come easy to them. Little in life gave them as much pleasure as their work. They tolerated Christmas for my sake, but I was not convinced they enjoyed it.

Such then were my thoughts as I peered at the contents of Nancy Peters' skip. Looking at the furniture and knicknacks, I could not bear to think of them being sent to the tip. They might be crushed or broken up; covered with potato peelings, grass cuttings, dustbin bags. They would be bulldozed into the ground. Buried. Forgotten.

I thought of my own family. How I had preserved their memory. How I had honoured them with fires. I decided to set light to the skip. It would be a spectacular blaze. A giant candle to commemorate Nancy Peters' life.

# Chapter 5

I waited for an evening when Aunt Rose was working late in Colchester and Uncle Harry was studying in his office. I crept outside to the garage to look for the can of petrol kept for emergencies. It was hidden behind some faded deckchairs. The handle was rusty and covered with cobwebs. The flies trapped there were white with age. I wrapped a carrier bag around it and lifted it into the wicker shopping basket on my bike.

I was certain Uncle Harry would not miss me. We rarely saw each other before bedtime. When I got home from school, his office door was usually shut. He ate alone. As a result, we could go to bed without wishing one another goodnight – this was considered normal. As a precaution though, I stuffed some cushions under the quilt and left one of my old wigs on the pillow.

It was still light as I cycled across Dunwich Heath, and a heron rose up spindly and elegant in front of me. The air was still. The gorse, heather and ferns barely shivered as I passed. A lone starling shuffled on a telegraph wire but made no sound. Even the trees seemed to be standing to attention.

The sound of a car engine broke the silence as I was approaching the lane leading to Nancy Peters' house. I had anticipated this. Before I set out, I had promised myself I would turn back if anyone saw me. The engine hummed for a long time before I saw it – so much so, that I had time to wheel my bike to the opposite side of the road and start pedalling back in the direction from which I had come.

As the car passed – a black Morris Minor – I turned my head slightly to see who was inside. If it was a stranger, there was still a remote hope that I might go ahead with my plans. Isobel Franklin stared back from the passenger window, and I caught a glimpse of her latest boyfriend at the wheel. Her hair was pinned up and she was wearing lipstick. She gave me a thin-lipped smile which was crueller than any scowl: a mixture of scorn and pity. A look which said, 'I smile at you because I *can*; because I don't give a damn whether or not you smile back.' Then, they were gone. Off, no doubt, to meet friends from the Swimming Club.

I should have gone back to Four Winds, I knew I should. But there was something about that encounter which made me turn around. That smile would have erased me had I let it. If I had turned back, it would have confirmed everything the look implied: that I was a nonentity.

So I cycled back towards Nancy Peters' house full of defiance. I wanted to feel alive. To exist.

By the time I cycled up Nancy Peters' drive, I did not care who saw me. I propped my bike against the front wall in open view. What would it matter if I was seen by anyone passing by? Better to be seen, than to be invisible.

When I lifted the petrol can out of the basket, it made a seductive slapping. The weight shifted from one end to the other as I carried it. I felt invincible. As if I was carrying a magic potion. It had been raining for three days in a row and many of the items in the skip were wet. The tapestry cushions on the chairs were soggy and the wood had stained a darker shade. Normally, rain would snuff out a fire before it managed to take hold. But with petrol in my hand, it meant nothing. Everything would light without any effort at all.

I placed dining-chairs on all four sides of the skip. I stood on each of them in turn, carefully drizzling petrol over Nancy Peters' possessions. The petrol can was heavy. The handle was at an awkward angle and the spout was too short. I doused some furniture, but just dribbled petrol in other places. I was careful not to spill any on my clothes.

Once I had finished, I wiped my hands with a tissue. Then, I reached inside my coat for my matches. I struck one and flung it.

Setting fire to the skip was like casting a gold organza cloth over a dining-table. There was a sudden glimmer, a glitter, a glow. Then I wanted to rub my eyes. The skip disappeared, and in its place was a banqueting-table laid for a feast.

A glazed goose was steaming upon a silver platter, the skin crisp and brown. Next to this were jugs of white sauce, plum sauce and gravy. Beside these were so many tureens of roasted potatoes, parsnips, carrots, sweetcorn and peas that the tablecloth could barely be seen. The far end of the table was covered with desserts: a raspberry Pavlova, chocolate profiteroles, brandy snaps, whipped cream. There was even a Christmas pudding bathed in violet flame. There were no places laid at this feast: no cutlery, plates, goblets nor napkins. But there was enough food for several families.

The enticing scent of roast meat and plum sauce wafted towards me. The goose looked so succulent, that I reached out for my favourite part: the parson's nose. Yet as I came close to the crispy tail, I felt intense heat and snatched away my hand. In that same instant, the feast vanished. I found myself standing beside a fiercely burning skip. The flames were no longer incandescent gold, but violent yellow. Black smoke scratched my face and throat.

I was not surprised by what I had seen. I was accustomed to seeing things hidden to the eye. I considered what had happened to be a gift from my parents. My heart was singing as I swung my leg over my bike and pedalled away.

Fifteen minutes later, as I was free-wheeling down the hill into the wind, my new-found confidence gusted away. I wondered how much trouble I was going to get into. One thing I knew for certain: no worse person could have seen me than Isobel Franklin.


## Chapter 6


I was careful to hide the notebook detailing my experiments with fire. I changed the hiding place in accordance with Hilary's house-work routine. Mondays were washing days. Tuesdays were for dusting and polishing. Wednesdays for ironing. Thursdays were for hoovering. Fridays were for cleaning out cupboards, washing windows, mending and repairs. On a laundry day, I hid the notebook down the back of a chest of drawers. On a hoovering day, I hung it over a coat hanger with a shirt over the top. On an ironing day, I tucked it under my mattress.

The housekeeping timetable was taped inside the larder door: Hilary rarely deviated from it. But one Wednesday afternoon, I arrived home and found pillow cases flapping on the washing line like seagulls on a wire. It was less than a fortnight after the fire in Nancy Peters' skip. I ran upstairs, my heart fluttering, and reached under the mattress. The cotton sheets were cool around my fingers. But I did not find what I expected to find. I searched the middle of the bed. The head of the bed. Finally, in frustration, I heaved the entire mattress on to the floor to confirm what I already knew. My notebook was gone.

I once heard a robin crying for its chicks after a cat had eaten them. The ground was scattered with fledgling feathers; the cat was licking blood from its whiskers. Yet the robin hopped around the nest, trilling for chicks it must have known it would never find. I was like this disbelieving bird. Not content with pulling the mattress off the bed, I started searching between the sheets, blankets and quilt. When I did not find it, I moved the bed frame away from the wall. After this, I pulled off the pillow cases. I repeated the same searches several times.

I was about to haul the mattress back on the bed when I noticed a pile of fresh laundry on an armchair on the other side of the room. My notebook was on top of the stack, its russet cover camouflaged against a woollen jumper. Hilary must have put it there.

I sat down heavily. How long had Hilary been in my room? Ten minutes? Fifteen? Twenty? What had she seen? Hilary had always taken such a keen interest in my school work. She could not have resisted peeking inside. I leafed through the pages as if they might give answers. The disguised handwriting, the coded letters which once seemed sophisticated, now looked simplistic. Did I really hope to fool anyone by dropping certain vowels and consonants? Was I really so naive? Even if Hilary had not deciphered the words, she would have seen the newspaper cuttings. There was no mistaking what this was: the diary of a fire-raiser.

Hilary was mashing potatoes at the draining board when I finally went downstairs. The windows were open and the room was smoky. The sausages were two-toned: pink and black. A knife, fork and spoon had been placed at right angles on the kitchen table. A glass of milk had been placed on a pottery coaster. I sat down.

'Are you hungry?'

'Not really. I had a big lunch at school.'

'Well, eat what you can and leave the rest. Would you like baked beans or peas?'

'Peas please.'

Hilary pulled a bag of peas out of the freezer and let them rattle into a saucepan. She poured boiling water over them. Her movements were calm, controlled. She was not going to say anything without the words being carefully considered.

I took *The East Anglian* from the rack, pretending to read the sports on the back page. A Wimbledon victory in three straight sets. An athlete with a banned substance in her blood. I turned the page.

Hilary brought my plate to the table. The mash was flecked with bits of black onion. The sausages rolled over so that they were pink-side up. I folded the newspaper and picked up my cutlery. I was about to start eating when Hilary joined me at the table.

'Pass the paper. I'll have a quick flick through while you're eating,' she said.

The sausages were soft on one side, crunchy on the other. The onion crumbled in my mouth and got stuck between my teeth. I smothered everything in ketchup, but it still tasted of charcoal. I ate as much as I could, then hid the rest under my knife and fork.

I was pulling the lid off my yoghurt, when Hilary finally spoke.

'You read anything about the lad on death row in the States?'

I licked the lid of my yoghurt. Little cat's-tongue licks. Working my way around the edge of the lid. Circling inwards. I avoided her eyes.

'No. I must have missed it.'

'Maybe it isn't in this paper. I read it the other day. He killed his girlfriend's parents. They were trying to stop him seeing her, so he set their house on fire.'

'Weird.'

'His solicitor's trying to get him off saying it stems back to his childhood. His parents died in a car crash when he was little and he was brought up by foster parents.'

I dipped my spoon into the yoghurt. It was strawberry flavour. Lumps of fruit dotted the surface like little red hearts. I balanced one on the spoon, lifted it to my teeth.

'Looks like he's going to the chair anyway. The state governor won't give him a reprieve 'cos he's in favour of capital punishment. What a tragedy! What a waste of a life!'

Hilary peered over her glasses like a magistrate, caught my eye, then looked away again. She licked a finger, turned a page and continued reading in silence. I coated the back of my spoon with yoghurt. Sucked it. Dipped it in the pot again.

We sat at the kitchen table for some time. Me, scraping imaginary yoghurt from the bottom of an empty pot. She, gently flicking pages which she may or may not have been reading. And still, I could only guess what she might or might not have read.


# Chapter 7


The kitchen was full of steam and there was a bucket on the floor. Three crabs with pastry crust frills on their shells were twitching beneath the magnifying glass of water.

'You're not going to cook them, are you?' I asked.

'I thought they'd be a nice treat. Your uncle likes crab salad.'

'I'm going upstairs then. I hate it when they scream.'

'That's just air coming out of their shells. It's so quick, they don't feel a thing.'

'All the same, I'll give it a miss!'

'Before you do anything, you'd better go and see your uncle. He wants a word.'

'In his office?'

Hilary smiled. 'Consider yourself truly honoured.'

Since I arrived at Four Winds, I had only ever been in Uncle Harry's office on a handful of occasions. The first was to discuss the contents of my father's Will. Another time was when my uncle congratulated me on my 'O' Level results. The most recent occasion was when he discovered a page ripped from his atlas.

The office was the sort of room which was unwelcoming to all but its owner. A large ammonite fossil and a pitted cannon ball were the only frivolities in a space otherwise dedicated to study. The chairs were spartan. There was not an item of comfort apart from the white blanket under the desk which my uncle wrapped around his legs when he turned down the heating.

The floor was a patchwork of papers. Piles of assorted sizes hid the carpet from view. My uncle carried a pencil behind his ear and wrote notes whenever the inclination took him: on the backs of envelopes, bills, beer mats. The wall surrounding his desk was covered in scribbled notes. Maps, photographs and diving grids had been pinned to a noticeboard. The floor either side of his desk was scattered with rubber shavings. The room smelled of damp skin, stale breath and hair cream.

'Come in, come in. Make yourself at home!' Uncle Harry said.

There are certain sea captains who know the drift of the ocean bed, who have knowledge of the hidden channels leading to a quayside. So it was with my uncle and his office floor. To reach the chair, I first had to navigate my way across the carpet, careful not to disturb any papers.

Uncle Harry indicated a route and I tiptoed across. There was a pile of books on the chair. He scanned the room for a space, then finding none, bundled the books on his desk. I perched on the edge of the chair and waited for him to begin. I was curious whether it was good news or bad.

Uncle Harry rubbed the bridge of his nose. He wiped his forehead with his handkerchief, then blinked.

'There's a can of petrol missing from the garage. I only bought it a couple of months ago. I was wondering if you knew what'd happened to it?'

My heart lurched as if an inexperienced rider had settled on its back. I had forgotten about the petrol can. I could not remember where it was. Probably somewhere in Nancy Peters' garden. Somehow I managed to answer.

'Why should I? I never go in there except to borrow the bike. Maybe you used it and forgot about it?'

'No. I haven't touched it since I bought it. I haven't needed to.'

'Maybe Aunt Rose used it?'

'I've already asked her. She didn't even know it was there.'

'Why are you asking me? I haven't got a car. What would I do with petrol?'

There was a strum of galloping hoofs which I knew to be my pulse. I felt as if I was heading towards a dyke or a fence. I braced myself for weightlessness. A sense of flying. Hard earth.

My uncle's face hardened. 'Now look here, there are only three of us in this house. Rose hasn't had it and I haven't had it. So that only leaves you. I don't know what you've taken it for, but I want it back. If there's any funny business going—'

'What about Hilary?' The words careered out of my mouth before I could stop them. 'How do you know it wasn't her?'

Uncle Harry's eyes narrowed. He stroked the dog-eared corner of his diving log book. He turned half towards his desk, half towards me. His lips twitched.

'Now why didn't I think of that?'

I stumbled out of the office with rather less care than I had entered it. As I went out, I grazed a pile of papers with my heel. They splayed untidily across the floor. I did not stop to pick them up. This was not my first lie, but it was my first and only betrayal.

## Chapter 8

A middle-aged woman was peeling carrots in the kitchen when I arrived home the following week. She had a dark mole on her cheek with hair sprouting from it.

'Hello, I'm Mrs Appleton. You must be Angela,' she said. She shook my hand. Her skin felt like defrosted chicken.

I marched to Uncle Harry's office and tapped on the door.

'Where's Hilary? Is she ill?'

'She's gone.'

'What do you mean? *Where's* she gone?'

'We decided to let her go. The agency's sent a replacement. Not a moment too soon.'

My voice rasped, 'Why?'

'Well, I'm sorry to say you were right about the petrol. She did take it. At first, she pretended to know nothing about it. Then I suggested calling the police and she soon changed her tune. She said she'd "borrowed" it – she was going to buy some more, but forgot about it. So she said! Thought she'd got away with it, until I mentioned the other things which've gone missing . . .'

'What other things?'

'Half a bottle of brandy. Aftershave. A bottle of meths. To be honest, I thought you had something to do with it, so I turned a blind eye. But once I knew about the petrol, it didn't take much to put two and two together.'

My uncle sniffed, then wiped his nose with an ironed handkerchief.

'You're not really going to call the police, are you?'

'Over a can of petrol? Don't be silly. I was just trying to frighten her!'

It was obvious he knew nothing about the fire at Nancy Peters' house. His dislike of 'gossip' and the 'village grapevine' had kept him in ignorance. Or perhaps he did know, but had not made the connection. Hilary had remained loyal to the last: sacrificing herself to protect me. But coward that I was, I did not tell my uncle the truth.

In the kitchen, Mrs Appleton was serving lamb chops for tea. The meat was lightly browned, the potatoes were evenly roasted, the carrots were a vibrant orange.

I ate my tea in silence while Mrs Appleton washed the saucepans. I felt numb. My only friend. Gone. Hilary had been a mother to me. She had nursed me, entertained me, helped me with homework. She had made my bed, ironed my clothes, cooked my meals. Talked to me. Listened. Cared. Selflessly. Expecting nothing in return. This was how I repaid her. With betrayal.

Other thoughts crept in too. Base and selfish thoughts. I remembered my mother warning me that there was no such thing as a secret. 'Even if you think it's safely locked up, someone'll always find the key,' she said. She told the story of Pandora. How she could not resist opening the box, unleashing demons and dervishes on the world.

I wondered why Hilary had lied about taking the petrol. What Isobel had told her. *If* Isobel had told her anything at all. If Hilary knew my secret or merely suspected it. Whether she had lifted the lid of the box or peered through the keyhole into darkness.

# Chapter 9

It was late August. The wind was pummelling the windows, tossing salty water at the panes. The grass, which had not been cut for some time, flattened against the land. Shrubs squatted like cats, claws drawn, clutching the earth. At the back of the house, the dustbin fell over. The lid span, rattling, down the drive.

As the wind wailed outside, a smaller squall was blowing up in the kitchen. Aunt Rose's jaw tightened and her lips quivered at the edges. She shut a cupboard door with more force than necessary, and tugged the cutlery drawer so hard it came off its rails.

I ate breakfast with my head down, trying to make myself as

small as possible. My aunt had broken her ankle after a fall at work. She had been working from home for several weeks, restless and tetchy. I had tried to help her as much as I could: making cups of coffee, relaying messages on the telephone, fetching books, and letting her lean on me as she hobbled up the stairs. The rest of the time, I tried to stay out of her way.

Aunt Rose peered out of the kitchen window down the sloping bank of the lawn towards the North Sea. Perhaps because of the rain, perhaps the grass was rolling and rippling, it seemed that the house was not on land but afloat on water.

Finally, my aunt could no longer contain herself.

'Are you still planning to go out this evening, Harry?'

'Of course I am. Why shouldn't I?'

'I'd have thought that was obvious! Look outside.'

'It's just a squall. It'll die down by tea-time.'

'But a *night* dive! Harry, please!'

'You're not going to make a fuss are you? I don't do them very often.'

My uncle tipped coffee from the pot and picked up the cream jug. He did not do as my aunt did, pour delicate spirals of cream over the back of a teaspoon; instead, he stirred briskly after adding two spoons of sugar. He liked his coffee almost black.

'Just be sensible – for once in your life!'

'If I'm not back by eleven, then send out a search party. You're always like this when I go without you. I'll be fine. I promise.'

'Can't you call anyone? There must be someone you can trust.'

Uncle Harry looked exasperated. 'We've been through all this before!'

'I'd feel better knowing someone else was there. Even if they only waited on the beach.'

'There's no one I can trust. I don't want the whole village knowing my business!'

Uncle Harry drained his cup and poured another coffee. He had a habit of leaving his wet teaspoon on the table rather than in the saucer, so that it stained the wood. This always annoyed my aunt.

'What about me?'

Both Aunt Rose and Uncle Harry turned to stare. I had never taken part in their expeditions before. Nor had I ever shown any inclination to join them. I had always been too frightened of the sea. They were drawn towards water like tides towards the moon. I, on the other hand, was ruled by the sun. I stayed away from water as much as possible. I was as surprised by my offer as they were. I had acted impulsively to prevent an argument. I had not considered the consequences.

'Are you sure?' my aunt asked. Already, the tension in the air was diminishing.

'She won't even dip in her toes, let alone swim!' my uncle spluttered.

I suppose I wanted to punish myself in some way for what had happened to Hilary. To atone for my betrayal. But mixed in with this was the desire to please. I wanted my aunt and uncle to be proud of me, to notice me. For though we lived in the same house, we were strangers. There was a vast chasm without Hilary. I wanted to fill it, but was not sure how.

'She doesn't have to go anywhere near the water. You're only diving on All Saints. You aren't taking the inflatable, you said so yourself.'

'I know. But . . .'

My aunt picked up the wet teaspoon from the table and placed it on my uncle's saucer. She wiped the drop of coffee with her finger. Then, she looked across the table at me and beamed. It was the first time I had seen her smile in weeks.

'Take her with you, Harry. She's only got to sit on the beach and keep an eye on your gear. What could possibly go wrong?'


# Chapter 10


We trudged three-quarters of a mile along the beach with the diving equipment. We staggered over peach and black shingle, flint cracked and split open like hard-boiled eggs. The bags grew heavier with every step. The stones slowed our progress.

The cliff face was pitted with holes. White flints flecked the sand where land had fallen away. Sea wrack, seagull feathers, pink tellins, saddle oysters were scattered across the shore. Eventually, we stopped at the spot marked by a gravestone high on the cliff. This was the site of All Saints' churchyard, before the church tumbled into the sea.

My uncle undressed to his underwear and pulled on his wet suit. He did this methodically, eyes on the sea, oblivious to the wind clawing around us. After this, he stood examining his maps and charts. He worked on a grid system, scouring certain areas and avoiding others. No matter how many times he searched the same spot, it always revealed something new due to the shifting of silt and sand.

'How long will you be?' I asked.

'About an hour.'

'What happens if you don't come back?'

'Don't *you* start! I've already had all this from Rose!'

'Really, Uncle Harry: what if you don't?'

'I will. Don't worry.'

'But what should I do? I ought to know.'

'Just run along the beach to the coastguard's cottage. Give him a knock.'

'And what'll he do?'

'He'll send out a lifeboat I expect. But if I'm gone, I'm gone. There won't be much anyone can do.'

I felt increasingly apprehensive as my uncle continued with his preparations. I recalled Mrs Jackson collecting me from school on the day of the fire. I remembered lying in bed at the Queen Alexandra Hospital, wondering why my father had not visited. I remembered the bouquet of sunflowers in the sink, Hilary's smile which wasn't a smile at all. Tragedy came on ordinary days. Unexceptional days. It punched you when you were least expecting it. It always took your breath away.

'Cheer up! You're not regretting coming are you? You can go

home if you like. I won't mind,' Uncle Harry said, cheerily.

'I'm just cold.'

The wind had spurs in it. I had a coat over my T-shirt. But the gust slipped inside, finding its way through zips, poppers and buttons.

'Not enough fat on you, that's your problem.' My uncle patted his own ample torso. 'There's a blanket in the rucksack. Or you can run up and down the beach a few times with me. That's the best way to warm up.'

'No thanks.'

I searched for the blanket while Uncle Harry jogged along the beach. He lumbered across the shingle, grunting and heaving, like those other creatures – walruses, sea lions and penguins – which are graceless anywhere but the sea.

He returned red-faced after his warm-up and attached a torch, compass and depth gauge to his belt. There was a hiss of air as he checked the valves on the air tank. He spat into his face mask and rubbed the glass, then picked up his grappling hook.

'All right then, I'm off. Wish me luck!'

'Good luck.'

'And rich pickings!'

'Rich pickings too.'

Impulsively, I jumped up and followed my uncle as he walked towards the sea.

'Take care!' I said. What I really meant was: 'Don't go.'

'See you in just over an hour. Remember not to light the lamp until it gets dark. The batteries are low. I'd have brought some more if I'd been on my own. I usually put it on the tripod and leave it on. But since I have a helper . . .'

I felt helpless. I understood now why Aunt Rose was so bad-tempered whenever my uncle went diving alone. It was fear. My uncle had dived hundreds of times before and had always returned unharmed. But every dive was different: an uncharted experience. There was no guarantee he would return.

As Uncle Harry waded into the surf, the waves bowled, knocking him like a skittle. He lost his footing for a split second, then recovered himself. This happened four or five times. Every time he attempted to dive, a wave hit him. I was relieved when I saw this. I thought he would have to turn back.

A large swell started rolling in, growing in height and force as it rushed towards the land. My uncle would have to submerge or be overwhelmed by water. I ran towards the edge of the sea, yelling, 'Take care! Come back safe! Don't be long!'

He did not hear. The wave was curling over him, licking his wet suit like a massive tongue. He was swallowed almost instantly. After this slathering wave came crashing in to shore, the swells diminished again. I scanned the water for any sign of a bobbing head or air tanks. But the surface was clear as if no one had ever been there.

# Chapter 11

There had been a fresh cliff fall on the beach. The earth had split into pieces like slices of a huge yellow cake. A tree had fallen down the side of the cliff and lay with its roots pointing at the sky. Dusk was settling in and the air had a grainy ethereal quality. A couple of miles out to sea, a small fishing boat cut through the waves heading towards Southwold. It scurried across the water bouncing on the swells. In the remaining light, I scrambled over the rubble hoping to find something of interest.

I was interrupted by a noise on the cliff top above. A man was waving his walking stick to attract my attention. A black labrador was standing beside him.

'You all right down there?' he shouted.

'I'm fine!'

'I suppose you know what this spot is?'

I shrugged. 'I suppose.'

'You shouldn't be here on your own. A young girl lost her life here a few years back. It isn't stable. You never know when it's going to fall.'

The labrador was restless. It bounced away and bounded back again, urging the man to follow.

'I'm waiting for my uncle,' I yelled.

The man squinted at me. 'You Harry Burnett's niece? That's all right then. Sorry, didn't recognize you.' He touched his cap and ambled after his dog.

I picked up a stick and idly started to inscribe my name in the sand. A-N-G-E-L- But then I stopped. Something about the shape and colour of the stick made me pause and examine it. I was hold-ing a human bone.

It is surprising how the eyes see what they expect to see. Once I knew what was in my hand, I took a fresh look at the debris scat-tered around the base of the cliffs. What I had imagined to be twigs, driftwood, boulders, revealed their true forms. Thigh bones. Ribs. Vertebrae. A pelvis. Two shattered skulls. I dropped my stick with a shudder.

I cannot easily explain my reaction. My aunt and uncle had always been matter-of-fact about the unearthing of the dead at All Saints' graveyard. There was a skull in my bedroom which Uncle Harry had picked up from here. I had even researched the area for a history project. Yet there was a world of difference between visit-ing an ancient burial ground with an adult and being in the spot alone at nightfall.

My immediate impulse was to run away. But I knew I had to wait for my uncle. I had promised to switch on the lamp so that he could find his equipment. I was needed to raise the alarm if he failed to return.

I hurried back to the spot where the bags were left. I hardly dared look what I was treading on, as if at any moment the shingle might produce an unearthly groan. When I reached the bags, instinct kicked in. I rummaged through them, pulling out my uncle's clothes as I searched for the items I would need. I opened the Tupperware boxes, unwrapping the greaseproof paper from the sandwiches and slices of fruit cake. I grabbed the diving log book and maps. I found a crumpled tissue, some sweet wrappers, a wallet stuffed with paper money and credit card receipts. Anything that would burn.

I made a small mound from this paper, wedging it down with stones. I fumbled in my jacket for my matches. I tried my left pocket first. My right. Then, I tried my jeans. There was nothing there.

As darkness crept over the beach, the shingle shifted and shimmered. Sticks seemed to quiver. Rocks pulsated. Everything – even the smallest pebble – looked as if it was alive. My skin was tingling, electrified. There were ghosts here, but not comforting ghosts. Not the ghosts of my parents.

I huddled underneath the blanket and screwed my eyes tight. I wanted to switch on the lamp, but did not dare. The battery was too low. I told myself it would not be long before my uncle returned. All Saints was the closest part of bygone Dunwich to the shore. Only the previous November, the wind had pushed the sea along the beach so that the waves piled up like snowdrifts. In this extra low tide, I had been able to see the ruins. All Saints was not so far, I told myself. I had seen it from the land.

To distract myself, I tried to imagine the city that once stood at this spot. I tried to visualize shops, homes, hospitals, windmills and church towers. I tried to imagine people – merchants, sailors, fish-wives, peddlers, beggars – wandering down the main highway to the city gates. When this failed, I thought of what remained: the walls and foundations on the sea bed. Rather than comfort me, this only reminded me of the sea's appetite. It seemed incredible that the water could devour so much. And that it was still hungry.

There were no matches to conjure up my parents. Instead I tried to summon their spirits by thought alone. As if by merely thinking of them, I might protect myself. I tried to recall the creaminess of my mother's face; the leather lines of my father's. But my parents had become more sensation than memory, more dismembered parts than people. My father was an emerald-veined hand which ruffled my hair; a chin which felt like sandpaper; a shirt which smelled of horsehair and iron. My mother was a pair of chafed hands with coal dust under the nails. She was uncooked cake-mix on the back of a wooden spoon; diamond-cut coal; a lilting fairy-tale at bedtime.

I pulled the blanket tighter and tried to imagine myself elsewhere. But time and again, I was pulled back to the beach by the rattling of stones: the sound of the sea sucking at the shoreline, pushing the shingle in and out, in and out. I promised myself I would wait five more minutes. Until the hour was up, no more. After that? After that did not bear thinking about. The graveyard was a hundred yards wide. I would have to cross it in the dark to return home. My only other option was to attempt the cliff.

Until this moment, I had avoided thinking about the dangers my uncle faced underwater: the undercurrents that could drag him out to sea; the snagged fishing nets that could wrap around him like serpents. To say nothing of faulty air tanks, compasses, and pressure gauges. I recalled that Aunt Rose had once brought back a sample of water off the sea bed. It was thick as oxtail soup. It seemed impossible my uncle would ever return.

I flicked on the lamp and examined my watch in its pale circle of light. One hour and fifteen minutes had passed. I remembered too late that I was supposed to shine a beam of light at the water to guide my uncle back. In my panic, I had forgotten. I was trembling as I aimed the lamp at the waves. I saw nothing but blackness and cruel white crests. I tried to convince myself that my watch was fast; that I only had to be patient and my uncle would appear. But my heart was fluttering like a lark beating its wings at the bars of a cage.

Then, about a hundred yards out, I spotted a light bobbing between the swells.

I held the lamp high and waved it frantically, yelling at the top of my voice.

'Over here! Over hee-eeere!'

As Uncle Harry emerged from the waves, I ran to greet him. He brushed past me, tugging off his face mask and flinging it angrily on the shingle. His grappling hook followed.

'What happened to the bloody lamp?' he stormed. 'You only had to do one small thing! *One small bloody thing!*' He punctuated his rage by tugging his fins from his feet. By unfastening his air tanks. By hurling his diving belt along the beach.

'I should never have listened to Rose. I should bloody well have left you at home. If I'd been on my own I'd have used a tripod. I'd have brought some batteries! I could've been swimming up and down for hours!'

He unzipped his wet suit and fumbled in the rucksack for a towel. Then, finding it missing, he tried the other bags. These too were empty.

'What's happened to my clothes?'

He shone his lamp at the beach. Its bright aura picked up scattered shapes on the shingle – a jumper, a pair of trousers, a shirt, a coat – huddled like frightened lambs.

'What the. . . ?'

The beam of light swung round. I was momentarily dazzled. I froze, trapped in its bright light.

'Jesus!' he said. 'Jesus – you look in a bad way.' His voice was calmer now. More reassuring. 'Just hold on there, girl, and I'll get you home.'

# Chapter 12

The sound of the living-room door being clicked shut always signalled that something important was about to be discussed. I padded out of bed and put my ear to the floor. The settee and armchairs were directly beneath. I lay on the carpet, listening.

'You did what?' Aunt Rose exploded. 'Have you no sense at all?'

'You knew where I was going. You could've stopped me. You didn't say anything,' my uncle protested.

'I didn't know you were going to the graveyard!'

'I was diving on All Saints! Where else would I leave my gear?'

'You scared the poor girl out of her wits!'

'How was I to know she'd react like she did? She didn't say

anything. She could've said *something*!'

'She shouldn't have to. You should never have taken her there! She shouldn't have been put in that position.'

'You're right. I should've gone on my own like I intended in the first place!'

'So it's *my* fault?'

'You're the one who was so keen for me to take her!'

'As a precaution! Not so you could frighten her to death!'

'She bloody well frightened me! You should've seen what she did to my rucksack! I was lucky to find my log book. It could've easily blown into the sea. God knows where my wallet's gone. And my maps! Years of work lost in a single night! She must've gone nuts!'

'Keep your voice down, will you? She might be awake. It's hardly surprising she's highly strung, is it – considering . . .'

I fell asleep on the carpet. When I woke up, I could smell fresh lacquer and pinewood. My legs were pinned together. My hands were folded as if in prayer. Two cold objects, which felt like coins, had been placed over my eyes.

A voice boomed, 'So we would commit this body to the Lord. Earth to earth. Ashes to ashes. Dust to dust. The certain knowledge that her memory will be kept alive within us all . . .'

I heard a roar which I took to be a furnace, but I was not afraid. Far from it. I knew my parents were waiting for me on the other side of the flames. We would soon be reunited.

There was a creaking. A rumbling as my coffin moved on metal runners. Then there was an enormous jolt. A splash. I realized with dull horror that I had been dropped not into fire, but into the sea.

My coffin rocked on the surface of the waves. Then, water started to seep in through the cracks. At first, it was just a puddle at the back of my head, legs and buttocks. But suddenly it was tickling my ears and chin. I was shrieking. Screaming. In my terror, I thought: 'This is a dream'. But when I tried to wake I could not.

I held my breath for as long as I could, hoping for a miracle – for the coffin lid to be torn off, to be rescued, for the mourners to discover their mistake. Eventually, I could hold out no longer. I inhaled.

The first breath was the most difficult. The briny water was a scorpion slipping down my throat. My body fought against it: gagging, coughing, spluttering. As the water skittered into my lungs and unleashed its sting, I stopped resisting. My last thought as I slipped away was that the fish would make a feast of my eyes.

I woke from this nightmare to the steady trickle of water. Not the crash of the sea, but the tinkle of tap water. A tap left dripping in the bathroom. My aunt and uncle had gone to bed: the house was dark.

I stumbled across the floor to switch on the lamp. The light hurt my eyes. But the fear of Dunwich beach was still with me. I was relieved to feel carpet under my feet rather than shingle. To see walls rather than waves. I turned around, slowly taking in the shoes toppling out of the wardrobe; the corduroy trousers sprawled over the chair; the patchwork quilt with its lacework of threads between the seams. Then, I looked at the things that pleased me least. The shelves lined with historic artefacts. Lumps of masonry, ancient coins, a pilgrim's badge, a skull. The haphazard collection of photographs and sketches. The pictures of All Saints Church, Greyfriars Monastery, the Leper Chapel, St James's Church.

I climbed back into bed and sat up. I did not want to sleep, to dream. My gaze was drawn back to the middle shelf: to the skull which had been there since the day I arrived. Parts of the nose socket had been eaten away and there were unusual protrusions on the cheeks. The skull should have been sent to St James's for reburial, but Uncle Harry had kept it as a curiosity.

I had never really looked at this skull before. I had never questioned the logic of keeping it in my room. Now, it struck me as odd to find it there: a dead person's head. The skull stared back. And I realized that I had not left the beach at all. I would never be free of the sea in Dunwich. It seeped in through every crack.

I pulled the quilt over my head, just as I had the blanket on the beach. I wrapped my arms around my stomach, hugging myself, longing for daylight.

As I was falling asleep, I heard my aunt's voice again. Or perhaps I dreamt it: 'It's hardly surprising she's highly strung, is it – considering . . .'

Considering. Considering *what?*

How much did she know?

# Chapter 13

I decided that I had to leave Dunwich. There was nothing to keep me there. I doubted if my uncle would ever forgive me for losing his maps. My aunt would always have 'considering' between us. However much I loved them, I could not live with them. The incident on the beach had separated us forever.

So I dreamed of a home surrounded by land. A garden that stayed the same length year after year. Trees and shrubs that did not disappear with each storm. I dreamed of still water. Water in puddles and lakes and ponds. Water that only stirred when the wind grazed its surface. I dreamed of a city where houses stayed up for hundreds of years. Where the dead stayed buried. Where shoe leather never had salt crusts. Where the street lights stayed on all night, every night. Where it was never dark. Where the only roar was the surge of traffic, rather than sea water.

I opened a map and looked for the inland spot furthest from the sea. I already knew the answer. It was engraved on my heart. The Midlands. The heartland of stone and metal, furnaces and fires, chimneys and smoke. Place of my birth.

I rifled through my possessions to find the cutting Hilary had given me from the Appointments Section. It seemed fitting and right that I should become a trainee reporter at *The Birmingham Bulletin*. I felt as if I owed it to Hilary to get the job. It would make amends to her. It would prove (to myself as well as her) that I was capable of change. That I was not destined to be a fire-raiser. That I could cross to the other side of the fence. I could report on fires, rather than create them. It would just be like documenting them in my notebook.

All job applicants were required to write a 500-word feature on a subject of their choice. I knew exactly what to write about. There had been a series of fires at beach huts and fishermen's sheds along the coast that year. The article was easy to research because I had cuttings on every fire in Suffolk for the past five years. I was able to calculate the frequency of the fires; the cost of the damage caused; the number of hours the Fire Service spent putting them out. At the end of the article, I suggested a list of people to interview: the Head of the Fire Service; beach-hut owners; fishermen; the Suffolk Coastal MP.

It occurred to me when I had finished, that my article might easily fall into the wrong hands and arouse suspicion. So I went to the library and photocopied the stories published about the flood in Walberswick and the appeal for the Robinsons. I put these cuttings in the envelope together with my application form and a covering letter. I gave myself a *nom de plume*: Sandra Angel: a blend of my mother's christian name and my own.

The interview at *The Birmingham Bulletin* was preceded by an hour-long written test. There were questions such as: 'Who is the Education Secretary?' 'Who is the captain of the English rugby team?' 'Which country is hosting the next Olympic Games?' 'What does ACAS stand for?' 'Who is the Prime Minister of France?' 'What is the capital of Indonesia?' 'Which Hollywood actress recently married husband number six?'

I had expected to sit a test, so had spent the previous weeks revising. The only questions I could not answer were, 'What is the difference between a government White Paper and a Green Paper?' and 'Who is the leader of the NUT?'

The test made me realize how much I had to thank Hilary for. Most of my general knowledge came directly from her. My aunt and uncle made it a point of pride that they never read national newspapers, listened to the radio, or watched television. Hilary, on the other hand, revelled in news.

There was a rolled-up newspaper in Hilary's handbag every day: she picked it up on her way to Four Winds. She often sat at the kitchen table leafing the pages while I ate my supper. She had an opinion on every subject: the abolition of the monarchy; the price of petrol; church ministers with mistresses; plans to reduce coastal erosion; match-fixing in football. She spread her net wide, sometimes buying the *Sun*, sometimes the *Daily Mail*, sometimes *The Guardian*, sometimes *The Times*. There was little Hilary loved more than to discuss news and gossip. In the process, she had educated me.

After the test, I was taken for interview in a featureless room with smoked windows. There might have been torrential rain or bright sunshine outside: I would never have known. This, and the reassuring whirr of an air conditioner controlling temperature and circulation, rather pleased me.

The news editor, Miles King, was sitting behind a desk as I entered. Miles King had a handsome but brutal face. He had black hair, hollow cheeks and blowtorch eyes. The wrinkles around his mouth might have been mistaken for laughter lines had I not spotted the brown stain of tobacco on his fingers. He sat with one ankle resting on his desk. At first I thought he was wearing long johns. Then I realized that the white patch between his trousers and socks was, in fact, skin.

Miles King did not stand up or shake my hand. He gestured towards a chair with one finger, then sat examining me. Three minutes must have passed, and still he did not speak. I had borrowed *How to Break into Journalism* from the careers library, but was unprepared for his behaviour. I wondered if this was another test to see how I would react in an awkward situation. My hands started moving independently: chafing together, picking bits of fluff off my jacket, smoothing down my skirt. Eventually, I had to wedge them under my thighs to keep still.

Miles King drew a tobacco pouch from his shirt pocket. He pulled out a ready-made roll-up and tapped it on the edge of the desk. He balanced it on his lip, then took it off again without lighting it. Finally, he spoke.

'You wrote a cracking article about the arson attacks. It was a bit puffy in places, but the structure was sound. On a sliding scale though, it's pretty soft stuff. I want to know if you can cover the hard news. If a man died in one of these fires, would you have what it takes to stake out his house? Would you be able to doorstep the neighbours? Could you get pics of his wife and kids?'

I was taken aback. The careers manual had warned me to expect a difficult interview. Even so, I had not expected such an assault, such aggression, from the outset.

'I think I'd be a good listener. Both my parents are dead, so I know what it's like. I'd try to draw people out,' I stuttered.

He smiled in a way which suggested that he was not accustomed to being friendly. He placed the roll-up on the edge of his lip again and flicked his lighter. It was on its highest setting – a large flame suddenly speared the air, illuminating his chin. He lit up with a practised skill which revealed this was no accident.

'Good. Very good. Now tell me why you want to become a reporter. How do I know you're not going to get trained up, then change your mind? I don't want you pissing off once I've gone to all the trouble of training you.'

'I don't want to go to university, if that's what you mean.'

'You know it's a full-time job. You're on call most nights and most weekends. You can forget Bank Holidays. And if you get Christmas or Easter off every other year, you'll be lucky.'

'As I said: I don't have family. Holidays don't mean a lot to me.'

As I was speaking, the door opened and a woman with a severely cut fringe and a tailored suit strode in. She introduced herself as the chief reporter, Lydia Thistle. Miles ignored her. If anything, he seemed to stretch out his legs to take up more of the available space.

No sooner had Lydia Thistle sat down, than he began firing a series of hypothetical questions: 'If you could interview anyone in the world who would it be?'; 'If you were given a helicopter and unlimited budget for a story, where would you go?'; 'If one of your friends was working at a children's home under investigation for abuse, what would you say?'; 'If you saw a fatal car crash on your way to work, what would you do?'; 'What are your strengths?'; 'What are your weaknesses?'; 'Where do you want to be in ten years' time?'

Miles King did not give the impression of listening to my answers. He ignored most of what I said; concentrating instead on thinking up the next tricky question. This might have set me at ease. Except that every now and then, Miles would seize upon something and tear it to shreds: 'Why would you say that?' 'When?' 'Where?' 'Rubbish!'

I was relieved when he fell silent and started poking at the ash in his foil ashtray. This, it seemed, signalled the end of my interrogation. Lydia Thistle held the door open and shook my hand. She had said very little throughout my interview.

I was half-way through the door, eager to escape, when Miles King spoke.

'One more thing before you go: you realize we have two intakes – one in September, the other next January. Which would you prefer? Hypothetically, of course.'

'September please.'

'Personally, I think January's more appropriate. It'd give you a chance to kick your heels. Take a grand tour of Europe. Feed the poor. Save donkeys. Whatever your *thing* is.'

'I'd set my heart on September. That's what I'd prefer.'

'We'll have to see how much you want this job then, won't we?'

As I left the building, Miles King's voice was still resonating in my ears. I shuddered involuntarily as if to shake off the memory of the past hour. I was unsettled. I had never met such an unpleasant man before.

Then there were Lydia Thistle's hushed words as I left the room. Whispered conspiratorially, not to frighten me, but to warn me: 'In case you're wondering, his bark's as bad as his bite.'

I rather hoped I would fail the interview and never have to meet him again.

# Chapter 14

The letter from *The Birmingham Bulletin* arrived during the first week of my A level exams. By this time, I had applied to several universities to study English and had been offered places at Bristol and Exeter. I was also toying with the idea of taking a year out – working as an au pair in Vancouver.

> *Dear Sandra Angel,*
> *I am writing to offer you a position as a trainee reporter, subject to obtaining your expected A level results.*
>
> *It is important that journalists should be able to type quickly and accurately. It is therefore a condition that you learn to touch-type to a speed of 50 words per minute before starting work. (A teach-your-self typing manual can be obtained from most bookshops.)*
>
> *You should also read the latest edition of* British Constitution Made Simple *and* McNae's Essential Law for Journalists. *Shorthand (Teeline system) will be taught on Wednesday evenings – you will be expected to reach a speed of 100 words per minute. You will also have to pass preliminary examinations in journalism, law and public administration.*
>
> *On joining the company on 10 January* (I groaned aloud) *you will serve a six-month probationary period during which we will assess your suitability for the job. If at any time your work or conduct is judged unsatisfactory, you will be suspended immediately.*
>
> *Acceptance of these conditions is requested within seven days. Failure to do so will result in this job offer being retracted.*
>
> *Yours sincerely*
>
> > *Miles King*
> > *News Editor*

I experienced a mixture of emotions on reading this letter: excitement at being offered the job; anger at the January entrance; a rush of dislike for the man who wrote it; confusion, because I had got used to the idea of going to university.

My main reaction though was triumph. A summit reached after a rocky climb always has an extra sense of worth. I never stopped to consider what it might be like on the other side of the mountain.

I had planned to spend the morning doing last-minute History revision. Instead, I wrote my acceptance letter, then knocked on Uncle Harry's door to ask for a stamp.

'Does it have to be first class? What's it for?' he asked.

'I've been offered a job!' I said proudly.

'Oh yes? And what might that be?'

'A job as a trainee reporter. Remember? I went for the interview ages ago.'

Uncle Harry rummaged in his drawer and took out a stamp steamed off an unfranked letter.

'That's the latest plan is it? I thought you were set on Vancouver. And what about the place at Bath?'

'Bristol,' I corrected him. 'That was just a safety net in case I didn't get the job.'

'Well, it's your life. It's up to you what you do. You're an adult now.'

I could hear the relief in his voice. The girl who was too afraid to dip her toes in the sea, the girl who forgot to switch on the lamp, the girl who went nuts and lost his precious maps, preparing to depart. The cuckoo in the nest flapping its wings and taking flight.

'When do you start?'

'Next January. I have to teach myself to type before then.'

'Unless you change your mind and buy a plane ticket, eh?'

The tube of UHU was rolled in a tight spiral. Glue had hardened around the nozzle like amber resin. Uncle Harry broke the seal, then prodded inside with a pin. A tiny spot of glue appeared. He dabbed the stamp, then pressed it on the envelope.

'The job's conditional on me getting two As and a B,' I admitted. 'But then so are the university places.'

'So nothing's decided then.'

'I got straight As in my mocks.'

'Ah yes. So you did.'

He stared just long enough for me to see that he resembled my father. The realization jolted me. I had always imagined them to be different. My father with dark hair, he with red hair. My father glorying in fire, my uncle prizing the sea. Yet there was something about the illumination behind Uncle Harry's eyes, the way thoughts flickered over his face like images over a movie screen, that reminded me of my father. I had the same sense of watching from afar; of seeing but never touching; of meeting but never knowing. No, it was not the two men who were different: it was the quality of my feeling towards them: the quality of their feelings towards me.

As I negotiated my way across the sea of paperwork on the office floor, I realized how much I wanted to leave. To leave this house with its damp walls and damp floors and damp affection. I would find a home with unstained window sills; with carpets that smelled of wool rather than mould; with curtains unmottled by mildew. The only time windows rattled would be when lorries drove past. The only time I wore two pairs of socks would be if I stepped outside. A red morning sky and a storm forecast would not set my heart stampeding. I would fill my fireplaces with coals rather than dried flowers. I would start each day laying the kindling in my own hearth.

# Chapter 15

I could have left Dunwich immediately after my exam results arrived (three As, as predicted). Perhaps if I had travelled the world or moved to another part of the country, I could have averted the disaster that followed.

Maybe it was lack of imagination which led me to apply for the temporary job at Blyth's Bookshop in Westleton. Maybe it was laziness. Or maybe, it was the lingering suspicion that once I left

Dunwich, I would never see my aunt and uncle again.

Brenda Blyth, the owner of Blyth's Bookshop, was one of those people who believed they could tell whether a person was trustworthy or not just by looking at them.

'I can see you're honest,' she said. 'Which is just as well – considering what I'll be asking of you.'

She hired me on the spot. Then, she trusted me with the bookshop's biggest secret.

That summer had been a wet one. Water soaked into the bricks and rendering, and stayed there as if in blotting paper. Autumn arrived. Mrs Blyth had smelled the aroma of sodden birch leaves outside her shop and made a mental note to rake out the drains.

Then one day, as she was taking a hardback from a bottom shelf, she had discovered her fingers coated in pale green powder. She had tugged out a paperback and discovered the same green dust on the cover. A fine fur was sprouting from the spine.

She pulled out an entire row of books and found a band of black mould speckling the outer wall. The books were valuable. Some had been on the shelves less than six months. Rather than throw them away, Mrs Blyth had placed them in leaning towers in the storeroom. She had closed the shop for 'refurbishment' while she whitewashed her walls.

'It'll be the end of me if this gets out. Don't breathe a word to anyone!' she warned.

I was officially employed as a shop assistant. But in addition to this, were more clandestine duties in the storeroom. It was my job to wipe each damaged book with a soft cloth then lightly brush the pages with a feather duster.

I worked alone with the door shut so that no customers could see me. A three-bar heater was placed beside my desk and left on round-the-clock to dry out the books. Mrs Blyth gave me gloves and a surgeon's cotton mask.

'Just to be on the safe side. I don't want you breathing it in.'

'You mean it's poisonous?'

'It's supposed to affect people with asthma.'

'I should be all right then.'

'I'd rather you wore it. I don't want you taking risks.'

The heat in the storeroom was crushing. It was a dry electric heat which made my skin feel as if it was cracking like parchment. I would arrive at the bookshop wearing tights, trousers, two jumpers and a coat. By lunchtime, I would have taken off my shoes and tights, and changed into a T-shirt.

One day, I lost my cotton mask and worked without it. The dust made a fine mist in the air with every stroke of the feather duster. Since I had no mask, I reasoned, it would make little difference if I went without my gloves. So I 'lost' these too.

I dusted thousands of books during my time at Blyth's. Thousands of books with thousands of pages. Thousands of pieces of paper damaged by damp. Page after page after page after page. Sometimes I experienced a sort of snow-blindness from seeing so many white pages one after the other. I would forget where I was and become absorbed in the simple task of feathering them clean. Unflinching whiteness. Without edge. Without end. I would become lost. Disorientated. Then, I would look up from the blizzard and realize where I was. In a hot cramped storeroom surrounded by mould spores and decaying books.

So it was that I was always alternating between different temperatures, between fiction and reality, between the world in my head and the world outside. Cold and hot. Damp and dry. Ordinary and extraordinary.

By the start of December, the last of the damaged books were back on the shelves. The expensive bowls of pot pourri placed at strategic points throughout the shop were removed. The walls no longer smelled of compost and mildew.

Mrs Blyth pulled out a bottle of amontillado sherry and poured two glasses.

'Here's to you,' she said. 'My saviour. You may not know it, but you've saved me from ruin.'

'Thanks. To tell the truth, I enjoyed it.'

'Well, "enjoy" isn't a word I'd use. But just the same, you've saved the day. Just in time for Christmas too.'

I had never had sherry before. I drank it as I would have milk or orange juice: gulped, rather than sipped. It burned my mouth and throat, before making a pleasant heat in my stomach. I felt that I had made a friend.

Mrs Blyth beckoned me to follow her into the storeroom. There, she hauled an old Remington typewriter from the cupboard.

'A little surprise for you – an early Christmas present. You start at that newspaper in just over a month. You better get your typing up to scratch. I don't want you blaming me for falling behind.'

After this, I left the storeroom. Instead, I spent most of my time answering the phone and dealing with customers. Because the shop was quiet for long stretches, I was able to practise typing several hours a day. I started off with: *The quick brown fox jumped over the lazy dog*. The drum on the typewriter was stiff. The *R*, *S* and *Y* keys grazed the surface of the paper, leaving gaps instead of ink. The ribbon was temperamental and sometimes entire words were printed in red rather than black. At first, my fingers would not move as I wanted them. But eventually, they learned to dance together; to strum in time.

Mrs Blyth gave me index cards, invoices and letters to practise on. She did not seem to mind if the odd letter was missing or if the words were two-toned. In fact, she seemed to accept this as inevitable. The regular clackety-clack, clackety-clack, ping was the song of our friendship. A tune of triumph over the dampness, the loneliness, of Dunwich.

In no time at all it seemed, I achieved a speed of 44 words per minute. Most difficult were the final six words required to build my speed to the required 50 words. I was practising one afternoon – typing sections from *Teach Yourself Typing* against the clock – when the doorbell carolled. There was a murmur of cold air as the door closed, but I did not look up. Most customers needed time to settle into the antiquated atmosphere of the bookshop. Any intrusion made them feel hassled or harassed. Even a misinterpreted glance could send them scuttling back into the street.

I was typing the final sentence of a three-minute exercise when I became aware of another person in front of my desk. I picked up speed. Typed a full stop. *Ends.* Glanced at my watch. Three minutes, twenty-one seconds.

'Sorry. How can I—'

It was Isobel Franklin. She was wearing a sweat shirt, jogging trousers and trainers. Her hair was tied back in a pony-tail which was dry at the ends but wet at the roots. A towel poked out of her bag. I thought of the chill outside and wondered if she had been swimming in a pool or the sea. An unpleasant memory came back of Dunwich Heath. The bicycle bouncing over the potholes. Isobel in the passing car. The enticing gorse which smelled of coconut, but had hidden thorns.

'Can I help you? Are you looking for a particular book?'

I could think of nothing else to say. I could only treat her as I would any other customer. Her eyes were black and clouded as dock water. In the same way that dock water does not slap or lap or swell, her glance did not flinch.

'Mum sent me.'

I felt a familiar twinge of nostalgia. Longing. Guilt. I thought of Hilary's loyalty. Her love. My ridiculous plan to persuade her to adopt me. How I had imagined I might replace Fiona. How I had wished to become Isobel's sister. How miserably I had failed.

'She knows I'm working here?'

'News travels. There aren't many secrets round here.'

Isobel emphasized the words. Was this an accusation or a statement?

'How is she?' I asked quietly.

'Same as ever. Still packing fish. Still hates it. Still looking for a housekeeper's job closer to home.'

An accusation then – and deservedly so. I tried to imagine Hilary at Lowestoft fish market. Sometimes, when I caught the early bus to school, I would sneak through the gates to see what the boats had brought in. The fishermen were preoccupied, so I was able to saunter around looking in the plastic pallets. The fish nestled on beds of ice like rose quartz. Occasionally, there was movement.

Flailing. A mouth gasping. Gills flickering.

I thought of Hilary lifting the fish by their tails, their bodies slippery in her hands. Laying mackerel in neat lines and covering them with shovels of ice. Her hands pink with fish blood, shimmering with scales. I thought of her dislike of the cold. The damp concrete of the market.

Many months had passed since Hilary's dismissal. Occasionally, I passed her while I was on the bus. Or I heard about her via Mrs Appleton. I often thought of phoning her, but never got past dialling the first two digits. I tried writing, but screwed up the letters as soon as they were written.

Isobel moved to the side of the desk where the amontillado sherry had been placed on a circular silver tray for pre-Christmas customers. She poured herself a glass. Downed it. Then poured herself another. She wiped her mouth with the back of her hand.

I wanted to say, 'Isobel, can't we be friends?'

Instead, I said, 'What are you up to now? Are you at college or working? Didn't you always want to train as a diver?'

'Something like that.'

Mrs Appleton had told me Isobel was taking a course at Lowestoft College, sponsored by one of the oil companies. There was an emergency simulator there. A pool in which students pretended to be escaping from a capsizing boat or a burning oil rig. I imagined her being tossed about in total blackness, waves lashing the sides of the boat. She would have been the perfect student: in her element. Survival through wits and stamina rather than class tests and exams.

'I'm only temporary here. I've got a job as a reporter. Your Mum suggested it. She gave me the idea ages ago. I start in the New Year—'

'As I said: news travels.'

Isobel glanced around the bookshop, taking in the shelves in one brief sweep. Her expression was contemptuous. As if to say: *How deadly dull. Just like you.* She, so vivacious, full of life. Me, living life second-hand. Little had changed since school.

I faltered. A saying sprang to mind. *Still waters run deep.* A cliché, but true nonetheless. Years had passed since Hilary had given me Fiona's clothes and shoes. Since I had frightened Daisy while she was playing hide and seek.

We went to the same schools, shared the same classes, the same teachers, her mother – but we led separate lives. Isobel was the class troublemaker; successful at sport and swimming, weak at academic subjects. I was the girl who always got the highest grades, but flunked at sports. While Isobel was busy captaining the swimming team, the netball team, the hockey team, I had resigned myself to life on the sidelines. I never took part in after-school clubs or sports events. Instead, I studied hard and made fires to stave off the loneliness.

'Just for the record,' Isobel said, 'I know you had something to do with Mum being sacked. She won't talk about it – and she usually talks about everything – so I know it must've been you. If I ever find out what happened, you won't know what hit you.'

I fiddled with the typewriter keys. The lazy dog jumped over the quick brown fox. The quick brown fox bit the lazy dog. I wanted to tell Isobel that the sacking was a mistake. That I missed her mother, loved her. That I regretted what had happened. That I had changed now, was mending my ways. But, of course, I could not. She would never have understood.

Isobel thrust a package at the desk. It was wrapped in white tissue paper and tied with gold ribbon. It was flat and square; small enough to hang from a Christmas tree.

'Mum sent this – God knows why.'

She slung her sports bag over her shoulder and, with a spring in her step, her pony-tail slapping her shoulders, she opened the shop door to the cold December darkness.

'Remember what I said: Mum might forgive and forget, but I don't.'

The doorbell twitched for a while after she had gone. Then, I was left with the trembling of my heart; the wing-beat of my breath. I was filled with conflicting emotions. Fear. Sadness. Frustration. And joy. Yes, joy. Hilary had not forgotten me. She still cared enough to send a gift before I left.

I clawed at the ribbon; tore the white tissue paper. As the paper separated, something silver and sparkling tumbled into my lap. It was a trinket shaped like an angel. It had a delicate face and sturdy wings. Bare feet. I unclasped the chain and fastened it around my neck. The angel pressed against my rib cage, thudding softly, cold silver, where my own heart should have been.

I set about replacing the till roll. But I was so flustered that the paper bounced out of my hands on to the floor. I tugged the end. But this only served to make it unravel all the more quickly. Eventually, it disappeared beneath a bookshelf out of reach.

I bent down to grab it, eyes level with the carpet, arm outstretched. Then I spied it: a rubber circle, brown-yellow in colour, with curled edges on the skirting board. I tugged the books from the bottom shelf, piling them on the floor. Finally, the wall was exposed. I had discovered a toadstool.

I realized then that you can never turn your back on anything. Minor triumphs are misleading. They confuse you into thinking all is well, but you can never afford to assume the best. You might think you have got rid of something poisonous, but there will often be something more deadly to take its place.

# Chapter 16

It was impossible to ignore Christmas. There were wreaths on every front door – traditional holly wreaths; dried oranges with cinnamon scrolls; birch twigs with mistletoe berries – as if the villagers were vying with each other for goodwill. Row upon row of unplucked turkeys were strung outside the butcher's shop. The bakery filled its window with spiced gingerbread, cream meringues and mince pies. The newsagent's had a display of chocolate novelties, foil decorations and paper angels.

At night, when I cycled home from Westleton, there were exuberant displays of festivity. A Christmas tree decorated with weatherproof tinsel was erected in the High Street. A nativity scene, with a baby in a manger, was set up outside the church. Families who normally kept to themselves left their curtains open after dusk and shared the brilliance of their lights. As if joy was a substance like angel dust which might be sprinkled on every passerby. As if by bathing in the pearl of these lights, one's soul might be similarly illuminated.

At Four Winds, the atmosphere was more sombre. Aunt Rose had been asked to mark a colleague's end-of-term dissertations in addition to her own. She was determined to complete as many papers as she could before Christmas. She had set up a makeshift office in the living-room, and the slightest noise – even a footfall – disturbed her.

Uncle Harry was irritable because his publisher had brought forward the deadline for his book, and he was struggling to finish on time. In addition to this, there were cards to be written and gifts to be wrapped. There was a tree to be decorated and groceries to be bought. The roads were busier and the shop queues were longer. If it had not been for me, I doubt if Christmas would have been celebrated at all.

My uncle was a man who hated deviations from his timetable. The thought that he would have to stop work for a week, that none of his research contacts would be available, panicked him. His constant refrain was, 'I don't have time for this. I can't wait till this is over. Roll on the New Year!'

On Christmas Day, my aunt and uncle gave me a card with gift vouchers. There was double the usual quantity.

'We thought you could buy a smart suit when you start work,' Aunt Rose explained.

Three days later, Christmas was over. The decorations which had been so hastily put up, were bundled back in the loft again. My aunt moved her desk to where the tree had been. My uncle, clearly relieved, returned to his office to write his final chapters. But for a few strands of tinsel on the carpet and a turkey carcass swinging from the bird table, Christmas might never have taken place.

With Christmas over, there was just over a fortnight before I moved to Birmingham to start my job. I had handed in my notice at Blyth's, so I had nothing to do except iron clothes, pack a suitcase, and write a thank-you note to Hilary. I lingered over the card, trying to find a coded way to apologize, to explain. I wanted to promise to behave better in future, to never strike another match. Eventually, I gave up.

I was a hypocrite. It was less than a fortnight since Isobel had confronted me in the shop. But the firebug was pummelling my insides again, demanding food. I tried to ignore it by distracting myself, by trying to keep busy. But I was frightened. The firebug needed flames like I needed food, oxygen, water. Its demands were overwhelming. I could not resist it for long.

# Chapter 17

It was New Year's Day. The sky was white alabaster and the sun a distant light shining through it. The aspens were marbled with frost and the arched back of the road was slippery. I cycled through Dunwich, then Westleton. I saw no one in either village.

I waited until after lunch, then headed for Plumstead Farm. I decided to turn back if I was seen. Fortune was either on my side or against me. The roads were empty.

A couple of brown chickens strutted over as I arrived at the farm. When they realized I had no grain they flew back, wings whistling, to the rafters. The farmhouse was silent. Julia and Jeremy Harrison had flown to Edinburgh to celebrate Hogmanay with friends. They were arable farmers: this was the only time of year when they took a break from the relentless cycle of planting, cultivating, and harvesting. Jeremy Harrison had ordered a book from Blyth's, with specific instructions for it to be delivered in the second week of January.

I wheeled my bike past a mound of sugar beet, a stack of straw bales, freshly hewn logs, grain silos and rain barrels. I hid it beneath some loose tarpaulin. I still had to cross a field without being seen.

The field was a plain of churned-up mud. It would have been impossible to cross had it not been for the frost. The chill had hardened the earth, fixing it to concrete. I set off at a steady pace, heading for a caravan in the corner near the road.

The caravan had been there for as long as I could remember. During the harvest, it was used to accommodate seasonal farm workers. It had two small bedrooms with bunks and a dining-table which opened into a double bed. Up to five labourers stayed there at a time.

At other times of year, the Harrisons' daughters, Charlotte and Lucy, used the caravan for sleepovers. Friends were invited from school and lads from the village would secretly slip across the field to join them for murder in the dark and kiss or dare.

At close quarters, the caravan had a neglected appearance. The white paint had discoloured to curdled buttermilk. There was moss on the roof and a thin layer of lichen clung to the rubber seals around the windows. Thistles poked through the steps leading to the doors. Many years previously, someone had planted a spruce next to the caravan, perhaps to give it a more homely appearance. The tree must have been small when it was planted, but now it leaned heavily against one of the rear windows.

The curtains had been left half-open. A salt cellar and pepper pot coupled in the centre of the dining-table. Saucepans were stacked in a pyramid on the rear ring of the gas cooker. A muddy newspaper was spread as a welcome mat just inside the front door.

The first window I tried – the one above the dining-table – would not budge even when I levered it. So I tried the bedroom window. After two sharp thrusts, the latch flicked up and the glass swung outwards.

I would not say I gave in to temptation, so much as succumbed to the inevitable. It was pure instinct. It was like being underwater and needing oxygen: bursting, almost exploding, with need, then surfacing into toxic air. I could not have stopped myself even if I had tried. There were three paraffin bottles in my rucksack. I had bought them from separate shops to avoid suspicion. I lined them up and started to unscrew the tops. They were safety lids, supposedly childproof.

The back bedroom was empty except for the bunk beds. Some blankets had been folded at the end of the lower bunk. The door had been wedged open with a tin kettle, but the room smelled of mothballs. The mattresses looked stiff and unyielding. I guessed they were made of foam. Highly flammable.

The first bottle emptied with a steady pulse-pulse-pulse. Air displaced paraffin: paraffin displaced air. Bubbles pushed through the liquid, rushing to the opposite end of the bottle. It was miraculous, I thought, how something that looked like water could be so different. The bottle was pliant beneath my fingers, responsive. I squeezed the ribbed plastic: paraffin fountained out. One bottle, then another, then another. Soon they were lined up at my feet.

I had already constructed a detonation device for this fire, ingenious in its simplicity. It consisted of an unlit match inserted into the filter end of a cigarette, with a piece of paper folded around it. It was designed to delay, then accelerate ignition. It was ideal for paraffin, avoiding the danger of an immediate flashover.

This fire – my last in Dunwich – deserved something special. The *England's Glory* box was frail now. The drawer had collapsed and the box was a flattened envelope collapsing at the seams. The glorious red and blue battleship had faded and the lettering had rubbed away. The sandpaper strip was less sandpaper than worn emery board. In spite of its antiquity, the box still had the scent of smoked kippers. There were two matches left. I took one of them.

I flicked the match several times without raising a flame. The sandpaper was too flexible. I scoured the ground for a large stone and eventually found one sugared with frost. I dusted it off and placed the matchbox on top.

I tried striking the match slowly and deliberately. I swept it feather-light over the surface. When this method failed, I struck it with a rapid flick of the wrist. This only succeeded in knocking the pink head from the match.

One match left.

I shut my eyes and called for my mother to help me: for her expertise, her skill to be mine. I imagined her hand guiding my hand; her eyes seeing as mine; her heart beating in mine. When I opened my eyes, I struck the match so hard that the matchbox collapsed. This time – miraculously – a flame appeared.

I lit the cigarette as quickly as I could. This was a special flame, passed from one side of the Divide to the other. If I set fire to the caravan, it must be with this flame or not at all.

I balanced the cigarette on my lip and held the match to the end. I had never been able to smoke. I associated it with the glowing butts in the car outside our home in Elm Road. But the moment called for selflessness. There was a strong breeze and I did not want the cigarette extinguished as soon as it was lit.

I sucked until the tip glowed amber. Twists of tobacco squirmed with life. A disc of grey ash formed. I dropped the device inside the folded paper. I tossed it over the windowsill.

Theoretically, that should have been that. I should have high-tailed it across the field and by the time the fire erupted, I should have reached my bike. But my plans were unexpectedly altered by the fate of my *England's Glory* matchbox. It had broken into five pieces and no longer bore the slightest resemblance to a matchbox. There were merely five bits which were neither white nor coloured; neither straight nor rounded; neither card nor paper. Even the sand-paper might have been dried soup.

There was a weight, a significance, to the moment. There was a crucial decision to be made – whether I kept the matchbox or cast it into the flames, was more, much more than that simple act. I was not just deciding the fate of the matchbox: I was deciding my future. So I faltered near the caravan, rucksack at my feet, unable to decide. Knowing that so much was at stake. Yet reluctant to commit myself one way or another.

Finally, fire, as it had always done, decided my destiny. An exquis-ite mane of yellow flame hurled itself at the caravan window. A fiery paw mauled the air. A brown nose pressed against the glass. A tail flicked out, whisking the paintwork. There was no blast, no roar, no shattering of glass. But it was spectacular nonetheless. It had fur like gold velvet. Hot smoky breath. Teeth of polished ivory.

I knew straight away this was no ordinary fire. I could feel the heat of its breath, see the hunger of its eyes. This beast would not be tame for long. It was trapped behind the glass. Caged. But it would soon start flinging itself at the walls and roof. Yet, like a child standing before a DO NOT FEED sign at a zoo, I could not resist gathering the pieces of my matchbox and aiming for the window. The fire caught them in a single snap, devoured them whole.

A window shattered in the adjacent bedroom. There must have been something flammable in there: a tin of flyspray, hairspray or maybe perfume. I grabbed my rucksack, tugging the straps over my shoulders. I should have run. But even with so much danger, curiosity overcame caution. I darted to the other side of the caravan to see what damage had been caused. Flame reared from the window, clawing the spruce. The lower and middle branches were already alight. The effect was of tiny candles on a Christmas tree.

The wind turned. A thick smoke was upon me full of talons and teeth. It made rivers of my eyes. It tore at my nose and throat. I ducked below the smokeline. The taste of paraffin in my mouth. Tears oily. The wind changed direction and I was able to breathe again. I rubbed my eyes, smearing away the tears. Blinking. I could not believe what I was seeing.

The spruce was no longer covered in flames, but flickering fairy lights. The foliage was twined with tinsel and baubles. Angels, bearing harps and bugles, clung to the branches. Beneath the tree was a stack of presents wrapped in yellow, blue and green. One of the gifts had been opened: the wrapping paper had been ripped apart. I was incredulous. I knew this was an illusion. But I believed it, too. I wanted to find out what was inside the gift. Who had left it here? Why?

I crawled forward. Moving not on mud but carpet. Through the confusion of tears and smoke, I spotted a striped scarf like a fabulous sunset. Scarlet wool gave way to crimson, crimson to orange, orange to gold, gold to yellow. Stitches had been dropped in the middle of gold purls. The fringe had an an uneven edge. The tassels were different sizes. I had knitted this scarf for my mother the

Christmas before she died.

Smoke whisked across my face again. It was less talons than the flip-end of a tail. My vision blurred momentarily. When it cleared, the Christmas tree and gifts had vanished. In their place was a blazing spruce. Dazed, I turned and bolted across the field.

Half-way to the farmhouse, I heard the unmistakable hum of a car engine. I started to sprint – stretching my legs wider, wider still, hoping to fly. I knew it was impossible to reach the house, to hide. Yet this did not stop me attempting the impossible. As if I would get there by willpower alone.

I glanced back. A red Mini was beetling along the road. The driver would have spotted the seething smoke by now. They would have spied fire rearing from the caravan windows. They would have seen me, a dark silhouette fleeing across a frosted field.

The hum of the engine became a drone, the drone became a buzz, and so the volume of my thoughts increased. My mind was a whirlwind of ridiculous and irrational escapes. If I could reach the farmhouse, I could pretend to be one of the Harrisons' daughters. I would hide in an outhouse. I would hide under the straw bales. Eventually my thoughts deteriorated into clamour. I ran hearing everything and nothing. The sound of my own panic.

The air felt as if it had broken glass in it. Every breath so jagged it hurt. My lungs were ripping. I could feel my breath splintering. I pushed myself to run even faster. I stumbled. Fell. I was staggering up from the icy soil, when I heard the yowl of tyres. A squeal like a birth cry. Brakes. Metal rolling over and over. An explosion. I did not look back. I took this event to be a gift from God. Divine intervention.

When I reached the farmyard, I mounted my bike in such a hurry that I tore the seam of my jeans. I reached for the pedal and missed it, the metal prongs hitting the side of my ankle. I found the pedal before the pain had time to register. Then, I was cycling away in a frenzy. I did not stop until I reached Four Winds. My head took somewhat longer to stop spinning.

## Chapter 18

The paperboy arrived early. He had been late all week. Now, as if to make up for lost time, his bike rolled on to the drive an hour earlier than usual. *The East Anglian* slapped on the mat while Uncle Harry was shaving and Aunt Rose was in the shower. I slipped down the stairs, snatched it up, then bolted back to my room.

The headline on the front page was: MOTORIST INJURED IN ARSON BLAST. Beneath this was a photograph of a mangled car, and a small picture of a man playing darts.

> A PENSIONER *is fighting for his life after a blazing caravan exploded in front of his car.*
>
> *Bill Lambert, 74, was driving along the B1125 near Dunwich yesterday afternoon when the blast happened, hurling debris in front of his car. The caravan at Plumstead Farm, Dunwich, had been set ablaze by an arsonist only minutes before. The explosion was caused by a gas canister which overheated. Superintendent Dave Hughes of Suffolk Police said: 'Mr Lambert didn't stand a chance. His car was blown straight off the road.'*
>
> *Firefighters spent over two hours freeing Mr Lambert's body from the wreckage and putting out the blaze. Villagers living nearby have reacted with shock to the accident. Mr Lambert, who lived in Blythburgh, had been a regular at The Ship Inn in Dunwich for many years.*
>
> *Police are still trying to contact the owners of Plumstead Farm, Jeremy and Jenny Harrison, who are thought to be on holiday in Scotland. They are appealing for anyone with information to contact them.*

I must have lost track of the time. Aunt Rose was suddenly rapping at my door.

'Are you up yet? Breakfast's on the table. You'll have to get a move on if you want to catch this train. I thought you wanted a lift to the station!'

'I'm not hungry. I'll skip breakfast today.'

'At least have a glass of milk. You can't go looking for lodgings on an empty stomach.'

When I entered the kitchen, my uncle was finishing a plate of toast and my aunt was putting on her make-up. I was convinced they only had to look at me to see my guilt. I sat down at the table and sipped my milk. I knew I should behave as normally as possible, drain my glass, and get out. But my tongue seemed to have swollen. It was impossible to swallow.

Uncle Harry twirled a plate under the tap, then placed it on the draining board with toast crumbs still sticking to the glaze.

'The paper boy's late again. I could've fetched it myself by this time,' he grumbled.

'Probably got up late,' my aunt answered distractedly. 'Better late than never.'

'Yes, but if you pay for a service, you expect a service. If they're offering to deliver your morning paper, that's when you expect it – not at lunch-time!'

Aunt Rose licked a tissue and removed a spot of mascara from her cheek.

'I don't know why you bother. You never read it,' she said.

'I'm only getting it for the interview about my book. As soon as it's printed, we can stop again.'

'If only you'd asked when it was going in the paper!'

'What's that got to do with the delivery?'

My aunt twisted up her lipstick and applied it to her lips. She sighed a light, almost imperceptible, sigh.

'He is only a kid!' she said.

'Then they should sack him and find someone more reliable. If there's one thing I can't stand, it's incompetence!'

'Cancel the order then. Collect the paper yourself.'

'I think I will. But if I catch him first, I'll give him a piece of my mind.'

On an ordinary day, Uncle Harry's moods did not bother me. I had learned to do as my aunt did – to flex and yield like a willow in the wind, until he had blown himself out. On this day, though, I felt myself going rigid. Every time my uncle spoke, it was as if a clockwork key was being turned. An elastic band winding tighter and tighter.

As my uncle paused for breath, the key stopped turning. There was a moment of strained calm. I got up from the table and emptied my milk down the sink.

'Hey! Don't tip that away! There's half a pint in that glass!'

I ignored my uncle and walked over to the door. Words rushed out of me in someone else's voice.

'I don't want the milk, OK? I don't have to drink it if I don't want to!'

'I paid good money for that milk. I don't want it going to waste!'

'Bill me then. I'll send you a cheque when I get my wages.'

'That's enough, Angela!' Aunt Rose said. 'I don't know what's got into you. But if you want a lift to the station, I suggest you apologize.'

'Don't bother! I'll catch the bus! I'll be glad to see the back of this place.'

I ran upstairs to finish packing without waiting for a retort.


# Chapter 19


There was still one last thing to do before I left Dunwich. I cycled to Greyfriars with a spade to unearth the cuttings I had buried so many years before. I could not find my clover-leaf marker. A single white pebble beneath the gargoyle remained.

I hurled the spade at the soil. The metal bounced off the earth with a slight chime. But eventually the ground yielded. I did not dig so much as scratch away the layers of frost and soil. After nearly two hours, I spied a corner of tattered plastic.

One of my fingernails was torn and my palm was wet with blisters, but I redoubled my efforts. I levered a large section from one end of the hole and scooped out the remaining earth with my hands. Eventually, the package shifted and was free.

I did not open the plastic bag. It would have been pointless. Inside the clouded cellophane, the paper had merged into a seamless whole. There was no separate envelope or cuttings – just a shrunken brown form. As for distinguishing a single word, it was impossible to tell whether this mummified object was made of paper, clay, marl or loam.

By the time the train pulled in to the platform at Ipswich Railway Station, I felt calmer. *The East Anglian* was in the bottom of my suitcase wedged beneath T-shirts. I had originally intended to hunt for lodgings in Birmingham, then return to Dunwich to pick up my belongings. Instead, I decided to leave for good. I scribbled my aunt and uncle a note on the back of an envelope. I promised to write when I had a forwarding address.

I got on the train and found an empty carriage in the non-smoking section. I stacked my suitcase in the luggage holder overhead and stuffed my ticket in my purse. I settled into my seat and twisted the top off a bottle of Coca Cola.

As the whistle shrilled and the train began its jolting journey along the tracks, my eyes shifted focus from the platform to my reflection in the glass. My image had a shadowy outline as if twin sisters were standing one behind the other, slightly off kilter. As if the darker sibling was obscuring its paler sister.

As the train picked up speed, I refocused my eyes. There was a knack to gazing out of moving windows. If I stared straight out at the sidings nearest the rail tracks, it was impossible to see anything at all: the landscape blurred. The trick was to peer ahead at the countryside the train had not reached, always looking to the future. There, every bramble, every pebble, every blackbird, was clearly defined.

In a few days, my new life would begin. The old life would be left behind. Birmingham. I made a solemn oath – and this time I would keep it – never to strike another match.

I believed myself cured.

PART IV

# Chapter 1

*The Birmingham Bulletin* was housed in a tall glass building on Exchange Street. Its mirrored windows dissected the sky so that its grandeur was reduced to a hundred small squares of blue light. Even the scudding clouds were interrupted: leaping like ruffled sheep as they made their way, pane by pane, from one side of the building to the other.

Outside the main entrance was a fountain with an abstract bronze sculpture at its centre: two boulders with holes in the centre such as one might spit through as a child and make a wish. These had been so highly polished that the light caught the scratches and made them dart like glistening minnows. The water made no sound: it seeped rather than spurted over the sculpture.

Two palm trees stood in the entrance foyer which felt warm after the chill outside. The floor was white marble. The walls were covered with framed front pages from *The Morning Bulletin* and *The Evening Bulletin*. I perched on the edge of a leather sofa while the receptionist telephoned the news desk. A bowl of courtesy matches embossed with *The Birmingham Bulletin* crest had been placed on the coffee table. The envelopes were white, with wording in gold bas-relief. The cardboard matchsticks were white; the phosphorous heads, the same tasteful white. The temptation was great, but I averted my gaze.

Fifteen minutes later, I heard my name being called. The chief reporter, Lydia Thistle, was standing in the lift, her foot wedged between the sliding doors, as if reluctant to step into the reception.

Her eyeliner was smeared below one eye, making it larger than the other. She was agitated. The poise which she had shown at my job interview was gone. Her hands kept fluttering up and clawing her neck. Her skin was raw. She garbled rather than talked.

'You're going to be thrown in at the deep end, I'm afraid. There's been a fire in Edgbaston. One person injured already. Three reporters are off sick, so it's all hands on deck. Best thing is to stay out of the way until things have calmed down. I'll find a desk for you, then crack on. We'll do the guided tour later.'

I felt a pang. No escape from my sins, even here. I was not involved in this fire: I was not even interested in it. No excitement. No curiosity. Yet my conscience stirred. The lift had carpet on the walls and floor: a military blue thread interwoven with gold heraldry. The buttons were polished brass, smudged with finger-prints. It ascended with such ease that you were hardly aware you were moving. Yet, I smelled smoke. Burning rubber and singed iron. So strong, I wondered if there was something wrong with the mechanics. The electrics perhaps? The cables? I looked at Lydia, but she was unperturbed. My imagination then. I was looking for a link, perhaps anticipating one. Yet there was none. This was a newspaper office after all. It covered the whole of Birmingham. They probably had a housefire every day. There was nothing unusual, nothing out of the ordinary. It was just my mind playing tricks.

When the doors eased open, we were in the open-plan news-room. Here, perhaps, was the source of the smell. All the reporters were smoking. Cigarettes flickered like excited fireflies. Glowing. On off. Off on. Quivering on lips. Resting on the edges of desks. Corkscrewing wisps of smoke from the sides of typewriters. Perhaps this scent had snared in Lydia's hair, her clothes, her skin. My guilt had transformed it into smouldering rubber and metal. Unusually, there was no haze; no brown sheen to the walls or ceil-ing. The air conditioning (or air extraction) must have removed all nicotine from the atmosphere.

Lydia strode across the newsroom and pointed at a wooden desk where a middle-aged man was strumming a typewriter. Wiry hair sprouted from his nostrils and ears. His face was tucked with folds which might have been either laughter or worry lines.

'This is your desk. But as you can see – *someone*'s sitting at it.' Lydia put a playful emphasis on the words. 'Eric's writing up the housefire for the front page.'

The man glanced up. 'Welcome aboard. Be with you in a minute.

If you could just bear with me.' His fingers, gliding over the keys, were long and elegant, the nails manicured. There was a dignity about him; an elegance. When he smiled, his mouth was kind.

'There's some Polos in my pocket if you fancy one.' He gestured behind him to a hound's-tooth jacket on the back of his chair. Then, he added to Lydia, 'You look tense. Don't let him get to you. There's more important things. . . .'

Lydia's face relaxed momentarily. She slipped her hand into the jacket and pulled out a green and black tube. She eased the foil away, popped a mint on to her tongue. She rolled the sweets over the table towards me.

'How are you getting on? Has he OK'd it yet?'

Eric shrugged. 'Fourth rewrite. I don't think he's going to be happy until he's sobered up.'

Lydia's face tensed. 'Then we've got a long wait.'

She was already crunching her mint. As she spoke, I could see bits on her tongue like tiny stones.

'So be it. I can't change him and you can't change him. We've just got to do the best we can.'

I slipped a mint in my mouth and sat down. I usually liked to suck Polos, letting the tip of my tongue slip in and out of the cold centre; rubbing the ridges of sugar lettering until they were smooth. But, I found myself crunching the sweet so that the bits stuck to the crevices in my teeth. There was something contagious about the tension. Or perhaps it was the thought that the man sitting opposite me was writing about a housefire. The atmosphere felt unreal as if I was inhabiting a dream. I wanted to ask who was injured. Man or woman. Girl or boy. Why had it happened? How had it happened? When? Where?

Yet it seemed wrong to ask questions. I should not show too much interest or this would draw attention to myself. What was I afraid of? That this would highlight my guilt? But I felt as if my crime was etched across my forehead.

There were half-a-dozen journalists in the news room. On an adjacent desk, a man was twisting a coil of telephone cable around his wrist as he gabbled into the receiver. On the other side of the room, an agitated cranefly of a woman was trying to listen to two radio news bulletins, while simultaneously watching Central News on the television. Another man was trying to fold a long ribbon of paper helter-skeltering to the floor.

There was a blue energy, a crackle, a buzz, to the room. The same sort of unhealthy electricity that hums around pylons and power stations. As if every sharp corner, every chair, every table, was super-charged. As if the slightest change would lead to thunder or a lightning flash.

In the midst of the chaos – the ringing telephones, the flapping paper, the raw intensity – a diminutive man, barely five feet tall: Miles King.

Eric Hewitt freed his paper from the typewriter with a *zip*. He dropped his cigarette into a coffee cup. He ambled towards Miles. The paper was flapping like a flag of truce. Wordlessly, he handed it over, his body folded in humility.

Miles snatched the paper without looking up. He leaned back in his chair and put his feet on the desk. He gave a dismissive flick of his fingers indicating that he wanted to be left alone.

Eric did not even manage to get back to his chair. The ball of paper hit him before he sat down. It bounced off his elbow, rebounded, and disappeared in the shadows beneath an adjacent desk.

Miles lowered his feet to the floor, but did not bother getting up. 'It's crap, Hewitt! This is a paper you're working for – not a woman's weekly! Give it some more topspin. If you can't get it right, I'm going to have to let you go. We're running a tight ship. There's no room in this office for slackers.'

Eric Hewitt raised his eyebrow slightly. His lips tightened. He lowered himself into his chair. Then, he rolled forward on the castors, using his heels. He bent down and retrieved the paper ball. He pulled a packet of Marlboroughs from his pocket and flipped the lid. Then, catching my eye, he gestured with the packet.

'I've survived here twenty years. I think I'll be here a few more.'

'No thanks! I don't smoke.'

He smiled grimly. 'You soon will! Can I interest you in another Polo?'

'Thanks.'

There was something reassuring about Eric, as if he was the axle at the centre of the wheel. I did not crunch the mint this time. I would suck it until the edges were washer-thin.

Eric scrolled a piece of virgin paper into the typewriter and realigned the ink ribbon. He set to work again, fingers tapping the keys.

A large typewriter took up most of the space on the desk in front of me. Scattered around it were papers (news releases, council agendas, clippings), two leaking biros, a bulldog clip and a ball of rubber bands. A tatty list of numbers had been sellotaped next to the telephone. Handwritten comments were scrawled next to each of the names – such as *Good contact* and *Off the record*. Beside this was a foil ashtray brimming with chewing gum wrappers and a disposable cup half-filled with coffee. A cigarette butt floated on the surface of the water. As I moved the plastic cup, the butt scudded across the surface like a waterboatman.

The typewriter was heavy and awkward. I pushed it away to make more space. Beneath it, the table top was tattooed with a single word: Help!

Was this what had happened when my parents died, I wondered? A journalist trying to save his job by hammering a keyboard, transforming tragedy into sensational words. Trying to give it more 'topspin'. A news editor hurling a typed story at him like a cricket ball. I was appalled.

I leafed through *The Morning Bulletin*. I tried to focus on the headlines, the words, the photographs. But I could not help stealing occasional glances at the news editor through the crook of my elbow.

Miles King's roll-up kept extinguishing itself so that he was forced to relight it two, three, four times. His lighter was still on its highest setting: the flame flared three inches high. As he held it to his lips, his face was illuminated.

'Have you got that contact for me yet?' he barked.

'We've got the name, but no address,' Lydia Thistle answered.

'Get someone to look through the phone book.'

'But the surname's *Smith*. We don't even know their address.'

'Then someone's going to be busy, aren't they! Edgbaston's not that big.'

Lydia raked her neck. Livid streaks hatchworked her skin. She heaved a telephone directory on to her desk and began scanning it.

'I want condition checks every half-hour. I want to know the instant she pegs it!' Miles added.

He leaned back in his chair, his body in perfect alignment. Stiff and straight as those people magicians leave hanging in mid-air. His roll-up was balanced on the edge of his desk, the glowing head facing outwards. Ash dripped on to the floor. Every now and then, Miles would inhale. The roll-up would be shifted a little to avoid scorching the wood.

There was paper everywhere. Not single sheets. Not bundles. Not even books. But bales and haystacks of it. Today's newspapers. Yesterday's newspapers. The day before yesterday's newspapers. The day before the day before yesterday's newspapers. Newspapers from the last month. Newspapers from the last year.

As I looked around the office, I realized this was a fire waiting to happen. A roomful of preoccupied smokers. A news editor who lined roll-ups on the edge of his desk. All it needed was a nudge of an elbow or a careless twist of a wrist. An ember dropping unnoticed. These thoughts were interrupted by the slam of a desk drawer. A woman reporter was standing in front of Miles King. The paper was not balled this time, but ripped in half.

'I'm surrounded by idiots!' Miles shouted. 'Can't anyone get me a fucking interview? Someone else take over news desk. I might as well do it myself!'

Lydia jerked to her feet. She scratched her neck again. Five red weals appeared. A scratch for every day of the week.

'I'm leaving you at the helm. I trust I can leave the office for an hour without everything going under,' Miles sneered.

I felt a stab between my shoulder blades.

'You!' Miles's finger jabbed a second time. 'Yes, you! Grab your coat and come with me.'

It was a mistake. This was my first day in the newsroom; I had no experience. Moreover, I wanted nothing to do with the fire. I wanted a different story. A car accident perhaps. Or an environmental campaign. Even a golden anniversary. But Miles had already slung his jacket over his arm and was pushing the button on the lift.

'Come *on*! We haven't got all *day*!'

On the other side of the newsroom, the woman reporter was already starting to empty her desk. She looked strangely relieved.

I grabbed my coat.

# Chapter 2

Miles's car was in an underground car-park. It was a cold airless place which smelled of urine and exhaust fumes. The stairwell was stone, but the floor of the car-park was lined with black rubber. It squeaked with every step we took as if we were wearing new shoes.

The car – a silver MG – was brimming with yellowing newspapers. The passenger seat was covered with *The Evening Bulletin* up to window level. The shelf in the back of the car was stacked high with *The Morning Bulletin*.

'Just leave them by the side of the car,' Miles said.

'Is there a bin?'

'We've got monkeys to deal with things like that. You'll be keeping them in a job.'

I did not argue, but started stacking the papers as neatly as I could against the wall.

'Leave them! Just get in!'

Miles had shoved the few remaining papers out of the door, and shouted over the hum of the engine. He reversed out of the space even as I was getting into the passenger seat. The wheels squealed as I put my seatbelt on. They continued to do so until we reached the exit barrier. I wondered why he had kept the back issues all this time, only to throw them away. It made little sense. But then I reasoned, newspapers were dispensable. You could bin them or archive them. There were plenty more copies in the office.

Above us, the sky was like a huge slab of concrete pressing down upon the city. Miles's temper did not improve. It was as if he thought by sheer belligerence he could force others out of his way. His driving in heavy traffic was of the stop-start variety. Rather than ease forwards as Aunt Rose or Uncle Harry would have done, Miles accelerated, braked abruptly, then accelerated again. I lurched backwards and forwards in the passenger seat, the seatbelt tightening and loosening across my shoulders.

Something kept knocking against my heels every time Miles braked. When the object finally rolled out from under the seat, it was an empty bottle of Jack Daniel's. I wondered whether it was safe to be in the car with him. As the traffic thinned and he accelerated again, I glanced at the speedometer. I could not remember how fast you were supposed to drive in a city. I knew the top limit for motorways was seventy. Miles was driving at just over fifty which seemed reasonable enough. Perhaps he was sober after all.

Miles did not speak to me directly, but continued muttering under his breath as we swerved around cars and buses. He gave an exasperated sigh as the lights changed to red. Then, he spat 'Fucking idiot!' as a moped cut in front of us.

We had been on the main road for about ten minutes, when Miles braked fiercely outside a row of shops. There were no parking spaces – there were double yellow lines in the road – so he mounted the pavement and parked at an angle. He dropped the keys in my lap.

'Move it if the warden comes – they're vindictive bastards around here. I don't want a ticket.'

I wanted to tell him that I hadn't passed my test, but he had already slammed the door and was marching towards the newsagents. I hoped he wouldn't be long.

When Miles came back, he was carrying a packet of Benson & Hedges and a bouquet of tiger lilies wrapped in gaudy orange paper. He tossed the flowers casually into my lap and tucked the cigarettes into his jacket.

'Let's hope we can find out which ward she's on or that's five quid down the drain,' he said.

It was then I realized where we were going.

Miles relaxed a little after buying the flowers. He had a roll-up lodged behind his ear. He slipped it between his lips and lit up. His cheeks hollowed as he inhaled. It was a cold day, but he lowered the window. He smoked with his arm hanging out, balanced on the edge of the frame. I kept thinking that the roll-up was dead as the side winds hit it, knocking away the ash, but Miles would bring his arm inside, and it would burst into life again. When he finished, he dropped the stub on to the tarmac. I saw it bouncing along the road behind us, in the wing mirror. The ember sprayed bright sparks, then faded into nothingness. I kept glancing back, expecting it to reignite. I did not ask who the cigarettes were for. I was relieved Miles's mood had improved. Some people were uncomfortable with silence, but I had spent so much time in my own company that I was used to it.

'I'm assuming you know how to take pictures,' Miles said.

'Pictures?'

'Photos! You know how to use a camera?'

Miles leaned over my lap and opened the glove compartment with his free hand. He pulled out a camera and dropped it on top of the tiger lilies. One of the flowers snapped off its stalk and dropped beneath the handbrake.

'It couldn't be simpler. Just point and press. I want as many as you can get. That way, we're covered whatever happens.'

'What if the woman's unconscious?'

'Of course she's unconscious – she's in a critical condition! It's not her we're after: it's her husband. Once we've found out which ward she's on, we'll head for the waiting-room. That's where he'll be. Mark my words.'

'Will they tell us where she is?'

Miles laughed. 'They will if you pretend to be her daughter.'

There were no spaces in the hospital car-park, so Miles drove on to a grass verge and turned off the engine.

'What about. . . ?' I gestured towards the notice: *All unauthorized cars will be towed away.*

Miles grinned. 'Don't worry. We've got diplomatic immunity.' He pulled a printed card from the sun visor and stuck it to the dashboard: DOCTOR ON CALL.

I was annoyed at his presumption. I did not want to pose as the Smiths' daughter. Miles must have sensed this.

'Of course, it's up to you. If you don't think you can do it. . . .'

There was no choice. Miles's tone made that clear. I recalled his question at my interview: 'If a man died, would you have what it takes to stake out his house? Would you be able to doorstep the neighbours? Could you get pics of his wife and kids?' This was an initiation: my future at the paper depended on it.

I wondered how many other reporters had been set the same test. Whether this was standard practice. I supposed it was my naïvety that made me feel so appalled.

'Don't forget,' Miles added, as we approached the automatic doors, 'if you're asked for a signature, do it with your left hand. That way, no one can prove it was you.'

The waiting area in Accident & Emergency was hospital standard. The chairs were black vinyl with rips where the filling was spilling out. Someone had attempted to seal a patch with gaffer tape. The magazines had pages hanging out and covers missing. The sofas stuck to the back of people's legs and farted when they stood up. The walls were decorated with paintings of water lilies at Givenchy.

As I waited for the receptionist, I had a strong sense of fate. I had just put a man in intensive care: now, I was tracking down a woman injured in another fire. Both were fighting for their lives. It was too much of a coincidence. Like the ripples from a stone. Or an echo bouncing back off a cliff face. There was such a sense of repetition, a pattern and order, that it had to be deliberate. It was a Divine lesson. Or Divine punishment.

The receptionist's hair was tied back in a severe bun, with wisps of grey showing at the roots. She had one of those transitory faces which can switch from friendliness to annoyance in one glance. There were soft blue sacks under her eyes.

I was nervous. I held the lilies in front of me like a shield. The orange and brown striped petals shivered. Reddish dust fell from the stamens.

'I've brought some flowers for my mother. I don't know where she is.'

'Name?'

'M-me!' I stuttered. 'I-I'm . . .'

The receptionist glanced up. She misread my fear. Her features softened. Thankfully, she smiled.

'Your mother's name?' she said gently.

'Smith. Mrs Smith. She was brought in early this morning.' I lowered my voice. 'There was a fire. A house fire.'

The receptionist hooked a clipboard off a nail on the wall and scanned it.

'Stella Smith? She's in theatre at the moment. She'll be in Intensive Care when she gets out. It's on the fifth floor. Follow the signs.'

I wanted to take the stairs, but Miles was already waiting near the lift. As we went up, I smelled smoke again. Was it guilt? Was my past catching up with me so soon.

'Wasn't so difficult, was it?' Miles said smugly.

I was standing over him, overlarge and stocky. I was tall like my mother had been: he was unnaturally small. It struck me that I could hit him; he would be able to do little about it. In a fight, we would have been pretty evenly matched. A thought, nothing more. A flicker, then it was gone.

Besides, I was nervous. I had never liked hospitals. Never liked the polish of them; the seering whiteness of them; the smell of antiseptic and pain. But there was more to it than that. Being here was too uncanny, too weird. I wondered if it was a trap. If Miles was toying with me. Flinging my past back at me. But no, this was paranoia. Projection. Miles knew nothing. He was unscrupulous and brutal. Anyone would have felt uncomfortable in his company.

I hoped the waiting room would be empty so we could go back. I would talk to Eric. Perhaps he could offer some advice on how to cope. I had made a mistake. I shouldn't have left Dunwich. I shouldn't have come here.

Then, I thought back to what I had left behind. I knew I couldn't return. It wasn't an option.

'What if he isn't there?' I asked aloud.

'He will be.'

'What if he won't talk to us?'

'Oh he'll talk all right – they always do. He'll be relieved to talk to anyone. Just try and stop him.'

We were walking down a corridor on the fifth floor. The windows on one side looked out over the car-park. Little patches of colour moved along the road – a reminder of life going on outside the building. That smell again – antiseptic and anaesthetized pain. And the whiteness! Not a reassuring white, but a stark frightening white. The walls and even the floor tiles. I never wanted to visit a hospital again.

Miles paused at a vending machine with a picture of steaming coffee on the front. He placed a coin in the slot and the machine whirred. A plastic cup clunked into the shelf at the bottom. Hot water trickled from an unseen spout.

'You find the waiting-room while I get my caffeine fix,' he said.

Perhaps there was a standard lay-out for hospitals. I knew intuitively where the waiting-room was. A royal blue door with a glass grid for a window. I approached quietly so I could see in, without anyone seeing me. There was one person inside: a man.

Attempts had been made to brighten the room. A child's drawing of a parrot had been taped to one wall. Sun-bleached silk roses had been stuffed in a vase on the windowsill. A heated lava lamp with orange oil bubbles had been switched on in a corner.

A cigarette was sending up smoke from an ashtray shaped like a gondola. But I could not determine the message. He might have been a relative or a stranger. Waiting for news of a wife, or a distant cousin. Sometimes smoke tells you everything; sometimes, it tells you nothing at all.

As I was peering in, the man spotted movement through the glass. He glanced up. There was no mistaking this was Mr Smith. His face was the same shade as the January sky.

There was something on the coffee table in front of him. Something not much bigger than a postage stamp.

Let this be a vision, I thought. Let me wake up.

It was a photograph – a baby who looked exactly like my brother Billy.

Miles was looking at his reflection in the vending machine, straightening his tie. His cup was empty; a brown silt lining the plastic base. He glanced at his watch. It was five past eleven. The first and second deadlines for *The Evening Bulletin* had passed. We had fifty-five minutes to make the final edition.

'Have you found our man?' he asked.

'You didn't tell me there was a baby.'

'A baby? Are you sure it's the right man?'

'There was no one else in there.'

'Fantastic. This is better than I thought.'

'You should have said there was a baby.' I was in a daze.

'Look, I haven't got time for this. Go and find a phone while I soften him up.' He thrust a scrap of paper and a ten pence piece in my hand. 'Give Thistle a call – tell her we've got a splash. Tell her to hold the front page and ditch whatever crap Hewitt's written. Wait outside. I'll let you know when I need you.'

As Miles entered the waiting-room, the man's face lit up. His clouded face, his bloodshot eyes, illuminated with hope. He saw Miles's sharply creased suit, the pens in his top pocket, his notebook. He imagined him to be a doctor.

'They're going to be all right, aren't they?' he asked.

Miles grasped Mr Smith's hand. There was a flash of gold as he pulled the packet of Benson & Hedges from his pocket. The door clicked shut.

It felt like a nightmare. The unreality of it shocked me. Or was it the reality of it? Yes, that was it. It was too real, too convincing to be a dream. The boundaries were blurring. Past and present, present and past. Maybe even present and future, future and past.

I must have blacked out. When I came to, my head felt like it did after the boiler exploded. Like when I woke up dangling in my father's arms. Chimney bricks and roof tiles scattered around me on the cold lawn. A line of neighbours watching. Except this time, I could hear my voice, the pathetic mewling. It was not frost but white tiles under my feet.

I was supposed to be doing something. Something important. I looked down and saw the notepaper, the silver coin. A phone call, that was it. I stumbled along the corridor looking for a call box.

I spotted a public telephone at the end of the corridor. I hadn't seen it there before. A woman answered at the other end. Her name? I couldn't remember. And the message? I garbled something about the man in the waiting-room and the baby.

'Slow down,' said the voice on the other end of the line. 'Take it easy. Take a deep breath and start again . . . Where's Miles?'

Thistle. That was it. Lydia Thistle. I remembered the fingernails raking her neck.

'He's talking to the man now. There's a baby. A baby was in the fire.'

'And the mother?'

'We haven't seen her. Miles hasn't spoken to anyone yet.'

'So how do you know about the baby?'

I paused to consider the logic of this. How did I know? Mr Smith hadn't told me; Miles hadn't told me. There was just the photograph and those spider-veined eyes.

'They're going to die,' I said.

'Look, I think it's best if I talk to Miles. We'll use the standby if he's not back in time. Otherwise, tell him I'll hold the front page.'

The phone started pipping so I didn't get chance to reply. As I replaced the receiver, I realized I was still holding the tiger lilies. I must have been gripping too hard, for a bloom dropped. As I knelt to pick it up, the stamens trembled like dancing shoes or ballet slippers. Pollen spilled on to my finger, dusting my hands. I wondered if there had been tiger lilies amongst my mother and Billy's funeral bouquets. Or in my father's. I suspected there probably were.

# Chapter 3

The news trolley arrived. The office runner wheeled around the newsroom handing out copies of *The Evening Bulletin*. There were three editions of the paper. This was the final edition. First and second edition were already on the news stands. There was a temporary lull as journalists stopped typing. I was handed my own copy. The paper was still warm – like a linen tablecloth just out of the airing cupboard.

Eric was sitting on the opposite side of the desk. He grinned so that his yellow teeth showed. He stood up and shook my hand.

'A front page byline! Miles is obviously impressed with you. Bylines are like gold dust around here.'

'I didn't do anything. Really.'

I hadn't even been able to take the pictures. My fingers had been overlarge. The lens was in the wrong place. The buttons wouldn't press. Miles had eventually snatched the camera off me and taken the photographs himself.

All that was left was to give the rustling tiger lilies to Mr Smith. The petals were a little crushed, translucent in places. But he did not seem to mind.

'You're too kind,' Mr Smith said. 'Too kind.' He was a genuine man and he thought us so, too. It never occurred to him that the flowers, the cigarettes, were cynically bought. Or that this charming female reporter had been devious enough to impersonate his daughter. He was not crying. It was as if his nose was weeping instead. A steady trickle on his upper lip. He dabbed it with a stiff handkerchief. Grief makes people do the oddest things. He attempted a forlorn smile as Miles clicked the camera.

The headline took up half the page. NEWBORN DIES IN HOUSE BLAZE. In smaller lettering underneath: *Mum Fights For Life*. There was a picture of the baby – the passport photo from the waiting-room. Then there was Mr Smith's haunted, and haunting face. The pathetic half-smile which made him look like a simpleton. 'Exclusive Interview by Miles King and Sandra Angel.' A two-page interview followed.

'Poor bloke,' said Eric. 'Imagine losing your kid like that. Was it a boy or a girl?'

'A boy, I think. I haven't read it yet.'

'Awful. Doesn't bear thinking about. Do they know what started it?'

'A spark from the fire,' I said automatically. 'While they were sleeping.'

'At least he's got one left. It didn't take all of them. And hopefully the mother will pull through . . .'

'She was quite badly hurt.'

'I thought you said you hadn't read it . . . Are you all right? You're not looking too bright.'

'I just need—' I realized I was still standing. 'I need to sit down.'

'Too much for you, huh? I'm not sure you ever get used to things like this. Well, with one exception.' Eric's eyes flickered momentarily towards Miles. 'Wait here a moment. Let me get you a coffee.'

I picked up the newspaper again. I had forgotten about the daughter. It was stupid really considering that I had pretended to be her. Yet I had not thought about her. Or rather, I had imagined her to be older. Miles had neglected to mention her age. Yet here she was. A pig-tailed girl gazing trustingly at the camera. In school uniform. I did not have to read to know she was twelve years old. Or that her brother was born just after the New Year.

The newsprint blurred. The words swirled. It was different and yet it was the same. The two events were separate, and yet intrinsically entwined. It was suddenly important that Mrs Smith should live. That she should break the chain. Our fates had to be severed.

By the time Eric returned, the newspaper had gone cold in my hands. There was black ink on my fingers.

'Damn machine's on the blink. How you feeling?'

'A bit better thanks.'

'Tell you what, I'll take you down to the gallery. There's another coffee machine there.'

'What about Miles?'

'He's just gone into paste-up. The pressure's off for an hour or so. Come on. It'll do you good.'

The gallery was a long corridor with one wall constructed entirely of glass. It was designed so visitors to *The Birmingham Bulletin* could watch the presses roll without getting involved in the chaos, the danger, the clamour, of the print room.

Below the window, was a place of violence and splendour. Huge rolls of paper, large as men, unfurled over cogs and rollers. Except it did not look like paper. One imagines paper to be soft and fragile.

This paper writhed and slithered, as if with a life of its own.

Eric grinned. 'If you stayed here long enough, you'd see your story printed ninety thousand times.'

'It's not *my* story!'

I realized the secret irony of this even as I said it. Miles had written the story. Yet perhaps it was mine after all. Perhaps this was my chance to change the course of events. Or learn something from them.

I squinted into the belly of the print room as if to find answers there. I could see nothing but coiling paper. We were too high up. It was impossible to read the words.

'Want to go down? See what it's like on the shop floor?'

I nodded. The coffee – the purpose of the trip – was forgotten. There was something mesmerizing about the presses. Something fascinating and appalling at the same time.

The noise hit us as soon as the lift reached the basement. *Thud-thud, thud-thud, thud-thud.* The pounding vibrated through the walls and floor. Pulsing. Palpitating. *Thud-thud, thud-thud.*

I put my fingers over my ears. But the noise still coursed through. Black and white paper. Huge ribbons of it. Jack-knifed. Sliced into a living stream of newspapers.

Three editions of *The Bulletin* each morning. Three each night. I multiplied these by days. Weeks. Years. Then, I considered the weeklies for each area. The free sheets. *The Handsworth Post, The Balsall Heath Times, The Edgbaston Gazette, The Solihull Journal.* The figures kept multiplying.

At the end of the line, the newspapers were bundled into bales tied with nylon string. A forklift truck manoeuvred them into neat stacks. After this, they were hauled into delivery vans embossed with *The Birmingham Bulletin* heraldry. As we watched, two delivery vans departed and another arrived.

The news vendors had already spent the morning shouting out the headlines. The sandwich boards had been out since seven o'clock. By late afternoon, no one could have walked past a news stand without knowing a baby had died in Edgbaston.

We were standing outside the sliding doors looking at the fleet of vans. There was a slight breeze. Wisps of stray paper, wrapped around our feet. The smell of ink, paper dust and exhaust fumes mingled. Above us, the imperial lettering for *The Birmingham Bulletin* was six feet tall.

I wanted to say something about the Smiths. About the house fire. About what had happened at the hospital.

'Do news editors usually go out and cover stories like Miles did this morning? I thought they—'

'. . . edited newspapers?' Eric finished. 'Yes. That's what they normally do. But Miles is a law unto himself. Don't let him put you off though. We're not all like that.'

'I used to have a friend – Hilary – who thought there was good in everyone. She said you just have to look for it.'

'Oh there's *good* in him all right. He's a *good* journalist. He'd sell his mother down the river for the right story.' Eric laughed. 'But I'm not sure that's what your friend had in mind!'

I had been hoping for answers. Some sort of revelation. Now I realized I had been asking the wrong questions.

'What happens if someone gets something wrong?' I said, hesitantly. 'If a reporter makes a mistake. If they write something that isn't true. Do they stop the press and start again?'

Eric started to walk back through the print room and I followed him.

'Once the press rolls, there's no chance of stopping it. Not for anything nor anyone,' he answered.

'Can't or won't?'

The machinery seemed to get louder at this point. Fresh ink perhaps. Or a new batch of paper. Eric's reply grated in my ear like a knife on a whetstone. But I did not hear it.


# Chapter 4


Miles was whistling 'I'm Dreaming of a White Christmas' as he arrived for the early shift the next day. The sun was already starting to poke bright fingers through the city, but the wind was bitter. The sort of wind that makes you dip your head into your collar and hug your arms a little tighter against your body. The forecasters were predicting blizzards over the next few days.

Miles took off his coat and settled into his chair. He was still whistling as he refilled his lighter. It was shaped like a pistol with a silver barrel. When he flicked the trigger, a flame appeared instead of a bullet. The ritual appeared to sooth him. There was a tin of lighter fuel in his desk drawer. As he unscrewed the lid, the oily scent wafted around the office.

'It's going to be a good day. I can feel it in my bones,' Miles said. 'You know anything about this pervert, Hewitt?'

'Only what was said on the radio.'

'Once you've finished check calls, I want you to go to the school gates and chat to some of the mums. See what they have to say about it . . . We'll need a photographer out there too . . . Angel what are you doing?'

'Checking the papers.'

'All right, ditch that. I want some comments from the governors. Get them out of bed. I want this story wrapped up by nine.'

Miles screwed the lid on the fuel and tucked it back in his drawer. He slammed a bundle of nationals in front of me. The headline on the top tabloid was SCHOOL CARETAKER – GAY ROMPS IN PUBLIC LOOS.

He pointed his lighter at me and lit a roll-up. His hands left a slippery sheen on the pistol's handle. He had not wiped the lighter fuel from his hands.

'Get to work then. We haven't got all day.' He sauntered back to his desk whistling '. . . just like the ones I used to know.' The 'know' quavered – 'kn-o-o-o-o-o-o-w' – lingering in the air behind him.

'I'm not sure which is worse: Miles on a good day, or Miles on a bad day,' Eric muttered. He rifled in his desk and pulled out a notebook, bound in leather. He flicked it open at the 'S' page, and passed it to me. *St Swithin's Public School for Boys – Governors & Teachers*. I was only a trainee, but I knew what this meant. A reporter's success or failure depended on their contacts book. No one shared names and telephone numbers. It was a golden rule.

'That's really kind—'

'Well, you look like you could do with a hand.'

It was approaching 7.30. We had been in the office for an hour and I had already helped Eric to make check calls to the police, ambulance and fire brigade headquarters. There had been a collision on the M40 (minor injuries); a mugging near the canal (a handbag snatched); a man impersonating a meter reader to enter pensioners' homes. Eric had condensed each of these stories into thirty words, typing them in what seemed like seconds.

'They're just fillers,' he explained. 'It's a busy news day. Lots going on in court. Miles won't be interested.'

This was my first lesson in 'hard' and 'soft' news. Reporters in favour were given hard news – murders, rapes, fatal crashes. Those out of favour were humiliated with soft news – theatre reviews, fund-raisers, and council meetings. It was possible to chart the rise and fall of careers by flicking through the week's bylines.

Eric pulled on a herring-bone jacket and tugged at the lapels. It was too tight across his stomach and wouldn't button. There was a strip a couple of inches wide where his tie poked out. He was going to be cold waiting outside the school.

'I'd phone them now if I was you. I'll be filing my copy just before nine. He'll want the quotes by then, so have them ready if you don't want a scene.' I must have looked worried, for Eric added. 'Try Jocasta Gatt. She's always got something to say.'

'What should I ask her?'

'Just what she thinks. Although you-know-who may have other ideas.'

I scanned the tabloid. The lavatories were a notorious haunt for gay men. The reporter had gone there and been propositioned. He had followed the man home. There, he discovered a wife and two daughters. It took a little more research to learn this was the caretaker of a reputable public school.

Jocasta Gatt was chair of the school's governors. There were children's voices in the background when she answered. Spoons and dishes clinked. She was washing up, with the phone gripped under her chin.

'What our caretaker does in his spare time is his own business. No one else's . . . No, I don't think he should be sacked. I think he and his family should be left alone.'

I wrote these words in darts and dashes of novice shorthand and repeated them to Miles.

'Keep phoning until you find someone who wants shot of him,' he said. 'That's the angle I'm after. None of this liberal bollocks.'

I tried two more governors before I got the answer Miles was looking for. It was a long-winded process as no one had seen the story. They received broadsheet newspapers anyway, not tabloids. So I had to read it to them line by line.

Finally, I called Anthony Rankin – an elderly governor, recovering from flu. I summarized the story for him and awaited his response.

'Someone in his position should be setting an example!' His breath bubbled like air through bathwater. 'Bloody poofs. Of course, I'll be looking into this. It's a bloody disgrace.'

Miles beamed when I repeated these words. 'Bingo!' he said. 'That's our man!'

At nine o'clock, as promised, Eric called in with his story. I don't know how he managed it. A 500-word splash for the front page. By this time, I had typed three paragraphs for the bottom, which consisted entirely of quotes from Mr Rankin.

Miles whisked Eric's manuscript away as soon as the copytaker finished typing. He stuffed it into a plastic canister and rubbed his hands.

'Beautiful,' he said. 'Just beautiful. Thank you, God – you've made my day.'

A giant tube spanned the office wall like a drainage pipe or sewerage outlet. This was the means by which stories were conveyed to the paste-up department on the floor below.

Miles gave the canister a lingering kiss. Then, shunted it down the pipe.

# Chapter 5

The night editor, Cliff Waring, was a placid man, calmer in nature, less tyrannical than Miles. His shirt hung over the back of his trousers like a bedraggled tail. There was a perpetual stain – egg, gravy, sauce – on his tie. His lank hair was badly in need of a cut. His Adam's apple bobbed disconcertingly when he talked.

The evening shift ran from 3 p.m. until midnight. Although it overlapped slightly with the day shift, it was slower and less frenetic. In the day, reporters were hassled, harangued, hounded. In contrast, the evenings had a holiday atmosphere. Cliff brought in bars of Dairy Milk and packets of ginger nuts. He made sure all night reporters had at least two coffee breaks. At 10 p.m., he encouraged one reporter to accompany him to The Woolpack, while the other stayed behind to answer the telephones.

Everyone was usually given a list of things to do and then left alone. There was no urgency. Day-shift stories were police raids, muggings, robberies, car crashes. Evening stories, on the other hand, were almost entirely generated by press releases, council agendas, local authority reports. That is to say they were soft stories. They were dull, predictable and carried no kudos.

There was no buzz on the nightshift. Miles, with his touchpaper energy, his merciless enthusiasm, went home at eight. Cliff would never match him for dynamism. But he induced no fear or panic.

I had just arrived for the night shift when I found a large buff envelope balanced on my typewriter. The name and address were typed: *Angela Burnett, c/o The Birmingham Bulletin, 23 Exchange Street, Birmingham.* There was a first-class stamp in the right hand corner, but no postmark. It was marked *Personal.*

'I thought it might be for you,' Cliff said. 'You know: Angel-Angela. Maybe they got your name wrong? Happens all the time.'

I prickled with apprehension.

'Maybe. I'll take a look.'

I shrugged in what I hoped was a nonchalant manner. But the

chill of the Dunwich wind was already inside me. Angela Burnett again. No longer Sandra Angel. I had hoped to slew off my old life. I did not want my old skin. The orphan. The arsonist. The killer.

I tugged the flap so that the tear zigzagged. Inside, was a sheet of paper. Basildon Bond blue. Typed upon it, the words: *Thought you might be interested in this*. There was no signature. Next to it, a folded page torn from *The East Anglian Daily Times*, the article about my uncle's forthcoming book.

I imagined Uncle Harry's office, the door open. The smell of hair cream, wood bark and decaying flesh. My uncle hunched over his desk, idly picking the wax from his ear with his little finger. I could see him huddled over the typewriter, pressing the grey keys. I could interpret this curt message in many ways: annoyance, concern, regret. A riddle like the engravings on the stones he found beneath the waves. It was odd. But then, the way that I had left was abrupt too. Perhaps he wanted to punish me. Or maybe he wanted to check my whereabouts.

I thought of Four Winds: the Virginia creeper tapping my bedroom window; the pockets of heat and cold; the fireplaces filled with dried flowers; the disappearing lawn. Then, I thought of Dunwich: the scouring wind; the sea slumbering over the cliff; the fires – the many fires – I had made in that lonely village. I tucked the cutting back in the envelope: I would read it later.

My lodgings were in a shared house in the city centre. Every bedroom door had a Yale lock; the communal rooms were utilitarian. The lounge was dominated by a chipped formica table, with plastic chairs usually used in village halls. The carpet had iron marks and the curtains were thin enough to see through from the outside. The landlord had attempted to board up the fireplace. But the hardboard came away without too much difficulty. I should have had the chimney swept. But there was no one to discuss it with. The other rooms were leased out to foreign students who had not yet returned for the new term.

I had already laid the coals. All that remained was to set light to the newspaper twists at the base. I made myself a bowl of late-night porridge, swirling it with Golden Syrup. Then, I sat down in front of the hearth on the stained carpet. I remained there until the skin on my face started to tense from the heat of the fire.

I fetched my bedcovers and a pillow from upstairs. I was about to switch out the light, when I remembered the envelope in my bag. I turned it upside down and the newspaper cutting tumbled out. This time, I saw the other side of the page.

FRIENDS *have been paying tribute to the motorist killed when a caravan exploded near Westleton.*

*Widower Bill Lambert, 74, of Blythburgh swerved off the B1125 when a caravan blew up in front of his car. The caravan at Plumstead Farm had been set alight minutes before.*

*Mr Lambert was a keen darts player at The Ship Inn in Dunwich. Pub regulars are holding a commemorative match in his memory at the weekend.*

*Darts champion Sam Heiney said: 'He'll be with us in spirit. It's what he would have wanted.'*

*Police are stepping up their search for the arsonist who caused the fire. They are appealing for anyone with information to contact them.*

The paper quivered as if with a life of its own. Then I realized my hands were shaking. I pulled my dressing-gown tighter and sat down. I turned the page over. DUNWICH HISTORIAN WRITES OF SUNKEN CITY. On the other side: FRIENDS PAY TRIBUTE TO BLYTHBURGH MAN. Which article had been intended for me?

I examined the letter again. *Thought you might be interested in this.* The words were ambiguous. They might have been blackmail. Or a warning. But who had sent the package? My aunt? Uncle Harry? Or someone else? The letter gave no clues. Nor did the envelope. Times New Roman, no signature. Except. Except my uncle never used first-class stamps. Who then? A neighbour? One of Bill Lambert's relatives? Hilary? Who?

# Chapter 6

I couldn't stop thinking about the Smiths. It was like a mudslide on a mountain. Every time I tried to get a firm footing, I found myself slipping again, until it was easier, much easier to stop struggling and let myself fall. To be pushed along by the flow. I might drown in this sludge. It might overwhelm me, but my chances were greatest if I stopped resisting it.

I imagined Mr Smith sitting in the hospital. The gondola filling with ash. The waiting-room swelling with silence. There would be no baby photograph in front of him. It was on Miles' desk, tossed under a pile of council agendas in his in-tray.

I wondered what Mr Smith did when he left the hospital. Whether he was still going to work. Or whether he was just waiting, trapped in the vacuum where there is no life, no normality. Whether he was sleeping at the hospital. Whether he was eating variations of custard.

I wondered where the daughter was. If she was still in blissful ignorance. Suspicious perhaps, but ultimately ignorant. How would he break the news to her? How would she react? Would she see her mother? Would she be allowed to visit her before—? Before— I stopped myself here. No, I should not dwell on this thought. There was still hope. There was always hope.

My fate was tied to the Smiths. I felt responsible for what happened to them. I was waiting for Mrs Smith to wake up. I *needed* her to survive. I wanted to break the cycle, for the nightmare to end.

I couldn't bring myself to read the front page of *The Evening Bulletin*. It sullied the event, degraded it. I was afraid the coincidences would cross over into reality. That I would learn something I would rather not.

I remembered a perfect rosebud I had plucked in the garden as a child. I had carefully peeled away the white petals. Each had revealed something new, something hidden. Greenfly with luminous bodies. Black beetles with shiny wings. At the heart of the flower, petals like brown wrapping paper.

I found myself idly doodling on my reporter's notepad. Over and over until the pen marks broke the paper. It was only on closer examination that I realized what I had drawn. A fawn like the one on Mrs Crawford's drive. Neck broken. Magpies pecking at the carcass. Where it had come from I did not know. How it had reached me after all these years.

'You want a cigarette?'

Eric kept forgetting that I did not smoke. It was not surprising really. My colleagues, each and every one of them, were smokers. Heavy smokers. So much so that the office smoke alarms had been disconnected to prevent them constantly summoning the fire brigade. Smoking was what united the office. If one journalist opened a packet of Silk Cut, someone else had struck a match before the cigarette reached their lips. Matches were tossed about and freely shared. There was a bowl of courtesy matches in the office, identical to those in the entrance foyer. Tiny cream envelopes with a sprawling gold lettering. They were left out like a bowl of elegant sweets.

It was common for reporters to play with these matches. In the same way some offices have executive toys: silver flicking balls and see-sawing woodpeckers with coloured oil in their bellies. Some reporters tore the matches from their envelopes and lit them one after the other, with no apparent purpose. Others stroked the shiny envelopes, tracing the gold braille, with their fingertips. Lydia had a habit of bending matchsticks around her fingers, creating imaginary rings with match heads as pearls. The sports reporter used them to pick bits from his teeth.

The flames, when they were lit, were rarely higher than a centimetre. But every scratch of the phosphorous was amplified. Each of the thousand subtle shades of amber was magnified. The lingering after-fragrance, wisping in the air, was sweet.

I felt like a pauper watching a feast from beneath a tablecloth. Waiting for crumbs to drop to the floor below.

I was in Miles's favour for the time being, but I knew it would not last. It would not be long before he noticed my preoccupation. He could not tolerate inattention. 'Slacking' he called it. Journalists were not allowed to slack. All focus should be on the job.

Miles prowled the office, shark-like and effortlessly menacing. He peered over reporters' shoulders, glanced at manuscripts, interrupted telephone conversations. Criticizing, carping, cursing. Interrupting and interfering. Constantly moving, as if to keep from drowning.

'There's no news! Find me some fucking news!' he groaned. 'What are we going to fill the paper with? Puffs and fillers? What have you got for me, Hewitt? What about you, Angel? Got any bright ideas?'

'I could do a check on Mrs Smith,' I suggested.

'The forensics report'll be out soon – let's see if they come up with anything. They're still going over the house.'

'Shall I call the police?'

'You know the drill – check calls every hour. I don't want anyone else scooping us . . . By the way, I've put you down to cover the baby's funeral the day after tomorrow. So make sure you're wearing black.'

I gasped. 'Do I have to? Can't someone else—'

'He wants you there. He took a shine to you. It's a delicate business. Not everyone wants a reporter at a funeral. I've booked a photographer to go with you.'

Outside, it was starting to snow. The flakes looked grey as they fell from the sky. Swirling like ashes. I wondered how anyone could dig a grave with the ground so hard. Then, remembered it would only be a tiny coffin.


# Chapter 7


Miles had been drinking. Even his peppermint chewing gum could not disguise the fact. Within minutes of arriving at the office, he had tripped over a fig tree and spilled coffee into Lydia's mock crocodile-skin handbag.

Miles was loud and over-friendly. He slapped reporters on the back and congratulated them on their copy, only to curse them minutes later.

'That's more like it. Why couldn't you have written something like this in the first place?' 'Send them a fucking box of chocolates – just get the story!' 'We don't tolerate clockwatchers in this office! There's no room here for dead wood!'

Without warning, Miles King heaved himself up and lurched towards the toilets. He left his roll-up perched on the edge of his desk next to his open drawer – the drawer where he kept his lighter fuel.

Lydia spotted the glowing ember and stubbed it out.

'I hate it when he does that! What an idiot!'

I was working on a story about refurbishment plans for the city's football stadium. There was no deadline to meet. The proposals were due in a fortnight's time. I phoned the chairman of the football club to arrange an interview, but got his answerphone. I left a message. I was grateful for the banality of the story. I needed something dull to steady me. I was finding it hard to concentrate.

I was staring at my desk, tracing the lines made by other reporters, when Miles reappeared.

'What you up to, Angel? That story about the soccer stadium? There's no rush on that is there?'

'I don't think so.' I knew so.

'Good girl. Give me a hand, will you? I need some figures on RTAs by eleven o'clock.'

The cuttings library consisted of row upon row of white filing cabinets with silver handles. It was impossible to know what was inside the drawers without looking at the subject index in a miniature filing cabinet.

I looked up ROAD TRAFFIC ACCIDENTS. There were various sub-headings: *Blackspots; Fatalities & Injuries; Joy Riders; Multiple Pile-ups; Prosecutions; Safety Campaigns; Statistics.*

I found the drawer I was looking for and tugged the handle. It juddered on its hinges. There was a glitch in the middle: a shudder as when a car runs over an animal in the road. Although the index was meticulous, the files were chaotic. Each taupe envelope was straining at the seams. Cuttings had been stuffed inside without any attention to place or date. I heard paper ripping as the drawer opened.

The *Statistics* file did not contain the information I was looking for. So I took *Blackspots* and *Fatalities & Injuries*. I began to look through them, still kneeling between the filing cabinets.

There were all sorts of headlines. A florist killed half a mile from her home; a businessman who fell asleep at the wheel; a hairdresser who lost his leg after swerving to avoid a rabbit on a country lane.

I felt as if I was trespassing. It was like rifling through a stranger's handbag, or underwear drawer. But this feeling soon faded. The deaths became indistinguishable. There was no beginning or end to the tragedy, only eternal repetition. Families trapped, injured, maimed. Bereaved, widowed, orphaned. The words lost their meaning. I saw only marbled columns of news print.

To hold my interest, I focused on the sensational details that singled out one story from another. A mother who somersaulted over the bonnet in spite of her safety belt. A lorry driver who stumbled from his cab unhurt, only to be hit by a car from the opposite direction. A teenager who lost all her teeth on impact.

I read one story after another until my senses blunted. I forgot Miles was waiting for the file; oblivious to the eleven o'clock deadline.

I was starting to understand the mechanisms behind each story. The hidden cogs and wheels beneath the text. I could tell when it had been a light news day, the journalist given a free rein. When it had been a busy news day, the story cropped with vital facts lost. I spied the headlines sensationalized to boost circulation. I spotted the 'hooks' which snared readers: the intrusion disguised as investigation; the false quotes attributed to 'family friends'.

I could guess which pictures had been 'borrowed' from relatives and neighbours; which poses had been feigned. I noticed when photographs were used instead of headlines: the subliminal visual messages when words would have been libellous.

'Is everything all right? Can I help you?'

I had a dizzying realization of the present. I was spinning. As if I had been staring over a precipice or a bridge.

'I'm just looking for some figures for Miles. He wants them for a story.'

The cuttings librarian, Helen Champion, was standing, hands on hips, in front of me. Her legs made an inverse V. She looked territorial.

'Miles sent me,' I repeated. 'You weren't here, so I got the files out myself. I've been looking for ages, but I don't seem to be getting anywhere.'

'What's he after? I'll see what I can do.'

Miles did not look up when I placed the *Safety Campaign* file on his desk. He was rolling a brown slug of tobacco. He tucked it inside a Rizla paper and sealed it with a trail of saliva.

'Ah, the wanderer returns! It's too fucking late now. The deadline's been and gone!' He fumbled under his papers for his lighter. The flints gave the chirr-chirr-chirr of a house martin. But there was no flame. He tugged open his drawer and pulled out the yellow can of lighter fluid.

'I'm sorry. I couldn't find it. There was no one to help.'

Miles threw the file at me contemptuously. It landed on the floor and split open. Cuttings tumbled out. I had been waiting for my fall from grace. Here it was.

'You'd better clear those up and put them back where they belong. Next time I want a job done, I'll do it myself.' Miles clenched his lighter between his knees. He unscrewed the cap on the fuel. Then, he attached the nozzle, tightened it, and poked it into the barrel.

'There's a news release on your desk about a sponsored walk. I want a fifty-word filler for the final edition. That's if you can manage it!'

I gathered up the cuttings and went back to my desk. The telephone was quavering. The chairman of the football club was calling back to arrange a time for an interview and a photograph.

I had gone to the darkroom to book a photographer, when there was a noise behind me. I looked back through the open door. Miles was jerking like a tin can hit by an air rifle, jumping and dancing to the tune of an invisible marksman. His jacket was on fire and he was batting it with his hands, twitching and convulsing.

Somehow, Miles managed to tug off his jacket. He threw it to the floor but was too confused to put out the flames.

Lydia was first to react. She grabbed her cup of coffee and tossed it. The flames hissed and went out. The air was filled with the stench of singed nylon.

'Are you all right? That was a close call.'

Miles ignored her. He turned and addressed the newsroom in general.

'Thank you everyone for your help,' he said sarcastically. 'Just as well my life wasn't in any danger.'

In the darkroom, the photographer, Nigel Harris, had been scanning the office diary. He looked up momentarily, as I did, hypnotized by the spasm of man and flame. He tutted and shook his head. Then, he scribbled an entry in the diary for three o'clock and tucked his pencil behind his ear.

'Stupid bastard,' he breathed. 'Serves him bloody well right! If he wasn't so rat-arsed, it wouldn't have happened. She should've done us all a favour and let him get on with it.'

# Chapter 8

The chapel was made of bleak breezeblock with narrow fingers for windows. It had been decorated with co-ordinating flowers: white chrysanthemums and rosebuds in sprawling pyramids of ivy. The mourners sat on wooden benches with tapestry kneelers tucked underneath. The wooden pockets in front were filled with prayer-books and psalm sheets.

The photographer, Nigel, was a frustrated artist. He spent his weekends driving to the country to paint landscapes in vivid acrylics. He livened his job by inventing extraordinary poses for ordinary pictures. He took delight in debunking self-important officials. He was infamous for deliberately elongating a city councillor's nose and for persuading the mayor to clean a toilet while wearing his chain of office. He was not the only person who hated Miles, but he was the only person who flaunted it. Miles would never get rid of him. Nigel was a genius at taking pictures.

'Don't try to interview anyone. It's too embarrassing. And it'll probably start a fight. The pictures should be enough. The rest is detail,' Nigel said.

'But Miles said—'

'I can imagine! Ignore that bastard. Say you tried, but no one was interested. I'll back you up. Just make notes – what people are wearing that sort of thing.'

'What about you?'

'They won't even know I'm here.' He held up a zoom lens. 'You go inside. I'll see you after the service. Don't forget your tissues.'

'It's OK. I never cry.'

Nigel shrugged his shoulders as if in judgement. 'Something wrong with your eyes is there? Each to their own.'

I hoped no one would notice me at the back of the chapel. I was wearing a black rollneck and a skirt so I would not stand out. But I felt uncomfortable. I did not take notes as there was no subtle way of removing the notepad from my handbag. There were no other journalists there – at least none I could see. I wondered if Mr Smith really had invited me. I did not trust Miles. This might be another trick.

The chapel filled quietly. Just the occasional rustle as a hat was tipped or a coat removed. A shuffle as family members spotted each other and shook hands or kissed. There was a photograph on an easel at the front of the chapel. A sleeping baby. His head nestled on one of those blankets which seem to have as many square holes as thread. As mourners arrived, they placed toys around this photograph. Winnie the Pooh. A fluffy lion cub. A blue rabbit. A wooden soldier.

A woman shuffled along the row beside me, her face covered in black netting. Her teenage daughters were either side of her. Her husband trailed behind, his arms loaded with coats and scarves. The chapel was full. These were the last of the mourners.

Mr Smith entered now: walking down the centre aisle as if his shoes were weighted with leads and his pockets filled with rocks, as if every step was torture. A wizened man, with the same mouth and nose, (undoubtedly his father) shuffled by his side. He kept reaching out, offering his arm as support, but Mr Smith brushed it off, determined to walk these last steps alone. I needn't have worried about him spotting me. His gaze did not flinch from the coffin. It was like a precious jewellery box. White. Tiny. A child could have carried it.

The vicar began. 'The Lord moves in strange ways . . . He moves in ways that we cannot always comprehend. When a baby is taken from the world, snatched from his parents' arms, we are left with the question, why . . .'

Nigel had gone into the foyer to take photographs of the wreaths. We had looked at them together when we first arrived. Not just the flowers, but the little cards hidden in the foliage. *Goodbye, sweet child. You'll always be in our hearts. Goodnight, little soldier. We'll never forget you.*

We had instructions from Miles to find the message from the baby's sister. We could not find it though and she was not in the church. Her father had not told her yet. I wondered what she was doing at this precise instant. If she had any premonition, any idea, of what was happening.

The woman with the teenage daughters was crying silently. Her face was wet, but she sang bravely and with determination. She held the hymn sheet in front of her. Her daughters peered in from either side, muffling sobs with their hands. They clung to each other for comfort. Their father's face folded in on itself like crumpled paper.

A woman, with pinched cheeks, walked to the front of the chapel. The baby's aunt. Her words were cracked and gravelly. They growled in her throat. Then, she found her voice and started to sing. A low floating melody. A lullaby.

> Rock-a-bye ba-by on the tree to-p
> When the wind blo-ws, the cra-dle will ro-ck,
> When the bough brea-ks the cra-dle will fa-ll,
> And down will come ba-by, cradle and a-ll.

There was a braying at the front. An awful sound. Like a donkey which has scented the slaughterhouse, or seen the meat hooks hanging from the ceiling. Mr Smith. He ran forward towards the coffin. He keeled over, clutching it. And now he was letting his father support him, for he could not stand. He could not stand at all. He was falling to the floor with the coffin in his arms. Now, a second man stepped forward to help. Together, they were prising his fingers apart.

The vicar – a middle-aged man with a slice of ginger hair – looked on helplessly. He tried to regain control. The Lord's Prayer was printed as final item on the Order of Service. But the service was over. There was no doubt about it. As if in mutiny, the mourners began to stand and filter out of the doors. This was a private moment. We had no right to intrude.

I followed the mourners to the children's graveyard. It was a forlorn place nestled in a natural valley, a grotto between banks of rhododendrons and horse chestnut trees. There were stone angels here. Marble monuments carved with baby shoes. Engravings of nursery rhymes. Words of love for children snatched too early from their parents. Not one of them over the age of ten.

In the city centre, the light snowfall had already been trampled underfoot. All that was left was a sludge which splashed against your legs as cars drove by. Here, the grass was still covered in white linen. Green shoots speared through in places. Snowdrops. It was impossible to step between the graves, without crushing them. A robin warbled. The trees stooped around us, as if offering comfort, their branches weighted with snow.

Mr Smith crunched up the gravel path with the vicar. He was in control now, striding stiffly without support. As he made his way towards the graveside, hands reached out. Family touched his sleeve, or patted his shoulder, or kissed his cheek.

He was staring intently at his baby's coffin. He seemed not to notice the trees, the snow, the gravestones. Yet suddenly he stopped in his tracks and looked directly at me.

'You! How dare you show your face here! Have you no decency?'

I took a step backwards. I could feel a mound under my shoes. I must have been standing on a grave.

'I'm sorry?'

The rhododendron bushes quivered. Snow fell from the leaves, revealing a glossy green sheen. Nigel appeared. He stepped forward protectively.

'Hey, leave her alone. She's only a trainee.'

'You can piss off, too. Let me bury my lad in peace. You're snakes, both of you. People like you deserve to be lynched.'

Nigel grabbed my arm. 'It's all right, we're leaving anyway. We're sorry. We didn't mean to intrude.'

'Don't insult my intelligence. Just fuck off out of here.'

Shaken, we went to look for Nigel's car. It was blocked in by a Rover in the car-park.

'Great,' said Nigel. 'Just bloody great. I'd better find a call box. Let Miles know we're going to be late.'

A sob rose in my throat and forced its way out. I tried to stop myself. But my chest was heaving. I felt as if my throat was tearing. Cries like broken glass. My cheeks were liquid. Not my cheeks at all.

Nigel opened the car door and helped me inside. He put his arm around my shoulders until I calmed down. He passed me a handkerchief.

'You take any notes?'

'No.'

'Good.'

He took his camera off the back seat. He clicked it open and took out the roll of film. He tossed it out of the window.

'OK, so this is the plan. I'll tell Miles I was jumped and they got the film. It was too hairy to stay, so we had to come back. Deal?'

'Deal.'

He smiled. Then, he reached out and wiped a tear from my chin with his thumb.

'You know, I wasn't sure about you at first. But you're all right.'

# Chapter 9

The snow melted as soon as it hit the pavements. Yet it clung to the roofs and windowsills. After dark, the streetlights stuttered and stammered, setting the buildings aglow. The roof tops shimmered as if with unearthly light.

At ten past ten, Cliff Waring and the other reporter went out for an hour. I stayed behind to answer the telephones. I watched them from the window. Black silhouettes shuffling in the direction of The Woolpack.

The cuttings library was in darkness. I felt something brush against my face like a cobweb as I fumbled for a switch. The light blinked on.

Back issues were in a room off the main cuttings library. Reporters only went here when they were researching items for *100 Years Ago Today*. Even the cleaners with their barrage of brooms, cloths and verbal bluster, seldom ventured here.

Inside, the room was like a large crypt. The walls were lined with shelves. Laid out upon each shelf were leatherbound volumes in varying conditions dating back as far as 1846. The covers were the size of table tops. The paper was as soft as a frayed edge of ribbon. The air was heavy with the scent of old leather.

I found what I was looking for almost immediately. As I opened the cuttings file, something shivered through the paper. A shock of energy. A bolt of grief, love, loss.

*Mum and Tot Killed in Tragic Fire.*
*Fire Horror – Why Didn't They Wake?*
*Funeral Special – Mourners Bid Farewell to Mum & Baby.*
*Police: Cigarette Caused Blaze Tragedy.*
*Smoke Alarm 'Had no Batteries' at Fatal Blaze.*
*Widower Quizzed Over Death Blaze.*
*Father Suspect in Fatal Fire.*
*£50,000 Comfort Money for Blaze Widower.*

*'I'm Innocent' – Blaze Father.*
*Inquest Verdict on Fire Deaths.*
*Blaze Widower Takes Life.*

And there were pictures: Mum, Dad, Billy, me.

My mother was beautiful. As a child, it was impossible to conceive of her as stunning, sensual, sexual. She was just my mother. I saw now what I had failed to see before. She was like a silent movie heroine. Bushbaby eyes. High cheekbones. Full lips. Frankly, starkly, beautiful.

My father too was handsome. Midnight eyes and hair. His nose and chin looked as if they had been carved from stone. His features were shadowed with anger – though whether for the photographer or for his wife, the reader would not have questioned. They would only have seen the fury.

There was a photograph of Billy with his cone-shaped head, soft dents where his skull was not yet formed. The cat's fur quality of his hair. His solemn gaze. No one looked inside Billy's pram without marvelling how adorable he was.

Then there was the little girl I had been. Pigtails, long lashes, eyebrows. A ski-slope nose with unblemished skin. A smile full of confidence and recklessness. A schoolgirl who enjoyed fire only for its warmth and light. The unknowing child I had been.

It was the sort of plot journalists and news editors dreamed about. A devoted mother and her baby killed in a house fire. A discarded cigarette down the back of a settee. A smoke alarm without batteries. A husband badly in debt. A high insurance pay-out. A murder motive.

The clever thing was to imply. To tread the borderline, the grey area between truth and libel, fact and fiction, analysis and accusation. To march across this no man's land, up to the frontier. To taunt. To lob accusations like grenades. Then dash for cover.

The accusations were cleverly phrased. They could have been revoked to prevent a law suit. Yet they were sufficient to plant seeds in readers' minds.

How many people have stared at a headline, a picture, and said with absolute conviction, 'I bet *he* did it?' Reading a story, perhaps 300 words long, without hearing a shred of first-hand evidence, without seeing the suspect, without hearing a defence. Yet saying with more certainty than a jury member after a six-month trial: '*He* did it.'

Never mind that the story was written by a reporter with an overbearing news editor. That the editor had an eye on circulation figures. That the journalist was seeking promotion and a pay rise. Never mind if a newspaper was renowned for salaciousness, trivia and gossip; if it had no concern for fairness or truth. The reader could still say: '*He* did it' without the slightest doubt.

Suddenly, I was back at Alicia Crawford's farm. Staring at the newspaper. *Farrier Quizzed Over Blaze Deaths*. The photograph of my father. Half-man, half-beast. My father's resignation and despair. The icy ground. The jittery horse. My skittish heart. The sweet smell of scorched metal. The searing stench of horse flesh. Burning coals. The story I understood, but did not want to understand; grasped but begged to be told a different meaning. The frost of my father's hands.

Confusion. Logic warring with fear and feeling. For those words were my thoughts: '*He* did it.' I had believed a stranger's words. I had doubted my own father.

# Chapter 10

After my mother and Billy were cremated, we decided to scatter their ashes. We drove to the car-park near the top of the Lickey Hills. Then we walked the short distance to the monument. It looked like a big clock with towns and cities instead of numbers. As if time was marked by distance travelled rather than hours, minutes, seconds.

A lone car arrived in the car-park behind us. Apart from this, there was no one. My father was carrying a pine box with a silver plate on the lid engraved with the words: *Sandra Angela Burnett 1945–1977 and William Burnett, 8 weeks old, 1977*. I was shocked at the size of the casket. It was too small for a woman and a baby. I imagined them curled up like genies. As if I only had to rub the box to conjure them again.

My father flicked the catch and opened the lid. I had expected to see tiny bones or crushed teeth. Instead, the ash was fine as flour or talcum powder. There was not a lump in it. There were two spoons on the top of the ashes. My father picked them out and wiped his fingers on his trousers. There were two oval dents where they had been.

'Should we say a prayer?' I asked.

'If you want to.'

'Not really. I just thought—'

'Maybe a minute's silence then? To remember what they meant to us.'

We stood silent with our eyes closed. At least, my father did. I could not take my gaze away from the casket. I tried to think what my mother and Billy meant to me. But all I could think about was the fact they were reduced to ash.

Finally, the minute was up. My father passed me one of the spoons. It was silver with a curved handle. My face was reflected in it upside down.

'Would you like to go first?' my father asked.

'No, you.'

At first, we were unnaturally solemn, cautious. I could not help wondering what each spoonful contained. My mother. The arms that rocked me. The belly that carried me. The lips that told countless stories. My brother. The trusting face. The curling fingers. The legs which had not yet learned to crawl.

We stood on the brow of the hill and scattered it over the edge. My father looked relieved. There was a slight breeze, blowing away the burden of the past days and weeks.

'What'll happen to Mum and Billy?'

'That depends what you believe. If you believe in reincarnation, they'll be reborn in a different form. If you're more scientific, I suppose you'd say their dust goes back into the earth and becomes part of the food chain.'

There was a lingering sadness to the words in spite of their objectivity. My father believed adults should always be frank with children.

'What do you believe, Dad?'

He did not answer immediately. He looked across the hills. At the pine trees piercing the sky. At the white earth sprinkled with ash.

'Dad?'

Eventually, he said, 'Don't look to me for answers, because I don't have any. I sometimes think there's a half-way place where spirits stay to watch over people left behind. I suppose it's what I want to believe.'

We started out respectfully. We spooned with as much deliberation as a Japanese tea ceremony. Every movement was loaded with meaning. Every spoonful weighed down by love and sorrow.

But the casket was seemingly bottomless. The ash did not diminish. The gaps lessened between each spoonful. We increased our speed. It was a cold day, but we had forgotten to bring our coats. As the cold seeped through our clothes, we scooped out the ashes quicker still.

At first, the wind on top of the Lickeys helped us. Every time we took a scoop, it dispersed the ashes like a fine mist. Then, unexpectedly, the wind turned. We tossed the ashes and the wind threw them straight back.

So the ceremony became an ordeal. A test of endurance. We continued for a while, struggling to maintain the dignity of the occasion. But the casket was a quarter full and there was no lull to the wind.

The ashes even started to rise from the casket: little flurries over my father's hands and wrists. We scooped the ashes still faster, but they came off the spoons as soon as they left the casket, smearing our clothes.

Eventually, my father said, 'Oh, what the heck! It wouldn't matter if we just tipped this out, would it? I'm sure your mum wouldn't mind.'

He put the spoons in his trouser pocket. Then, he turned over the casket and shook the ashes directly on to the ground. They formed a small heap like a melted snowdrift.

'What if someone walks on them, Dad?'

'They won't. The wind will see to that.'

My father held the casket upside-down and tapped the bottom.

He gave it another shake. Then he peered inside to make sure it was empty.

We were surrounded by pine trees. A pigeon was crooning in the branches. A family was strolling up the hill behind us. Two children were stamping footprints into the hoarfrost. A lone man was sitting on a bench nearby with a woollen hat pulled down to his eyebrows.

Suddenly my father's face changed.

'What's that slimy git doing here?' He took a few steps towards the bench. The stranger got up and started marching downhill towards the car-park. A camera was bouncing against his hip.

'Wait! I want to talk to you! I WANT TO TALK TO YOU!'

My father was still carrying the casket under one arm. He lolloped rather than ran. The stranger had the advantage. He picked up speed. Sprinted.

'I ought to kill you. You bastard! Can't you leave us alone!'

The stranger reached the car-park and ran to his car. He fumbled with his keys and climbed inside. He pushed down the door locks.

As the car was pulling away, my father threw down the casket to pick up speed. He caught up as the car was bumping over the potholes. He thumped the rear window. Once. Twice. Then the driver accelerated away. It was the white sports car that had parked at the end of our garden.

When I reached the car-park, my father was sobbing.

I see the photograph now amongst the scattered cuttings in the back issues room. My father is shaking the ash casket. The pine lid is flapping like a mallard's wing. Ashes flurry around him like belly feathers. He looks as callous as a butcher wringing a bird's neck.

## Chapter 11

*Michael King.*

I read the words as if they are hieroglyphs. Their true significance escapes me. My mind refuses to register their relevance, their enormity.

*Story by Michael King.*

I keep staring, imagining the words will rearrange themselves like scuttling ants. That I will see a different name.

*By Michael King, Investigative Reporter.*

Then I see the photograph. His younger face. Still brutally handsome, but without the lines. It takes my breath away. Fragments come back to me. Debris. I see shadows. Darkness. The unlit car at the end of the garden. The constant flickering of a cigarette. My father cursing the night air. Threats scrawled on our front door. An empty whisky bottle beneath the blue hydrangeas.

It can not be Miles; it has to be another journalist. The symmetry is too precise. Like neatly folded paper: patterned identically on either side of the crease.

Miles. A media name. More exciting, less ordinary, than Michael. He would have changed it to suit his career.

It has been easy enough to cross-reference what I found in the back issues room with the cuttings and files. Now I stuff the cuttings envelope in my handbag and turn out the light. When Cliff Waring returns from The Woolpack, I am sitting at my desk.

'Has Miles always been called Miles?' I ask. I tuck my hands in my pockets. They are quivering like leaves in a thunderstorm.

Cliff gives a lopsided smile. 'So you've found out his little secret! I'd keep it to myself if I was you. I've got a week's leave from tomorrow. He'll be night editor for the rest of the week.'


# Chapter 12


My father would creep down the stairwell like a thief each morning. At five o'clock. Before the milkman chinked up the pathway. Before the postman slammed the mail through our letterbox. Before the neighbours jerked back their curtains. Before I, his daughter, admitted to being awake. My father would dress furtively in the darkness – green sparks flashing as he pulled jumpers over his head. Then creak-craw, creak-craw down the stairs.

He never flicked the light on until he reached the hallway. By then, it was often too late. He would have trodden on dog turds, glue, eggs, chitterlings – whatever had been pushed through our letterbox.

Before he cleared this away, he would slip outside to see what new threats had been scrawled on our walls, windows or door during the night. He would fill a bucket with water, or get some turps from the shed. Then, he would set to work – rubbing, scrubbing, scraping – to hide his notoriety. As if everyone cleaned their windows before breakfast and repainted their front door once a week. As if everyone had pieces of pigs' intestines in the grooves of their shoes.

The newspaper boy needed his bag for our delivery alone. We had every local and national delivered. 'Rags', my father called them. He read every poisoned word that was written about him. Everything from casual mistakes to malicious falsehoods.

He was a blacksmith and he was a silversmith. He was a regular at The Ten Bells and a regular at The Silver Bells. He was sociable and he was a loner.

The fire that killed Mrs Sandra Burnett and her baby had been caused by a smouldering cigarette. It had 'mysteriously' (nudge, nudge) slipped down the back of a chair. An unnamed family friend claimed my mother had not touched a cigarette in years. Another source claimed she smoked like a chimney. The batteries in the smoke alarm needed 'replacing' and they were also 'missing'.

There were certain facts though that the newspapers did agree upon. My father – Mr Jim Burnett – owned a forge that was badly in debt. He was paid a large sum of life insurance. *Comfort money* the newspapers called it. As if his grief (wink, wink) was appeased by a deposit in his ailing bank account.

Then there was the picture. A story in one glance. There must have been rolls of film. Yet the choice was confined to a man with a grimace which might have been a snarl.

Shortly after my mother and Billy's funeral, a strange woman called out to my father in the street. An unremarkable woman with shopping bags tied to the handle of her pram, and a baby who looked like a boiled prawn. A boy, barely five, at her side.

'Jim Burnett? I've got something for you.'

She leaned towards my father as if to give an embrace, a kiss of condolence. Instead, she spat – her spittle like battery acid in my father's startled face.

'That's what I think of the likes of you!' she hissed. She marched off hauling her son after her, a chaotic pitter-pat of heels and wheels, as if afraid that we – the murderer and the murderer's daughter – might follow.

My father blinked. Dazed. He wiped his face with his coat sleeve. He rubbed my head. The fine spray had settled in my hair.

'Who was that?' I asked.

'I haven't the foggiest.'

'Does she hate us?'

'It's nothing to do with you, Angel.'

'Does she hate you?'

'She doesn't know me.'

'Why was she so angry?'

'Do you know what a scapegoat is?'

'Someone who takes the blame . . .'

'Not just the blame. All the bitterness too.'


More hurtful were the people who *did* know my father. Neighbours. Work colleagues. Friends.

Alf Marney, the coal merchant, had always stopped for a chat and a mug of tea. Now, he hurried back to his lorry without so much as ruffling my hair. Helen Cooper had collected our pools coupons for as long as I could remember. Now, she claimed she had given up her round, although later we saw her collecting money on the opposite side of the road. Loyal clients who had hired my father for years cancelled their orders. Eleanor Braithwaite, our next-door neighbour, who had borrowed cups of sugar, buttons and cotton reels from my mother, took plates of sandwiches and Battenburg cake to the sports car at the end of our garden.

My father would sit for hours in semi-darkness, staring into space, without switching on the lamp. I remember seeing whiskers on his chin for the first time, the apology of his shoulders, the defeat of his eyes. I could imagine him thinking: 'If that's what they want to think, let them.' He shrugged dismissively as a dog shaking water off his coat. First, its head and shoulders. Then, its haunches and tail. So many people. So much water. Just as he thought he was dry, being plunged into the lake again. And again.

When my father left newspaper cuttings instead of a suicide note, I was confused. I imagined the cuttings to be a confession, an explanation, an apology. I buried them at Greyfriars Monastery in a wordless panic. It was the sort of impulse which drives a vixen to eat her cubs at the sound of a bugle. I persuaded myself that I was protecting my aunt and uncle: that I was safeguarding my father's memory. In truth, I was protecting myself. I had felt tainted and implicated. I could still feel the spittle in my hair. As if my father's infamy, his crimes, were mine.

I understand now why my father left the cuttings. They are accusations. Protests of innocence. Pleas for vengeance.


# Chapter 13


For weeks, months, we were his obsession. He sat at the end of our garden: peering through binoculars; plying neighbours for tittle-tattle; pursuing my father's van. Sitting in a cold car in dark and daylight watching our windows and front door.

We are an intrinsic part of each others' lives. He has deprived me of a father, lingering on the edges of my nightmares. I have helped him in the passage from junior to senior reporter, from senior to chief reporter, from chief reporter to news editor.

I am different now from the child I was, but I suspect Miles would never remember me. I am not a person, merely a juggling of letters. He might recollect a story. The gratuitous details. The sensational events. The shocking headlines. But Miles would not recall a child. Not one among so many.

# Chapter 14

I am fourteen, standing on the threshold of my parents' bedroom in Elm Road. My aunt and uncle are in the garden. We have made a day-trip from Dunwich to collect my belongings before the house is sold. Uncle Harry and Aunt Rose have warned me to stay away from my parents' bedroom: not to open the door under any circumstances. I have made a promise that I have no intention of keeping.

As the door swings open, the room has a sweetish, yeasty smell like that of a bakehouse. The bed, wardrobe and dressing-table have already been taken away. The main thing which strikes me is the quality of the light. The room is bathed in an unearthly glow, as if orange filters have been placed on the windows.

My instant reaction is to reach for the light switch. The naked bulb emits a dull glow. It is coated in the same substance which is filtering the light through the window. The floorboards rattle as I walk across the room. The walls magnify the sound and cast it back at me. There is a shape on the floor like a target – a dark inner circle, outlined by a larger transparent circle.

The window pane is sticky to the touch. Like fly paper. Or toffee. I put one finger on the glass and pull downwards. The smear elongates and catches the light, but the substance stays. I put my finger to my tongue. I do not recognize the taste.

I scratch the glass and examine my fingernails. There are tiny threads like worms or maggots. They are not orange, but suet-coloured. Suddenly, it is important to make a spy hole, to let daylight into the room. I scratch again. Hard. Tiny fireworks spark over the glass. White light shoots through. Just like those drawings at school made with wax crayons and needles.

Something terrible has happened. Something nameless. As I leave my parents' bedroom, I look up. The plastic lampshade has come adrift from its fittings. The ceiling is the colour of soot.

# Chapter 15

For nearly two weeks, Mr Smith has been sitting at his wife's bedside listening to the machines keeping her alive. The steady wheezing, not of lungs but pistons. Plastic tubes instead of veins. He has waited not for a miracle as such, but for the promise of modern medicine.

We have both in our own way been waiting to find out what will happen; how the story will end. I realize now this is the end. For as the beginning starts to come around again, so the ending approaches. There will be no grand finale. Only circularity. The joining of two sides of a ring.

As I arrive for the night shift, there is a message on my desk. *Ring police – any charges yet on house fire?* The forensics report has just been published. Batteries missing from smoke alarms. Scorch marks suggesting a cigarette down the back of the settee. The motive? Only one person has one.

Miles appears behind me, stealthy and silent. He exhales whisky as he leans over my shoulder. Or rather, leans on to it. He stubs out his roll-up on the top of my typewriter, leaving a double burn mark in a figure-of-eight.

'Have you checked with the police yet?' he asks.

'The media line says he's helping with their inquiries.'

'The police are questioning him, you mean. He's a suspect. If his wife snuffs it, they'll upgrade the charge to murder.'

'He didn't do it. You only have to see him to know he didn't.'

'You're soft in the head – you and Nigel. That crap about being jumped at the funeral! You can't pull the wool over my eyes. I wasn't fooled for a minute.'

On the opposite desk, Eric is concentrating on a pile of paperwork, avoiding eye contact. It is his birthday. He wants to get home on time as his wife has cooked his favourite meal: sirloin steak and crinkle-cut chips. His sleeve catches his Polo packet and the sweets start to roll to the edge of the desk. He does not reach for them. He is very quiet and very still. I remember what Uncle Harry once told me: with a shark one has to move slowly. Any sudden movement will draw its attention.

'What are you up to, Birthday Boy? Got a scoop for me?'

'I'm working on the TV Listings. I want to be away by ten.'

'Well, you can call your wife and cancel dinner. I want you to knock up Mr Smith's neighbours and see how he was getting on with his wife. It'll all be *sub judice* if he's charged. We won't be able to print a thing until they nail him in court.'

Miles takes a bottle from his inside jacket pocket and fills a coffee mug. He downs it in one go. He fumbles in his shirt pocket for his tobacco, and finds it empty.

'As for you, Angel, if you're not working on anything important, you can pop out and get me some baccy. All this excitement has put me in the mood for some cancer sticks.'

Miles unfolds a five-pound note and drops it on my desk. He smiles drunkenly. His mouth is ocean-black.

'You got a problem, Angel?'

There is a low menace, a threat, in his voice. I pretend not to hear it.

Eric phones his wife, and pulls on his coat. His car keys chink angrily in his hand. Before he leaves, he bends near my ear. He breathes words into it like a gale gusting in a seashell.

'Any problems, call security! He's a mean bastard when he's sober. But he's evil when he's been at the bottle.'


# Chapter 16


It is snowing again. Snow upon snow. Just like the Christmas carol. I open my mouth and catch it on my tongue. It dissolves without a taste. The flakes catch on my eyelashes, making me blink. I have left my coat behind, so the snow blows against my jumper and skirt. I can see individual crystals, six-fingered delicate stars when I reach the Eight 'til Late.

The fountain outside *The Birmingham Bulletin* has not frozen over yet. The two bronze boulders are still seeping water. As I climb the steps, the ground shifts under my feet. My handbag spills as I fall. I scramble to my feet, but instantly slip again, legs skidding in every direction. I am wearing the wrong shoes for the weather: smooth soles without any grip.

I gather up my scattered possessions: the Golden Virginia; coins; a handkerchief. I take off my shoes. I set off again. This time, I am barefoot.

There is no sign of Miles at the news desk. I leave his tobacco and money on his typewriter. My tights are sodden so I peel them off and trail them over a radiator. I did not notice the cold while I was outside. Now, my fingers prickle. Chilblains. A creeping cold starts at my toes and works its way over my calves.

Miles enters the newsroom. Or rather, staggers. He scrolls a story and attempts to stuff it into a plastic canister. The paper struggles in his hands: refusing to crease where it is supposed to and creasing where it is not. Corners stick out at all the wrong angles. Miles makes three attempts at folding and curling, before the paper finally fits. He pushes on the lid skew-whiff.

'You called the police yet, Angel?'

'Nothing to report.'

'Bollocks, there's always something to report! They've got a suspect, haven't they? I want a fresh angle – those missing batteries in the smoke alarm. That'll liven things up a little. I want the story on my desk in ten minutes.'

'But that's not what they said—'

'Just do it.'

Miles stands unsteadily and walks across to the tube. He kisses the canister, then inserts it in the pipe and sends it whistling down to the floor below. He staggers back to his desk, and telephones the chief sub to inform her the story is on its way.

He flicks open the office diary while I am typing. He scans through it, scrawling amendments and comments in the margin. Absent-mindedly – perhaps unaware of his movements – he pats his shirt pocket. He unfastens the small pearl button and pulls out a roll-up. It balances on his lower lip, bouncing, as he finds his lighter.

Again, the same blind man's movements. Fingers creeping across the braille of the desk. Finding the lighter. Grasping it. Flicking the trigger. The flints whirring and chirring like a watch being wound. No flame.

The desk drawer is already open. Without looking at what he is doing, Miles places his lighter between his legs. He reaches for the lighter fuel and unscrews the cap.

I am shivering slightly. The heating must have been turned off or turned down. Or perhaps a window has been left ajar. A creeping cold starts at my toes and works its way over my ankles. Over my knees.

I unscroll my story from the typewriter and approach Miles. I do it quietly, hoping he will not notice. I leave it on the corner of his desk without saying anything. His hand swoops over it. He holds it up and reads.

'What the fuck is this? *A man is helping police with their inquiries. They're trying to rule out the possibility of arson.* That's not a story!'

'It's what they said.'

'Are you stupid or what? I might as well do the fucking thing myself.' He rips the paper into ticker tape shreds and drops them in the wastebin. As he does so, his lighter slips through his fingers and disappears under his desk.

'Dead wood. You're dead fucking wood. There's no room in this office for—' Miles bends down to search for the lighter, but cannot find it. While he is crawling on his hands and knees, he inadvertently knocks his desk. The fuel can topples. Fuel slides off the edge like water over a fall. His clothes are drenched, although he does not immediately realize.

He tucks the lighter in his pocket, and begins to mop the desk with tissues. He moves his telephone, his typewriter, his mug. He places the office diary and a pile of press releases on the floor. There is a spike at his feet covered in discarded agendas. He kicks this out of the way.

A dark circle grows at the bottom of his jacket pocket. The lighter must have flipped over on its side.

'What the fuck—?' he slurs. Then: '*Fuck fuck fuck fuck fuck fuck fuck.*'

He pats his thigh, feeling the wet patch seeping through the top of his trouser leg. He pulls out the lighter. Upside down. Still dripping. The effect is clown-like. Somehow, he manages to tip more fuel over the papers on the floor. Over his swivel chair. Over his socks and shoes.

'Angel!' he shouts, as if I am personally responsible. 'Pull a finger out, will you? Get over here and give me a hand!'

Miles kicks the pile of press releases at his feet so that they splay across the carpet. His shoes leave grey shadows on the paper. Wavy lines for soles, half-moons for heels.

'Now! Not next fucking week!'

Something flies across the floor and hits my leg. The wastepaper bin. Miles has booted it deliberately. The pain ripples in widening circles. I rub my knee.

'You can't treat me like that.'

'Don't get lippy with me. Just shift your arse.'

Suddenly I am standing by the bowl of white courtesy matches. There is a small envelope in my hand. I am ripping out a match and holding it to the strip. The match comes alive with a beautiful shiver. It trembles in the air between us.

'You stupid bitch! You'll start a—'

'Sit down,' I say slowly. I hold the match towards him. A flame no bigger than an eagle's feather. Speckled. Silky. Magnificent.

Miles backs into his chair and collapses into it.

'Now look, Angel! If this is about—'

I am already pulling another match from the packet. My hands are shaking. For some reason, I have lost my shoes. Everything has happened so quickly. I have left them under my desk. The flame flickers. I pass the match from one hand to the other. As soon as one flame is extinguished, I will light another. Then, another. I back towards my desk and reach for my handbag with my foot. I kick it forwards, bend down, unzip it. I pull out the cuttings file and toss it at him.

'Do you remember these?'

Miles plucks at the flap and tips out a handful of cuttings, the headlines face upwards.

*Fire Horror – Why Didn't They Wake?*
*Fire Blaze May be Arson.*
*Vigilantes Attack Blaze Widower.*
*The Verdict: His Suicide Says it All.*
*Guilty Father Set Himself Ablaze.*

Miles squints.

'They've got my name on them.'

'But do you remember them?'

He shakes his head. 'No.'

At least he is honest.

'Bromsgrove,' I say. 'This is my father.'

He peers at me. '*Your* father?'

'If it wasn't for you, he'd be alive.'

The match quivers. Miles runs his hand through his greasy hair. Fear flitters over his face.

'Look, I didn't mean anything by it. It was just a story—' The words trip off his tongue without the least thought.

'I'm not going to let you do this to anyone else.'

The strangest thing is that I know exactly what to say. The tone to use. The volume. As if my actions have been carefully scripted. As if I have secretly rehearsed this scene a million times.

Miles's fingers drift to his pocket, tugging the button like a piglet after a teat. He finds his roll-up and lifts it to his lips. It quivers. Tremulous. Then, he remembers the danger and lowers it again. The cardboard filter is a shade darker, moist with saliva.

He taps the filter-end on the table. Then flips it over and taps the other end. His fingers slide all the way down, as if slipping down a greasy pole. Then they flip it over and begin again. Slide. Flip. Tap. Sli-ide. Flip. Tap. Sli-ide. From cardboard filter to tobacco twist.

From tobacco twist to filter.

He looks pathetic. A pile of bedraggled clothes hunched in a chair. I almost feel sorry for him.

'Come on,' he wheedles. 'I'm sure you don't want to do anything silly. What do you want from me? Money?'

'An apology.'

'I apologize.'

'I want you to mean it.'

We stare at each other. Stalemate. Ironically, he is clinging to his lighter. He grasps it in his palm like a child's comforter. Not so much holding it as clutching it.

'I want you to know how it feels,' I say. 'To be helpless – for your life, to be in someone else's hands.'

Miles falls silent. An emptiness settles between us. I know now that I have frightened him enough. And I am frightened, too. For I do not know how to stop. Like a rolling snowball, it has gathered too much momentum.

My match goes out. I light another one. My eighth. Strange to think how I have perfected the technique over the years. Striking matches on the sole of my shoe, between my fingers, on walls, on glass. As if I was honing my abilities for this moment. I watch the flame burn down the stick. We both watch it. We both know that all I have to do is toss it.

There is a poetic and appropriate symmetry to our movements. His eyes dart, assessing his chances of getting to the swing doors in the time it takes to throw a match. My eyes shadow his, assessing the same facts. An intricate ballet in which we each pair the other. He, an unwilling partner. I, tight as a shadow. He tries to seem calm. But his nose betrays him. It is dotted with tiny beads of perspiration. His eyes circle the exit, the fire doors, the smoke alarms, the lift. Finally, his eyes swing back to me. I am his only real chance of escape and we both know it.

The telephone starts to ring. Miles looks relieved. The chief sub. I had forgotten the ten o'clock call.

'You'd better get it. But don't try anything funny,' I say.

'How could I? With you standing over me?'

Fear seems to sober him. He has more control over his facial muscles, his lips, his eyes. His personality, his mocking tone, returns.

My arms are aching. I have to hold the match near enough to frighten him, but not so near to start a fire. It is the fumes, the vapours, that are dangerous. I hold the match high.

The conversation is short, but dull. Captions for photographs. A spelling query. Sports results. 'Nibs' for the back page.

'No, hold it. I might have. Wait and see . . .' Miles says. He puts down the receiver.

Already, I am starting to regret what I am doing. To consider ways out of it. I have not planned this nor thought it through properly. I do not know where to go from here. I take another envelope of matches from the bowl.

'Look, Angel, why don't we put a stop to this right now? You go home and get some kip. We can chat about it in the morning when things have calmed down . . .'

I wonder how I have come to be here. Threatening this man with a match. Behind me, my past like an open diary. Pages fingered, crumpled, slightly worn. A diary slyly stolen and sneakily read. I wonder why I don't just put the courtesy matches back in my pocket and go home.

'I didn't mean for this to happen . . .'

'Exactly,' he says. 'Of course you didn't. Like I said: we can work something out.'

I do not believe him. But I am cold and tired. This has already gone further than I intended. I hoped to scare him, nothing more.

'You'll let me go?'

'You have my word.'

He is too calm, too collected. Suspicion settles like a dragonfly on the end of a reed. His diffidence. The way he spoke in code to the chief sub. The ellipsis that came after 'Wait and see . . .'.

Understanding suddenly dawns and I am amazed at my own stupidity. The front page. Even now, faced with his own mortality, he cannot resist the thought of a splash.

'Are you going to call the police?'

'No.'

Miles will write the story first. If the police are called, I will be arrested. There will be reporting restrictions. The case will be *sub judice* until it reaches court. Miles does not want a fifty-word filler; he wants a banner headline. He will not make the call until the morning; after *The Morning Bulletin* is on the news stands.

I back away from him and put on my shoes. The flame dances in my hand, but there is no real need. He is already fidgeting, glancing at the clock. The hands sweep towards the final edition. He is itching to start, to hammer out his story at the keys. HOW I WAS HELD CAPTIVE DOUSED IN LIGHTER FUEL. I edge towards the lift, and press the Down button. Whether I leave or stay is irrelevant. He has a scoop.

Miles takes a sheet of virgin paper out of his drawer and winds the typewriter. The barrel whirrs. He takes the roll-up from behind his ear and chews the filter end. He taps the keys.

'You better get going,' he says. 'Before I change my mind.'

As the lift doors slide open, the unthinkable happens. The roll-up jigs on Miles's lower lip. He lifts his lighter. Flints whirr into life. Grind. A spark flashes. Suddenly, Miles is aflame. Cloaked from head to toe in fire.

He stands up and lurches towards me, arms outstretched. Staggering. Hands grabbing at the air. He crashes into a noticeboard. Sends a swivel chair ricocheting. Knocks a stack of *Weekend Supplements* off a trolley. He reels about, as if blindfolded. Arms waving. Finally tripping over his spike. Crashing to the floor.

It only takes seconds. The many papers scattered across the carpet are alight: council agendas, letters, minutes, press releases, newspapers.

Already, the smoke is billowing in thick eiderdowns and pillows. Silky winding sheets of it. Great feathery clouds of it. The light is so bright I am forced to shut my eyes.

When I open my eyes again, I am in a deserted street. My feet leave no footprints in the snow. The blizzard is so bad it is impossible to tell if the snow is blowing down from the sky or upwards from the pavement.

A shop doorway looms under the gentle halo of a street lamp. There are snowdrifts against the door and windows, but at least it is out of the wind. I crouch down on the step and pull my jacket over my head. In the seam of my inner pocket, where the fluff gathers, is a small smooth envelope. My fingers trace the delicate heraldry, before lifting the flap and feeling inside. Stroking the delicate stems. The jewel-like heads. If I cup my hand around them, they will stay alight.

Even as I strike the first match, my parents step out of the swirling, curling softness. They stay just beyond the circle of light. I can sense them, rather than see them. Yet there are shadows reflected in the shop windows that were not there before.

The flame is only a small one and it will not last long. I protect it with my palm. My parents will disappear if I glance up. Yet, it is hard, so hard, not to look.

Then, the softest of touches like the trail of a cobweb. A woollen shawl is draped around my shoulders. Slippers of the softest fleece are slipped under my feet.

The match flickers and I know there is not much time. My voice is not much more than a whisper.

'Come into the light,' I say. 'Let me see you.'

There is no shuffle of footsteps nor rustle of robes. But when I look up, they are leaning over me. My father's face is radiant, as if he is still standing over his roadside furnace. My mother's is, too, as if she is still gazing at gleaming coal. Between them, a bundle is wrapped in a lacy shawl. Billy frees one arm and reaches out to me, tiny fingers curling and unfurling.

The match is dwindling. Already the flame is dimming and the light is fading. I take one last lingering glance. The eyes that wept and smiled. The hands that caressed and carried. The cheeks like frozen rosebuds. Beyond them, the driving snow.

One last glance. Then, I remove my hand and let the wind whisk the flame away.